WITHDRAWN
FROM COLLECTION
VANCOUVER PUBLIC LIBRARY

World Body

By the Same Author

A North American Education, 1973

Tribal Justice, 1974

Days and Nights in Calcutta, 1977

Lunar Attractions, 1979

Lusts, 1983

The Sorrow and the Terror, 1986

Resident Alien, 1986

Man and His World, 1992

I Had a Father, 1993

*Here, There, and Everywhere:
Lectures on Canadian, Australian, American Literature
and Post-Modernist Theory*, 1994

If I Were Me, 1997

Southern Stories, 2000

*Time Lord: Sir Sandford Fleming
and the Creation of Standard Time*, 2000

Pittsburgh Stories, 2001

Montreal Stories, 2003

The Selected Stories of
CLARK BLAISE
Volume Four

World Body

With an Introduction by
Michael Augustin

The Porcupine's Quill

Library and Archives Canada Cataloguing in Publication

Blaise, Clark, 1940–
The selected stories of Clark Blaise.

Contents: v. 1. Southern stories – v. 2. Pittsburgh stories –
v. 3. Montreal stories – v. 4. World body.

ISBN-13: 978-0-88984-284-7 (v. 4)
ISBN-10: 0-88984-219-1 (v. 1). – ISBN-10: 0-88984-227-2 (v. 2). –
ISBN-10: 0-88984-270-1 (v. 3). – ISBN-10: 0-88984-284-1 (v. 4).

I. Title. II. Title: Southern stories. III. Title: Pittsburgh stories.
IV. Title: Montreal stories. V. Title: World body.

PS8553.L34S68 2000   C813'.54   C00-932402-X rev

Copyright © Clark Blaise, 2006.

1   2   3   4   •   08   07   06

Published by The Porcupine's Quill, 68 Main St, Erin, Ontario N0B 1T0.
http://www.sentex.net/~pql

Readied for the press by John Metcalf.
Copy edited by Doris Cowan.

All rights reserved. No reproduction without prior written permission of the publisher except brief passages in reviews. Requests for photocopying or other reprographic copying must be directed to Access Copyright.

Represented in Canada by the Literary Press Group.
Trade orders are available from University of Toronto Press.

We acknowledge the support of the Ontario Arts Council and the Canada Council for the Arts for our publishing program. The financial support of the Government of Canada through the Book Publishing Industry Development Program is also gratefully acknowledged. Thanks, also, to the Government of Ontario through the Ontario Media Development Corporation's Ontario Book Initiative.

Contents

7 Introduction
13 Strangers in the Night
17 Salad Days
21 A Saint
25 Kristallnacht
29 Drawing Rooms
35 The Banality of Virtue
47 White Children
71 Doggystan
81 Dark Matter
105 Migraine Morning
113 Yahrzeit
119 Meditations on Starch
129 Did, Had, Was
145 Sweetness and Light
161 Man and His World
175 Dear Abhi
189 The Sociology of Love
201 Partial Renovations
213 Afterword

Introduction

THE FIRST TIME I met Clark Blaise was in September 1984. He happened to be the host of a party in Iowa City. The house and the garden were packed with bizarre people, beer and wine flowed freely and there was the sweet music of chatter and laughter. Quite a number of the guests had walked over here from a rather unremarkable concrete high-rise building of the University, which, however, bore the wonderful, resonant name 'Mayflower'. It was there, in a long corridor on the eighth floor, that a community of international writers happened to reside. About forty individuals had been invited for a period of three months. And here we were, in infinite celebration and dialogue: playwrights, poets, novelists, essayists and translators from all corners of the world, guests of the International Writing Program, invited by the legendary Iowan and citizen of the world, Paul Engle, and his Chinese wife, the writer Hualing Nieh. The crowd of celebrants in the house and in the garden of the writer couple Blaise and Mukherjee was made complete by an equally high-spirited group of students from the University of Iowa's famous Writers' Workshop, which in the past had been attended by aspiring writers such as Tennessee Williams, Kurt Vonnegut and Raymond Carver, as well as a young writer by the name of Clark Blaise. It was here that he met a fellow student from India, Bharati Mukherjee....

It was a party on Noah's Ark, so to speak, with remarkable couples: the writer from Taiwan talking to the one from the People's Republic of China (or as they used to say in America in those days, 'Mainland China'). There was the novelist from Israel and the short story writer from Palestine, my colleague and fellow countryman from the other side of the Berlin Wall and myself, the 'Westerner'. Constellations such as these require a special place, and here in this house and this garden there was such a place – radiating openness to the world, colourful diversity and curiosity.

I have to mention, by the way, it was at this party that I first laid my eyes on my future wife and co-founder of our family, the poet Sujata Bhatt, then a student, who unfortunately, at least at that stage, showed little or no response to my longing gazes. Like my host's wife, she happens to be originally from India. Fate or coincidence? (A blessing, I tell you.)

During numerous visits to the United States, some long, some short, I have realized that there are some unwritten laws of small talk. It may well happen, for example, that a host asks countless questions of a guest without actually caring about the answers. Indeed, it may even be impolite to give a proper, extensive answer to a very personal question. It didn't take me long, however, to notice that this rule by no means applied in the house of Blaise. Here was a host showing genuine interest in his guests, a polyglot contemporary who elegantly stood his ground in this multilingual confusion of tongues. He too, a constant traveller, a researcher, an investigator, someone making proper use of his eyes and ears – *ein Augen- und-Ohrenmensch*, as we say in German, someone who cannot get enough of the visible and invisible secrets of the world. It's no surprise that almost a decade later, this man became the successor to Paul Engle as the director of the International Writing Program.

Reading the short stories collected in this volume, I cannot help thinking of that first encounter in Iowa City, of the international writer Clark Blaise, who is more than just a sharp observer of North American realities and states of mind.

Dear God, how must these permanent repetitive questions get on his nerves: whether he defines himself as a U.S. citizen or as a Canadian citizen. Let the U.S. critics claim him for their country and likewise the Canadians. But please, let me raise my hand and claim his services for the rest of the world! Yes, ladies and gentlemen, there is life beyond your borders.

Brilliant how Clark Blaise (or rather Gerald Lander, his Faustian hero and anti-hero) shaken by mid-life crisis, moves about in that part of the world which I myself know best, which has fascinated me since my childhood, my family ground, which nonetheless, will always be full of riddles for me. With the stories 'Kristallnacht', 'Drawing Rooms' and 'The Banality of Virtue', he places us right in the centre of the Baltic microcosm. The ice

INTRODUCTION

of the Communist paralysis has melted, the submerged bonds of the neighbouring countries which had developed over centuries are finally becoming recognizable again. But so are the scars, the wounds inflicted on the neighbours by German guilt. Immediately, Czeslaw Milosz comes to my mind, as well as Günter Grass, with his *Danzig Trilogy*, and his Polish colleague, Stefan Chwin. And naturally, I have to think of the poet, short story writer and novelist, Johannes Bobrowski, a native of Tilsit (birthplace of my father), a town which is called Sovietsk today, and is a part of the Russian enclave, known as Kaliningrad Oblast. Like no one else, Bobrowski has made his ancient 'Sarmatia', these complicated, fertile, and often enough horrible neighbourhoods, into his grand theme:

Sprache
abgehetzt
mit dem müden Mund
auf dem endlosen Weg
zum Hause des Nachbarn

Language / exhausted / with the tired mouth / on the endless path / to the neighbour's house

There is an echo of all this in Clark Blaise's writing, when he makes his readers follow him to this cultural sphere, to a nameless city with Hanseatic features which reminds one of Riga or Tallin. In other stories, we find ourselves in Gdansk, Sopot or Pomerania. This is where they have always lived together: Estonians, Latvians, Russians, Lithuanians, Poles, Germans, Jews and non-Jews. This is where they have learned and profited from one another in times of tolerance and this is where they turned life into hell for one another when times were bad. Not only here, have people come to know from painful experience that the varnish of civilization is very thin indeed. So that it is not forgotten that this danger is always dormant, it is important to speak about it and to write about it. *If I Were Me*, the book from which most of the stories collected here have been taken, ranging from 'Strangers in the Night' to 'Yahrzeit' (with the addition of 'Migraine Morning', a strange, incredibly breathtaking story), shows us the 'world according to Blaise'. A patchwork novel, a novella composed of tales, an assembly of short stories, where each story taken by itself reveals great diversity in terms of style and perspective. Here is a master at work, a virtuoso taking us on a tour de force through time and space, and through the tricky history of the short story.

'I may be in all of my characters', he once confided in an interview with Derek Alger, 'but none of them are me.' And indeed, there seems to be a hearty portion of Blaise in Gerald Lander, the eternal seeker of sense and meaning – the incarnation of the mid-life crisis. Blaise, too, as Goethe would say, 'wants to know what keeps the world together in its core' – this shrunken world of bonus miles, airports and hotel rooms. 'The one thing he could not imagine was meaninglessness.' Clark Blaise has made his family trauma a theme. His grandfather and his mother died of Alzheimer's disease. Whoever knows this, whoever knows even one single person who has been in the claws of this incomprehensible disease will be touched especially by this aspect of the stories. 'Salad Days', one of the shortest pieces in this rich collection, belongs, for me, among the most exciting, disturbing and lasting texts he has written.

I have already mentioned the diversity of locations Blaise takes us to: Poland, the 'new' Baltic states (which have only recently become full members of the EU), North America, Japan, Israel … In other stories, (most of them published in his 1992 collection, *Man and His World*), we find ourselves in Prague, in Vienna, Bruges, Paris or Toronto. Places Clark Blaise captures perfectly in his sensuous rendering of atmosphere.

'Meditations on Starch' is one of those stories in which he enchants us with his magical power. As if one were sitting in a time machine, one is taken suddenly from the contemporary American everyday life and plunged right into the explosive 1930s of pre-war Central Europe, into the life-threatening years after Hitler's rise to power, when it became foreseeable that 'Old Europe' was only a step away from being extinguished, when this continent was about to lose its centre. A journey through time and space, encompassing three generations and three continents, ending in the present-day Vienna, Berggasse number 19, where once a certain Dr Freud dissected the soul of the world. 'Number 19 is just a flat, as it always was, squeezed between other flats and offices' – or is it? You must be dreaming.

'Meditations on Starch' is one of Clark Blaise's many stories connecting 'the West and the East'. Countless outsiders have had a go at writing about themes connected with India, ranging from Hermann

INTRODUCTION

Hesse, via Thomas Mann all the way to Günter Grass and his Calcutta poems, just to mention some of the most famous writers in my language, all three of them Nobel laureates. One could fill a library with all the stories, novels, travelogues, fairy tales, and poems of Western authors who have dared to explicate the Subcontinent. Clark, too, has written with unusual insight and success about India and its people. His early work, in collaboration with his wife, Bharati Mukherjee, *Days and Nights in Calcutta*, received great acclaim.

In recent years, new generations of Indian writers in the Diaspora have invaded the book market ('The Empire writes back') stunning readers and critics alike with unfamiliar perspectives of life in these times of multiculturalism and globalization. They (not unlike the Irish writers) are the ones who prevent stagnation in the 'traditional' literatures in English. This is how unjust history can be – awarding the undeserving former colonial powers with new ideas, new sensibilities, new perspectives! Clark Blaise, though, is probably one of the very few Westerners who manage to give readers insight into the complicated structures of the Indian Diaspora. If one takes, for example, the previously uncollected story, 'Dear Abhi', a highlight of this collection (which to me reads like a wonderful script ready to be made into a great film), one finds oneself exposed to the experiences of a certain Abhishek Ganguly from Bengal, a successful immigrant who has made his fortune in Silicon Valley. Abhi is married to a second-generation Indian from San Diego, they have two children and are leading a responsible life, eager to recycle at least part of their good fortune to the community they live in – an 'extremely well-adjusted' family. Abhi believes that 'my situation is not uncommon among successful immigrants of my age and background'. And yet: it's the background, the hyphen, the navel-string that hasn't been cut, the old family bonds with his native India, his relatives, and in particular, his Chhoto Kaku, his late father's youngest brother, which will shake the foundations of his existence. This is a beautiful, well-balanced story, full of surprising turns (which, of course, I won't give away here), it is a sad and moving story and yet, one that makes you smile and wonder ... A powerful story written entirely from the perspective of an Indian immigrant, a daring undertaking by the author – but one that proves fully successful (and this holds true for the other new story, 'The Sociology of Love', as well).

WORLD BODY

What I value about Clark Blaise is the way in which he perceives the world: his sensibility, his respect for *the other*, his curiosity and his almost scientific talent for going to the heart of the matter, revealing the hidden layers, connecting the seemingly unconnectable. And yet, Clark's scientific precision does not prevent him from being a man of beautifully weird fantasies and humour. One can also say: this man is not a globalizer – he's an internationalist. And that's exactly what the 'world body' needs. May there be many translations of his work!

— *Michael Augustin*

Michael Augustin lives and works as a poet and broadcaster in Bremen, Germany. He hosts a regular poetry program at Radio Bremen and edits a weekly radio documentary. He is the author of many volumes of poetry, drama and short prose. Some of his books have been translated into English, Italian, Polish, Gaelic and Dutch. Augustin has also done work as a translator of poetry and drama (Kenneth Koch, Pearse Hutchinson, Simon Gray, Adrian Henri, Roger McGough, Adrian Mitchell, Raymond Carver and others). He has read at numerous international literature festivals and is the recipient of the Friedrich-Hebbel Prize and the Kurt-Magnus Prize. In 1984 he was a member of the International Writing Program at the University of Iowa.

In 2003/4 he was writer-in-residence at Dickinson College, Pennsylvania where he also taught as a guest professor.

Strangers in the Night

IN THE NIGHTS OF HIS FIFTIETH YEAR, before sleep, Lander was assaulted by faces. Every few minutes he opened his eyes for a reality check. Judy was breathing shallowly beside him, as she had for twenty years. The front wheel of her exercise bike splayed window light in a giant metal florette, like the barred metal blades of the dangerous rotating fans of his childhood that really could chop off a finger. His alpine ski machine gleamed expectantly, ready for him to climb aboard, its chrome neck stretched forward in a parody of earnestness. The partially opened closet door caught the red readout of the clock-radio display and spattered it against the full-length mirror on the door's inside surface. It was his room, indisputably, in this time, it was happening to his body within his experience, yet the moment he closed his eyes he was taken outside it.

The perfect ordinariness of the nighttime faces, their clarity and specificness, the lack of a single grotesque, or of spectacular beauty or familiarity, bespoke a kind of urgency that he could not ignore. Surely, if they sprang entirely from his own will, or existed for his own mild amusement, he would have remembered or invented faces of old friends, comforting icons or enemies, a few delicious women from his past or present. These were not staged faces, there was nothing coy, familiar or attractive. Or if attractive, mildly flawed. They reminded him of atelier faces, faces cherished for their typicalness or eccentricity, tossed off by a gifted master and his school. Lifelike – there was no other word for them; he was being assaulted at night by an army of probable, interchangeable alternatives to the world he knew. He was sure that his faces were part of other people's lives, that he'd somehow crossed wires in this new fibre-optic universe, and was experiencing some neighbour's insomnia.

In Lander's intellectual tradition, Freud had taught him that dreams were urgent fragments of a ruptured past, personal and collective. They demanded attention, therapeutic resolution. Jung had taught, although Lander tried not to listen, that dreams were perfected futures, omens of uncompleted journeys.

A vast population had intersected his line of vision. They were not from his professional world. They were not American – if he could trust the flimsy evidence of haircuts and haberdashery – and many were not even European. Whenever he demanded their name or even a country, they faded, only to be replaced. Every night, he confronted a line-up of Latinos, Asians, Africans, middle-aged and old, male and female, poor and rich, like Roman busts, floating balloon-like above their own worlds, beyond speech, movement, or context, as though he were circulating in a vast professional cocktail party of tenured professors, without a proper invitation.

In the morning, or sometimes late at night, when he entered the visions in his notebook, as he habitually entered all his dreams and fantasies, he called them 'baseball cards'. A lavish pack of cards, shuffled and dealt by processes inside his skull, for mysterious purposes that he decided not to question. If he were to diagnose himself, he'd say he was going through a phase, he was part of something in development. There was no one he could share these half-sleeping adventures with. Judy, if wakened and informed, might have praised the interracial inclusiveness of his nighttime visitors, and the reassuring lack of younger women or troubled patients with robust transference problems. He'd learned years before not to discuss his patients with her, or to describe his research. He felt she was jealous of his involvement with patients, or at the very least that his emotions played a zero-sum game.

None seemed hostile. They seemed variants of probable faces, they reminded him, elusively, of names he couldn't place. They might have been the older brothers and sisters of people he knew well, parents even. They held still for a minute inspection, and he had the impression they were aware of him – as though they knew they were behind a one-way mirror. He wondered if this was the artist's 'fever of creativity', a tangible population of fully formed characters waiting for expression.

One night, in the crowd of nighttime faces, he saw a retreating figure, the broad, sloping shoulders and short legs, the fringe of curly hair. *You!* he cried with such force that Judy lurched beside him. The figure turned, reluctantly, as though apprehended in a theft, called to account. His double. Lander realized suddenly that he'd been waiting for it to happen. In his watered-down religious tradition, seeing one's double was not fatal. If anything, it was a sign of grace, the appearance of a personal genie.

The other Lander wore different glasses, and the jacket was unfamiliar, but it was Lander of the balding head and tadpole body, the sharp nose pulling against the flat planes of a Slavic face, a fuller beard than his, somewhat whiter. The bust was smiling, a little more accommodating than any who'd come before.

'That's right,' it said. 'You've found me. You're me.'

It was the first time a face had spoken.

'Where are you?' Lander asked. 'What is that place?'

He looked around, smiling, hands out in a familiar *can't-you-see?* gesture that reminded Lander of his father. 'This place?' he asked. In his double's world, there must have been props and other people and views out of windows, a common language, but none of it was available to Lander.

He spoke again. 'But I'm not you.'

By breakfast time, seeing himself at night slightly transformed seemed too small a thing to talk about, and Judy was too much involved in the inventory problems of the small boutique in a nearby shopping mall that she and two other women had opened. Both he and Judy were successful, which meant they had vast trust in each other, but little time, and their untended marriage was approaching a critical mass of unshared experience, uncommented upon, perhaps even unrealized. For the moment, they existed in the hollows and expectations each had carved out for the other.

Salad Days

'BY FIFTY, you have the face you deserve, the job you'll die at, the house they'll carry you out of ...' his father, the dry-cleaner, had insisted (then proved, at age fifty-five, from chain-smoking in a cloud of naphtha and acetone). Apart from his professional practice and his writing, Lander was involved with the reality of his mother's wasting away from Alzheimer's disease in a nursing home on the Yonkers side of Chappaqua. He tried to visit her a few hours every week, the first years as a dutiful, encouraging son, feeding her scraps of family information, safe memories, that might flush a response, a twitch of recognition. 'What a beautiful February morning,' he'd say, or, 'Wednesday, middle of the week.' Reality counselling, nurses called it, but if she answered, it might be a noun like 'bats' or 'butterfly', or a verb 'spilled' or 'swab', past tense or present, or any number of names of men and women he didn't recognize. '*Essie paint the chair*,' she said. She could not enjoy television, being unable to retain a plot, or even tolerate the intrusion of so many strangers. In the past year he'd been watching her slowly starve to death from an inability to recognize hunger or remember the taste of food, or to anticipate sweetness, heat, or cold, and finally, how to swallow. He watched her trying to communicate complicated ideas, judging from her frowns and gestures, before withdrawing; he watched her bat away food with her hands, swatting at the world like a baby. A world in which every second was intrusive, a world without context, life without antecedent or consequence. In the last several weeks, freed from all obligation to her, all guilt and the bonds of affection (he wished, profoundly, for her physical death) he'd begun thinking of his mother's silent dying not as personal loss, not as a philosophical vision of hell, but as a kind of clinical problem.

Still, Lander persisted. As a child of the Freudian method, he believed nothing issuing from the human mind was without form or purpose, particularly when others had declared it without merit or meaning. The one thing he could not imagine was meaninglessness. Alzheimer's word-salad was not random the way an infant's vocalizing might be. For

Lander, the word 'salad' conformed to a recipe, words never lost their meaning, and locked inside the vault of language were his mother's own Dead Sea Scrolls.

He worried about 'Essie', a name that recurred in her speech, but there had been no Essies in her life. Sadies, yes. Esthers, yes. *Painting the chair?* None of it made sense until another dream, this one of his mother, much younger, talking excitedly with a stranger. Lander strolled by, unrecognized, then suddenly became the stranger, his mother staring hard at him and speaking loudly. '*I say*,' she gestured, her arms flapping as though holding a brush and painting a wall, and Lander woke and stormed from his bed, writing out his vision in a fever of interpretation. *The chair* meant Lander himself, the person *in* the chair across from her. *Painting?* He hadn't a clue, except that it connected all her angers, her rage, at food being thrust at her, at strangers entering her room. Pain, perhaps, just plain pain. People thought of him as Freudian, unlocking meaning where there had been secrets. He thought of himself as Saussurean, a believer in the universality of language, its permanence, underlying all meaning and personality. He thought of Chomsky's theories, how language grows inside the brain, it is a human attribute, not a learned behaviour, and in the same parabolic function, language dies inside the brain, shedding its leaves, shrivelling. His mistake had been to look for content, for a woman named Essie, and for a special chair, and for a colour of paint, instead of approximate sounds. He was right, in that Alzheimer's had changed nothing of his mother, except that her content, her experiences, had become dead leaves. The leaves were still trying to speak.

Over her months, while language had persisted, he took notes. Then he recorded. The scraps of foreign language he took as an important clue – she was American-born, but she'd lived a life rich in others' languages, and she could at least make change and exchange pleasantries at the counter of the dry cleaning shop in five or six languages – it meant the words were not random, they belonged to her, they extruded from certain strata in her life. His mother couldn't locate herself in language; others in the nursing home who pressed Bibles on him, or hiked their skirts at the sight of any man, couldn't relate to society. *Oh, do watch the bed,* she'd say, *be a car and the cat won't slide, up the coffee hat and slippers too...*

He thought of his own occasional difficulties with names, or even at times with words, trying to apply his own common experience of word-retrieval, or name-recall, to his mother's problem with every sound and word in the universe. *It starts with 'M'*, and he began to wonder if the brain didn't store ideas as simple sounds, scanning a menu under the proper initial vowel or consonant, and then, by metre: it's a long word, tuh-dumm, tuh-dumm, an 'M' with three syllables, and then began throwing out words from his internal dictionary, like a computer's spellcheck: Morrison? No, not quite. Then social history kicked in: Jewish, Wasp, Italian? Morrison? Mendelssohn. Menotti? The idea appealed with its model of the inherent humanness of memory and consciousness, linked with the inherent human gift of language. *Cup* could mean anything, but it didn't mean nothing, and before it stood for a concave object for holding tea, it probably meant a short word starting with 'c'.

Music, mathematics and poetry – sound, length and symbol – slid together as the primal organizers. Even a baby's vocalizing made new sense: it was opening up the verbal pathways, hitting on opening letters, intonation and word-length. And when finally, by accident, a sound was understood to be a word, fitting a concept or an object, it was retained, stored, and other words quickly jelled. It made sense. His mother had simply reversed the process of language acquisition, dropping the sorter, then the menu. There was a mind still working, but it had lost control of first letters, opening sounds, and the salad was an infinitely complex rhyming game. She still had the intonation and metres of normal speech but she'd lost control of syllables and second and third letters as well. There was no way of knowing if the mind behind the salad was aware of the loss. The doctors called Alzheimer's a blissful stage of total mental rest, language without consciousness. There was even doubt that she felt physical pain, with her lessened brain functions. At the brain clinic the specialist, studying her charts, had told Lander, 'It's lights out for the old girl. Look at the dead nodules. It's like a bombed-out city in there.'

To quiet his guilt, to answer the tragedy of his mother's dying – not a personal tragedy by this time, but the awareness that the loss of any individual was the loss of an entire branch of human history – Lander began the process of translation of his mother's last words. The strangest translation process in human history, a kind of calculus, not algebra, of translation, in which all terms were functions, not equivalents. There was no Rosetta stone, he was adrift in a world of familiar words much in the way

Freud and Jung had wandered through the archetypes of dreams, each applying convenient meaning without the *click!* of final authority. Lander's mother had died, but her words – five hundred Alzheimer saladwords, translated into nearly three hundred pages of coherent text – became the basis of *Death Decoded: Language Acquisition and Language Loss*, a book, like *The Interpretation of Dreams*, that would link an everyday middle-aged event, memory lapse, with the continuum of language acquisition and language loss, the human process of birth and death. Some reviewers spoke of it as redemption; the first words from the Beyond. The dying still speak to us, nothing in human life is without relevance or meaning, we are human till the last breath is taken from us.

Harsher critics saw it as last-gasp yuppyism, baby-boomer possessiveness, vigorous middle age staking a claim even to old age and death. 'Gerald Lander, 51-year-old clinical psychologist, the sage of Chappaqua, boldly goes where no one has gone before,' wrote one detractor in the *New York Times Book Review*, 'claiming to have walked to the very portals of eternity. His translation of his mother's terminal babble is a curious labour of love and *hubris*, more a claim for his own immortality than a rendering of near-death experience. With his debts to Sigmund Freud all too obvious, Lander should be reminded of his master's words: "Sometimes a cigar is just a cigar." Harsh as it may seem to a humanist of Lander's obvious compassion, sometimes gibberish, even a beloved mother's gibberish, is just noise. For God's sake, let the elderly die in peace. There is, after all, a limit to what children might own of their parents, what the all-consuming present might seize of a parent's present agony and private past. Despite today's publishing climate, and the Wall Street mentality that fuels it, not everything can be – or should be – turned to vast profit.'

The latter, apparently, was a reference to Lander's surprise appearance – considering the difficult and uncompromising language of the book, as well as his own unglamorous self – for fifty straight weeks at the top of the world's bestseller lists. In international publishing circles, his name became linked with the improbable trio of other accidental bestsellers, Umberto Eco, Stephen Hawking and Salman Rushdie.

A Saint

MY SON HAD GRADUATED from college in Oregon, and I was on the way back to my midwestern life. A poet had delivered the graduation speech. I took pleasure in his words: *a baby tiger, just born, has an ox-eating spirit.* He did not mean, in the way of successful alumni addressing sleek young graduates, to leap upon the backs of oxen, though many seemed to take it that way. He meant for us to approach the world respectful of variety and of necessity, he meant to contrast appearance and appetite. My boy and I ate under a tent and listened to the projects of the new graduates around us, and to their proud parents. We watched the intact parental units dance to an orchestra, then the older successful men and much younger wives dance convincingly to the wives' music, and we left early. My boy had been happy there, had drifted into a counter-cultural community. He had no project in mind except escape, and though pleasant to everyone, hated his classmates. A friend once said of him, ah, Sagittarian. It is their nature to be adult in childhood, and childish in maturity. He seemed to be on course, and I wished him well. It was the traditional leave-taking of a father to a son: I have raised you, inculcated you, educated you, warned you, encouraged you, sent you every conflicting signal in the universe. You were in my arms for a couple of years, in my hands for five or six, in my house for a dozen more. You're bigger than me, stronger, you can slay an ox.

At the airport, I had noticed the woman in the waiting room. I sit in the smoking section though I don't smoke. In general, I prefer people who smoke, ox-eaters, fragile predators like cats. Maureen O'Hara on a bad day, I thought, green eyes – dating myself, like old guys dancing with younger women, like men my age with toddlers by the punch bowl. A honey-roasted blonde, lumberjack shirt and faded jeans, a backpack. Maureen O'Hara on a bad day, or a distracted day with the beacon of her beauty slightly broken, is better than Maureen O'Hara on a good day, when her helpless beauty could only bear down on you.

There would be no story if fate had not put us together in 10A and B.

Her name was Patty, her husband in Richmond went by the name of Terry. And she was returning to Richmond, a city she hated, from a ten-day camping trip with six male friends from Boston College. One of them said, 'This is what movies are made of.' My *Big Chill*, she said, Terry couldn't come. Too busy making the President's Golden Circle, writing up a million dollars in policies for the fifth straight year. She'd been married ten years, with him thirteen.

Her story is racing ahead, I want to slow it down. There are women who somehow make you feel and act and talk better than you are; others, much worse, even when they are the source of all your inspiration. Patty, whom I will never see again, is among the first. Two minutes with her, and I intuited nearly everything about her. Maybe not the four children, but the wistfulness about some briefly opened door, some recent transcendence. You were an actor, I said, quite confidently and it wasn't my intuition, it was her actor's radiance. Only some soaps, she said. I did soaps to pay for more acting and singing and dancing lessons. An agency sent me to Atlanta for some Coke ads. Three weeks for one of those Teach the World to Sing jobbies and I met Terry – he was in theatre then. He saw me in an ad and called the agency. I was thrilled. I acted in one of his plays. His father had an insurance agency in Richmond, and two years later the father died, and Terry...

Nothing happened in Oregon, she said. I don't want you to get the wrong impression.

But something did, I said.

I was raped in Richmond. Can you imagine, living alone in Boston and New York all those years, hanging out with models and actors, living in Hell's Kitchen, and I get raped in a parking garage in Richmond? I knew the name of every guy hanging out on the stoops on Forty-fourth between Tenth and Broadway. I was a soft touch, I gave them money, I talked with them, I got them tickets to some of my shows. They would have died for me. I know she's telling the truth, she is the sort that some men would kill for, some die for, but Terry would kill her if something had happened in Oregon.

Defending Your Life, I said, overcoming fear, doubt, insecurity is what separates men from angels. I'd seen *Wings of Desire* a few weeks earlier, and I saw through her with such clarity I almost said: Patty, it's no accident we're sitting together. I am the man put here to listen to you. But

I'm not a man. I was killed in a BMW crash two weeks ago, and you're my first case since I was sent down. Somewhere over Utah I said, 'A lot of men will be returning to their wives as dissatisfied with their marriages as you are.'

One of them said, 'Life has big plans for you. Don't close it off.'

You love this man, don't you, Patty.

I want to go back to New York, but one of these men – he lives in the woods, sort of a conservationist – he hates the city. He never married, he's a kind of soulmate. Knows the trails, knows what to eat, what to avoid. I feel safe with him, even in the woods. I don't feel safe in Richmond with all my cars and memberships. He says I'm closing my life. I lay in his arms at night – nothing happened – but I slept in ways I've never slept before, like a baby, with dreams I didn't want to leave.

One day, I was taking a bath in the river near the campsite and I didn't know the men were all watching me. They didn't tell me till we were sitting around the campfire and they started exchanging opinions on how I could improve my looks, starting out with my hair, or something, and then getting more and more intimate, you know, and I'm starting to get redder and redder. I mean, four kids, and thirty-six, you're not going to turn on many guys, especially not buck naked in a snow-fed stream.

A true angel, perhaps, would have kissed her then, or would have said like Willie Nelson if you don't want my peaches, baby, then why you shake my tree? Or he might have given up immortality on the spot, traded omniscience and invisibility for mutable, ecstatic flesh, moist members moving, and all its agony. A *Penthouse* fell out of one man's backpack, why do men buy it, is seeing pictures really more pleasurable than a woman's body? *Ever watch Dockers ads on television, I ask. Beer ads?* It was the only question I couldn't ask, I felt he was measuring those girls against me in the river and I didn't measure up, I'm all saggy, I've got a little roll, and Christ if my legs were bananas they'd be selling at half price. Well, you're a man, you've probably noticed it's downhill pretty fast from my eyes, but my eyes, I mean they need some shadow and all but I've still got a bit of it, don't I? Men were always in my power. Professors were in my power. God, this is awful, even priests, all the laps I sat in – we only hear about priests and little boys, but believe me, the Church isn't all that sick.

Patty, I said, you are beautiful, your eyes are the colour of thin caramel glaze over a crisp green apple and thoughts of your body rising from the waters leave me aghast with pleasure. You still have it, you are exactly halfway between my son and me, but life doesn't have any more big plans for you, maybe only one medium-sized one.

    Leap, Saint Patty. I present myself to you like a tethered bull in a pasture. Rip my stupid throat out.

Kristallnacht

THEIR SHOES MADE LOVE all night at the foot of the stairs, where they had kicked them off. In the bright early light the next morning he prowled her kitchen, looking for the cat food in her unreadable language. He'll remember the kitchen, the words on cat food labels – in German, Polish or Czech, and Serbo-Croatian, he couldn't tell – and where she kept the can-opener and his pride in not disturbing her, more, perhaps, than he'll remember the night before, the kicking off of the shoes, the famished rush to a bed before they magnetized the moon. He'll remember it all as something unexpected and undeserved. Maybe it could not have happened in another week, might never have happened a year before, or even a few months later. They'd clung to each other like Londoners in the blitz, seeking dark in the sunlit night, safety in her wooden cottage.

Out on the street in the white summer nights, prowling gangs controlled the city. No guns, the violence was more intimate; chains swung in an arc then down on a skull, tire irons clanking down the brick streets, echoing off the pastel canyons of Hanseatic housing. Blond young men in American T-shirts and blue jeans, squatting in the middle of ancient roads, holding their split-open heads as blood trickled between their fingers.

For her, perhaps, he was the man who appeared in her life in the weeks before history ended. He is the man she chose because he was new, and innocent, and somehow impervious to the local tragedies. A man who could appreciate her memories, she said, as she lifted crystal wine glasses from a satin-lined little casket with its Gothic lettering and swastika imprint, inside a carved-oak settee, the heavy furniture of the independence era, the glasses of the Nazi occupation, and poured the Moldavian wine of the dying present. 'This wine is too sweet,' she said, 'they can't do anything right,' toasting his glass nevertheless. Can you imagine these Germans, she asked, even in the War, even losing the War, turning out crystal so pure, so fine, that *Trockenbeerenauslese* could not be poured into the lighter *Rheinwein* glasses – too sweet, too heavy, you know – or else the *prosit!* would not chime?

They toasted each sip, and the sips lasted for hours.

He had stood all afternoon in line with her for pork, or rather the fat of pork, to make a broth for eggs she'd traded and vegetables from her garden. It had not seemed like three hours, though he realized it was privilege speaking, being the friend, the lover, of a beautiful woman – and she was that, dramatically so, with pale skin stretched over perfect bones, under her absurdly garish Romanian scarf – rare privilege being inducted for a day or two into the intimacies of her life, learning the only words in her language that he would ever have to know, some nouns for vegetables, some verbs for slicing them, some soaps, some nonexistent meat, anaemic cheese and watered milk, some endearments for a child coming home from school and finding a strange man in his mother's kitchen – there have been so many, she said, it doesn't matter except that you talk to him, show some interest, he's studying English, you know, and he likes to practise – and some verbs and nouns of intimacy, conferring a kind of giddy mastery that no classroom had ever taught.

They'd taken buses, and then a tram, though taxis hooted when they saw him, guessing his foreignness, shouting out entreaties, then threats in the nearest Western languages, descending from Finnish to German and finally Hungarian. Under the awnings of darkened stores, girls in leather skirts pushed their hips into him, boys in leather jackets with metal studs waited nearby on their bicycles. Two years before, the girls had been in high school preparing for college, their pimps had been playing football and trying to dodge the draft.

She would not permit herself the luxury of a cab ride, which she said she associated with visits to her mother in a bad part of town, near the public housing developments where the Tadzhiks and Uzbeks stayed, close to the barracks where Tatars manned a rim of tanks and anti-aircraft batteries, for protection against the likes of him. Decent women under seventy were not safe in those areas, where satellite dishes brought in Western television, and drunken bachelor Asians watched *Miami Vice*.

'But let me spend this money,' he said. 'I want to spend something on you, I want to make your life a little better.' It would be unspeakable to leave with a wad of rubles in his pocket, those worthless rubles that would have cost him a month's salary just a year before. 'Please,' he'd begged, 'you can use this, it's six months' salary for you.' She'd stepped briskly ahead while cabbies whistled, then she turned. 'Next, you'll want to take me to your hotel,' she said.

She had her pride, he learned that night, with her well-behaved boy speaking well-drilled English, and with the amazing soups of sour cream and rhubarb, potatoes and beets, pork fat, dill and eggs, rye bread and Moldavian wine in crystal Nazi glasses. Later, in bed: if you wish, you can send me books, she said, when you get back to your country. Books used to be stolen in the mail, but now it doesn't matter. And send me magazines. *Lear's*, she said, and *Apartment Living*, and maybe *California*. Oh, and some cat food.

He is in her kitchen, and a ginger cat rubs her whiskers on his naked leg. Just a minute, Sasu, he says. She, if it is a she, eats an egg, lightly whisked, in sour cream, lightly watered. In this country, house cats eat as well as foreign lovers. To a man, all cats are female: graceful, elusive, mysterious, and to a woman, they're always male: competent, agile, undemanding.

Is that a wad of rubles, or are you just glad to see me? Dear Abby: how does a gentleman leave the equivalent of twenty thousand dollars on a lady's bed without arousing undue suspicion over motives or morals, averting hostility or an international incident? The thought occurs to him: *this was all for her cat!* then he dismisses it, almost. Does it matter? And how will an American, ugly or beautiful, ever know?

He pulls out the settee drawer, the little sarcophagus of wine glasses nestled inside the Nazi shroud, and tucks every ruble and kopeck into a satin cavity where one glass, over the years, must have broken. He holds up a glass and raps it gently with his fingernail: *T-i-i-n-g!* and remembers the thunk of bicycle chains and the clanging of tire irons hurled down an empty street. It is the high, pure note of collective memory. He feels he has lived fifty years in two days and a night. The walls are down, the currency is melting, and he mounts the stairs wondering if there are not more ways than this of celebrating.

Drawing Rooms

AFTER HIS TALK to the city council, Lander and Jerzy Adamowicz, the assistant commissioner, took their brandies on the balcony outside the council chambers. If you can believe it, Dr Lander, this was once a prosperous city, before the war and before the Communists, Adamowicz was saying. As a distinguished visitor in a time of tumultuous transformation, Lander had been asked to contribute to a 'post-Communist urban dialogue'. He'd chosen this city in western Poland not just for its renowned medical college, where he'd conducted a seminar on his theories of language and memory, but to visit the town his family had come from.

Inside the council chambers, hollowed out from the splendour of an old private mansion, the walls had been hung with tourist posters of Gdansk and Krakow, Vilna, Riga, Smolensk and Minsk, Lvov, Pskov and Tatra mountains. All rather revanchist, the AC had admitted, as though the old Polish-Lithuanian Confederation were trying to re-establish itself now that the Russians were in retreat. The hallways and smaller bedrooms of the mansion were a warren of tiny offices with hastily erected drywall partitions, each whining with dot-matrix printers and fax machines. Lander had thought of the house as a schema of the brain itself, Polish liberation like a brain, recovering from a stroke. Being in the middle of it was a privilege.

The dominant landmark, of course, was the cathedral. Next, on a hilltop, the college and hospital. The Communist Party headquarters with its unilluminated red star was boarded up, with squatter families occupying the ground floor. There were the usual Stalinist sports palace and playing field, islands of ghostly concrete and patches of scruffy grass. Just below the balcony, in a tiny park, families of refugee Ukrainians and gypsies had spread quilts between tree branches, and propped up boards and cardboard slabs for a semblance of privacy.

'We were close enough to Germany in those pre-war years for a fanning out of German wealth and a taste for Mozart,' said Adamowicz, but remote enough not to dilute basic Polish decency. *Here you stand on the heart of Pomeranian-Polish culture, Dr Lander,* the place where Slavic Catholicism and Prussian Protestantism merged. And Jewish, too, of course, he'd quickly added, Jews supplying soul to the Germans and quickness to the Poles (quickness? Lander wondered), qualities now lost forever. 'We used to be the most cosmopolitan country in Europe. Now we're ninety-nine per cent Catholic and ninety-nine per cent Polish. We've been made stupid by history. How this country has suffered, Dr Lander!'

It had proven an ideal location for a cosmopolitan city, with its own Grand Canal linking the Baltic ports with the Oder and Berlin. The present-day canal wove through the foulest and most congested part of the city like a dirty string. The city council planned to dredge the canal and clean the waters, to rebuild the old promenade, to raze and rehabilitate derelict buildings and lease them to Benetton, McDonald's and Mövenpick.

In the council chambers, Lander had spoken against demolition. All things seemed possible in the new eastern Europe, why not a revolution of the soul? The best of all traditions – local, European, capitalist, socialist – seemed within reach. He'd suggested turning over the abandoned buildings rent-free to artists, dancers, weavers and publishers, for coffeehouses and cheap restaurants, printing presses, theatres and cinemas, subject to the tenants themselves doing all renovation. Charge rent only after they succeeded. Nothing makes an area more attractive, and more valuable, than a concentration of creative people. He'd felt he was being persuasive until he mentioned enlisting German aid. Council faces had drooped, eyes looked down, a few councillors had shaken their heads.

The town council had presented him with a gift book of Pomeranian etchings, circa 1910, featuring urban views of the prosperous old city. The cathedral, much as it was today; Sternfeld's Department Store, with families streaming in and out; parks, trams and the opera house; a synagogue, baths and the Lutheran *Heiligenkirche,* all of which had disappeared. Eighty years earlier, the canal had defined the centre of a compact, orderly city. The promenade was edged by trees along the waterside, like Amsterdam. Sidewalk cafés invited strollers. The shaded walks led to theatres and to the opera house, past docks tied up with decorated rowboats.

'They were such pigs, the Communists,' said Adamowicz, with sudden passion. He'd been trained in Australia, where local English had worked small wonders on his vowels. 'Communists were bysically pay-sants who took revenge on the city. They tore down the landmarks. They stuffed farm families into these old city houses, family after family. They hated everything the city stood for.' *Like Jews,* thought Lander. 'Culture, values, property, wealth, beauty – all of it had to get beaten down. That was the dirty war inside of Communism. Everything to humiliate the past, replace it with trash – out of vain-geance, not principle. How we suffered.'

'And the Germans are out, definitely?' Lander had been prepared to say that inviting German investment need not imply forgiveness. Germany was the nearest source of hard currency; logically speaking, they shouldn't be ignored.

'Pay-sants say pigs may stink but you can still eat pork. The pig is part of God's creation. We still don't know about Germans.'

Lander respected Poland's long memory. He trusted Jerzy Adamowicz. He had found a man he could stand on a balcony with, not having to talk.

His maternal great-grandparents, the Sternfelds, ghetto-sprung businessmen who'd educated their sons and daughters in Germany and France, had built a substantial residence – brick with white marble trim, on the London model – somewhere in this city, in the middle of an elegant block facing a private park. As a child in a third-floor Brooklyn flat, Lander had spent hundreds of hours staring at pictures of the house and of a little girl, his grandmother, tended by a nurse, riding a high-wheeled bicycle. Two old touring cars, with chauffeurs in livery, were parked in front of an unimaginably fine mansion, something belonging in Park Slope or the tree-lined brownstones of East Side Manhattan. Evidence, in Lander's helter-skelter New World, of having come from somewhere, 'from People', as his mother put it, of having had something substantial to lose.

No one in the current city council remembered such a park, or row of brownstones, although everyone revered the Sternfeld name. At the turn of the century, Sternfeld's Department Store was importing English porcelain, Paris fashions, Dutch cheese and German technology. Sternfeld agents, smart boys who'd married into the family, scouted every European city for quality and value, turning Sternfeld's into the biggest store between Berlin and Warsaw, and maybe the finest store of any kind between Vienna and Stockholm.

Before she'd lost her ability to remember, or to communicate, Lander's mother had spoken proudly of her mother's childhood with its loyal

Polish servants, horses stabled in the country, piano lessons and recitals, tea and cakes served in the drawing room. *Drawing room* was something Lander associated with Sigmund Freud or Sherlock Holmes: ... *showing the distraught young woman into my drawing-room ... Show the good inspector into my drawing-rooms, Watson ...* Even today the phrase evoked a cool, secretive, cavelike seriousness; a heavy velvet splendour in dark walnut trim where mysterious rituals were enacted. A place unseen, mysterious, but deeply felt, like the human mind itself.

One day in 1902 the Sternfelds had gathered in the drawing-room and submitted to a portrait photographer, an afternoon's vanity that became the only lasting proof of their ever having existed. The son in the picture was his great-uncle Henryk in a white student cap, on a visit from the medical faculty in Berlin. The three lively, dimpled daughters stood behind their bald, bearded father, whose one arm rested on a small table draped in fringed damask. One of those girls married the Vilna agent, came to New York, and became Lander's grandmother. His great-grandmother, almost frail and scholarly, with a Talmudist's face unreplicated among her children, seemed to be the only Sternfeld looking beyond that day, out of the drawing room into the future.

After Berlin, Henryk Sternfeld had gone to Vienna, become an apostle of Freud and set up the first psychoanalytic practice in western Poland. Sternfeld meant *field of stars*, and he'd used a starry comet-tail as an informal family crest on personalized stationery. As a wise, Freud-circle elder, he had lectured at Columbia in the year of Lander's birth, shmoozed with his old Berlin and Vienna colleagues at the New School, and turned down an offer to remain in New York. He'd found the city too trashy and Italian for his tastes. Henryk Sternfeld preferred *Don Giovanni* to *Aida*, Furtwängler to Toscanini. *I could not live in a country who listens to such a posturing little monkey without complaining,* he wrote on his field of stars, thanking his relatives: his widowed sister, her cultivated daughter and civil-servant husband, and their baby son, for hospitality in a Depression-dimmed, cluttered Brooklyn flat.

Lander's mother had a special name – Heinrich, sometimes just Heini – for her famous uncle.

In 1937 the great man, his wife, family, grandchildren and servants returned to Poland on first-class tickets. The return trip was curiously uncrowded. The captain's table was open to them every night, champagne was pressed upon them from breakfast till bedtime. The orchestra played all their favourite tunes. He was interviewed at dockside about the future of Freud's revolution in America, which he considered dubious, and their New York purchases were whisked through customs.

On *Blutsonntag*, September 3, 1939, when the German forces swept across Pomerania, all the Polish schoolteachers and doctors, all the professors, students and college graduates, every man with education, every unionist, artist, priest, communist, every nationalist, every politician, every policeman, every gypsy and Jew, every defective, every mental patient was taken to the back wall of the cathedral and shot. Thirty thousand died that Sunday, in actions that lasted from first Mass till after dark, the white-bearded analyst in his British tweeds – teacher, doctor, professor, nationalist, Jew – at the top of every list.

As a child, Lander had felt the same connection to the field of nighttime stars that he did, as a grown-up, to drawing-rooms, and as just minutes earlier he had to the Pomeranian etchings. The feeling was smallness, of standing alone on a hill in the dark, looking up. It was a feeling of wonder, close to exquisite heartbreak. Those families in the etchings under the umbrellas eating their ice cream staring at the canal could have been his, but they'd become stars, eighty light-years away. There had been a rupture in history, like his mother's memories and her ability to communicate them; nothing but shreds could be retrieved.

He turned slowly from the city view, then stared down at the dusty park studded with tree-stumps where refugee families were lighting their fires, and the string of dented Polish Fiats parked in the narrow street below him, then looked back over his shoulder into the empty council chambers. He realized suddenly where he was standing. Adamowicz drew closer, as though to help a stricken man. He recognized it now, everything. This is the balcony, underlined with dingy marble trim, that his grandmother had stood on, waving down to servants, looking out on an urban forest. The block of mansions had been destroyed. Wood mouldings and paintings had been carried out or burned, books and records destroyed, mezzuzahs ripped from the doorframes. He felt he had suffered a stroke. He gripped the iron railings of the balcony and held on until the roaring in his ears, the swirl of images, the weakness in his body subsided.

The Banality of Virtue

THE LETTER WAS WAITING at his Warsaw hotel. 'When you're in Gdansk, why not come to dinner in Sopot?' It was signed Tewfiqa and Slava. The hopeful sign was the greeting: *Dear Daddy*. Gdansk was on his government-arranged, Baltic itinerary, before Helsinki and Stockholm, after Bydgoszcz and a few other vowel-challenged provincial cities.

So: Rachel still noted his presence, perhaps even cared. At Wellesley, she'd started out a Black studies major, dropped out at the end of her junior year, worked a year in a Roxbury daycare centre, then enrolled at Hunter in Russian. Then graduate research ('It Ain't Just Pushkin: The African Presence in 19th-century Russia') had taken her to Moscow during perestroika. Knowing Russian isn't just a refinement, like French or Italian; it's a vocation, it becomes your life. You can write your ticket. As a Russian-speaking African-American woman with a suburban accent and social skills, she'd been offered places in business, in government, in the media, none of which had interested her. Rejection spoke well of her character, Lander had thought, her eventual prospects.

On a trip to Tashkent she'd married a Russian named Pyotr Shvartz, making her a real *shvartze* – what's new – she'd joked. They planned to return to the States, but when consular investigators swept through their apartment on a surprise visit, they found that Pyotr had left on an extended trip to the Caucasus with no forwarding address. The apartment contained no evidence of his underwear, no cigarette butts, no vodka – none of the sweet nothings of international courtship. The Shvartzes could not satisfy minimal standards of intimacy to warrant immigration through marriage. They called themselves Jews, but Pyotr knew no rituals and abhorred the very idea of Israel. ('I've been surrounded by Muslims all my life,' he'd said). She claimed Jewishness despite appearances, even reciting from the *haftara* and taking out pictures of her elaborate Chappaqua *bat-mitzvah* ten years earlier. Rachel had always taken to rituals. 'You don't look very comfortable in those pictures,' the official had noted.

Like many people in that time and place, the young Landers had felt their personal distaste for the war in Vietnam, and their country's failure to fight for racial justice at home, called for an act of positive, lifelong commitment. The prevailing ethos dictated: think globally, act locally; save one child and you've saved the world; if you're not part of the solution, you're part of the problem. They were liberal, concerned, suburban young professionals – *yuppie* had not yet been invented – Lander a clinical psychologist with academic connections in the city, and Judy just beginning to interest herself in the women's movement. She was debating a return to school – law, perhaps, or local politics.

One Sunday she did the unthinkable, threw the *Times* across the living room, tore up the 'Magazine' section and the 'Book Review', ripped the rabbit ears from the back of the television set and jerked the cord from its socket. 'I want to deface something!' she screamed. 'I want to scratch my name on the Lincoln Memorial. I want to blow something up!' Lander thought she was acting out, behaving badly, being just a little bratty, jealous of his life in the city and some early success. Like Lander, she was ready for a tango with the Zeitgeist.

He made the not unreasonable suggestion – in that time and place – that they look into adopting a baby. Judy had lost pregnancies in the third and fourth months; she couldn't tolerate a third. If you did observable good in removing an innocent life from hopeless conditions and resolving your own problems in the bargain, you were fulfilling the injunctions of the age. What fiercer act of good faith, of commitment, of engagement?

And so they pondered their choices: black, native American, Third World. Interracial adoptions were considered noble. Black parents couldn't take white or Asian babies, nor could they keep up with the avalanche of orphaned or abandoned black babies. The Landers never looked for children of their faith, or interracial children offered by Jewish orphanages. Although Lander was just a generation removed from the Holocaust, he and Judy were non-observant suburbanites for whom 'Jewish' was little more than a default position. He felt Jewish more strongly than he felt Other; it felt more a statement of what he was not than of what he was.

At the adoption agency the baby girls had been dressed in pink flannel nighties with pink ribbons in their nappy hair; the boys in T-shirts with cute, snarly sayings or team logos. Some of the girls were obviously bright, affectionate and pretty, potential Diana Rosses reaching out for an audience. But the Landers had wanted a damaged baby. They'd wanted a baby through whom the American holocaust had swept. They found her in a corner crib, still as a loaf of pumpernickel, wrapped in pink. She whimpered but didn't cry. The whimpering didn't change pitch or intensity even when she was picked up and held. Heroin, the nurse explained. Autistic, Lander thought. She's mourning something, said Judy. When the agency cautioned against taking her, of all the baby girls in the nursery, Judy clung to her even more tightly. She might never recover from the drugs in her blood, from suspect genes, the trauma of her delivery, the loss of a finger (they hadn't noticed) from frostbite. She'd been found in the garbage, not even wrapped in rags or a blanket. How could they resist? The whole world would go into her making.

Rachel (as they named her) did recover, even from the loss of a finger and the scattering of dead spots on her toes and the rim of one ear. They took extra care to wrap her warmly in the winter. She was slow in developing, at least by the standards of Chappaqua, but the Montessori school practically sent a limousine daily to pick her up – their only black child – and by three she had passed subtle developmental tests that indicated she was average or at least not handicapped. Average was not acceptable in the Lander house; the school allowed that she might even be slightly above average. As her suburban childhood progressed she was given the full range of skating and dance lessons, she learned to play the piano – passably, given the one-finger handicap – and a variety of stringed instruments.

Lander's father, a pants-presser turned dry-cleaner, had a low opinion of a *shvartze* granddaughter. Not race exactly, to which he was more indifferent than tolerant, but the sheer visual inappropriateness. The mismatch – how to explain her running around behind the counter when she was in the laundry? Who would push her in the stroller in the park and do the explaining? Rachel at six and seven messed up his ticket-recall system – his last great extravagance, his pride, the automated pulley-chain – in his laundry. She loved to watch a thousand shirts and suits march along an overhead track, emerge like trains from a tunnel and stop precisely at the cash register in her grandmother's hand. Lander's father would slap her hand. It costs, he said, each press of the button is like an elevator going up three stories. It was Lander's mother who put her on her lap and let her punch in each customer's ticket.

One summer day when Rachel, then seven, was playing in the front yard, Judy noticed something disturbing although she did not know exactly how to cope with it – or when, or if – to intervene. An old black woman shabbily dressed in an overcoat and watch-cap stood in the Lander yard talking to their daughter. Judy thought at first, I shouldn't disturb them. They must seem miraculous to one another. She's probably a maid in the neighbourhood, Judy rationalized, except that maids were better dressed and younger and would never be allowed to wear an out-of-season overcoat. By the time Judy got to the front door the old woman had seized Rachel and begun shaking her by the shoulders. Before she could intervene the old woman had reduced the girl to tears. 'Your name is Miz Lander? I believe you have stolen my granddaughter, Amber. I was just telling her about her real mama. And I don't reckon she's ever going to forget.'

Judy, ashamed of her reaction for the rest of her life, abandoned them both and ran inside and called the police, saying there's a horrible woman attacking my child who must be removed. Later she thought of it as the moment that ended Rachel's childhood and turned her from their daughter into something they always feared was present, like a hidden genetic malfunction that would take its time but surely announce itself. By the time Judy returned to her daughter the old woman had left and the girl had regained her composure and announced, 'My real mama's name is Latasha and she loves me and she's sleeping in heaven tonight but dreaming of me.'

They never saw the old woman again, yet they felt she had marked their house and was keeping them under some sort of surveillance. She noticed young black men – uncles? cousins? – in parked cars at the corner. Judy walked Rachel to school and picked her up until she got old enough to demand a bit of privacy. Rachel did appear to be naturally athletic, taller, faster, stronger, compared to most of the girls in high school and to poor myopic Sam ('Sam Lander the Salamander,' Rachel would call him), their son born five years later. Though the Landers tried to turn her away from the easy clichés of track and basketball, or discouraged coaches who salivated at the prospect of a fast-twitch princess on their team, she nevertheless excelled in sports and studies. In that ninety-percent-white, nine-percent-Asian suburban school, she was popular: Homecoming

Queen, three-sport captain, the lone black face in various activities and honour societies, naturally gifted in music and languages, Harvard early-admittee, popular with boys.

But Amber, or her reincarnations, had never died. When Rachel was eleven, attending a two-week summer camp, Lander had received an urgent call. 'Dr Lander, this is Tewfiqa's crafts teacher. We have to talk.'

'I'm a clinician, Mrs Tatum. What seems to be the girl's problem?'

'The girl, Dr Lander, carries a knife. She threatens everyone.'

'That's very disturbing – wait, has she harmed Rachel?'

'Rachel? Rachel, Dr Lander? I'm talking about Tewfiqa. My God –'

Back in the German times, when Danzig was the free city, Sopot had been a high bourgeois resort close enough for business, removed enough for graciousness. Up the coast was Königsberg, now Russian Kaliningrad, the capital, the city of philosophers and musicians, one-time cosmopolis of the Baltic. Further north, Riga, ancient home of Lander's paternal side. A few hundred miles west in Lübeck and several lifetimes earlier, Tonio Kröger had admired Hans Hansen and Ingeborg Holm and splashed upon the beach. German Danzig had been the city of Günter Grass; Polish Gdansk was the city of Pawel Huelle and the shipyards, Lech Walesa and the fall of Communism. Across the waters came Helsinki Watch and the Nobel Prizes. Lander approved of the Baltic. Something appealed to him about the cold, septic, eel-torn Baltic – now a toxic dump, its fumes sealed by oil slicks. It seemed to have an admirable, civilizing effect on a dozen disparate people. Unlike, say, the Mediterranean.

Even today, Sopot retained a bit of charm, some faded pastel on the stucco and wood trim, narrow streets following the ancient dunes of a wilder, cleaner Baltic coast, low buildings with language-school placards in the second-floor windows. Nowadays Sopot had its own identity as a distant suburb, far from the city's swirl.

Her name was on the door, just as she'd warned him: *Tewfiqa Nigadyke*. He spent a long time looking at it before ringing the bell. How dare she, his daughter, his New World Lander, his atonement. Don't get in a panic, she'd warned him. Here, they think it's Dutch.

He'd made a scene, holding the phone and a bouquet of flowers in the Gdansk train station. She'd given him directions, she'd been warm and funny, then she threw him her new name. 'Of all the insults,' he'd cried. 'I won't visit you. That's not a name, it's a vanity plate.'

'I didn't expect you to understand,' she'd said.

'Don't hand me that past tense, that "didn't expect" like you *always* knew. I understand perfectly. You want the world to pay attention to you. What's not to understand?'

'And you don't?' she'd countered.

'I never said respect. I said attention.'

'Well, forgive me if I'm a simple English teacher. Did you ever think this respect you've earned makes it very hard for someone like me to have to share your name?'

Slava was small, not ignorant and substantial the way Lander had been raised to think of Polish women. If anything, she seemed frail and scholarly, her hair chewed and blondish, glasses overlarge, ears prominent, teeth bad. She earned her living by translating French and German books and investment guides and how-to's for new profit-minded Polish publishers.

'Slava was the Polish translator of Cixous and Kristeva and Christa Wolf. Now they only send her crap. I'm teaching her English so we can collaborate on Toni Morrison,' Tewfiqa explained. His daughter had become the Pole: wide, strong, assertive.

They had three rooms, painted in red and blue and green enamels – a medley of Popsicle colours that made you think of licking the walls – a kitchen alcove with a sink and a propane campstove with an oven hood, a small refrigerator; a bed-sitting-dining room with Indian bedspreads and a round table, and a small study with a paint-flecked desk and an old schoolroom chair which overlooked Sopot's main street. Slava tended flower-boxes and hanging ferns, they had a cat, an aquarium, Polish movie posters, a stereo, and stacks of books that had outgrown various attempts at bookcases. On the small dining table, rescued, it would appear, from the same schoolhouse, they had arranged a bottle of wine, a ham, a bowl of greens, another of noodles. Suddenly he was back in 1955, in his undergraduate student apartment in Hyde Park, the details so inevitable, so poignant, it was almost as though he'd described it to Rachel in his memories and she'd transcribed it.

Rachel – strike that, Tewfiqa, the Russian scholar – earned her living teaching English in a country that had rejected its last word of Russian six years before. It wasn't easy, being black, despite having a U.S. embassy English teaching certificate. Polish businessmen took one look at her and asked, how can an African person know English? This is a joke, surely. They saw NBA games and black movies and heard rap – they knew that wasn't English. How could a black person teach the language of Grisham and Waller? It was like letting a Ukrainian teach Polish. What *kind* of English would she be teaching? Would they land in New York and be taken prisoner by Harlem gangs?

Yeah, she'd say, that's a good one.

Can you imagine, she told Lander that evening, they take one look at me and sign up with some Australian dropout instead. Some Canadian. Some slushy-mouthed southerner. Some *Indian*. Weird vowels. Wrong rhythms. Serves them right.

The ham was small and fatty ('Good Polish ham is exported to Germany,' Slava apologized); she sliced it in strips and stuffed them inside *pyeroguies*. She was the cook. Rachel had always avoided the kitchen. They were a natural couple, speaking Polish and sometimes Russian or French. When Rachel was growing up, Lander had dreamed of sophistication for himself and his family, of an easy familiarity with the currents of the world, its languages. Strange that he should be the one adrift in itineraries and official meetings, scratching the surface of the earth. His daughter had accomplished it all on her terms, the world was no more complicated to her than the contingency of her passions. It seemed to him at the moment that nothing could be more appealing than coming home to a cheaply decorated colourful apartment in a seaside Polish resort and listening to Polish music on a kitchen portable in the company of two women stranger and more intimate to him than any two people in the world.

'We may emigrate to Australia,' she said. 'They recognize gay marriage.'

'When I was growing up, Australia was the ultimate white man's country,' he said. 'Bad as we were, we could pride ourselves at least we weren't South Africa and we weren't Australia.'

'Now, just look,' said his daughter. Slava was spooning out gobs of whipped cream over a rhubarb compote. 'Many Polish people are applying for South Africa, too.' The rhubarb colour matched the walls.

'Daddy,' she announced, 'we have a favour to ask.'

'Anything,' he said, regretting it immediately.
'It's big. You'll have to think about it.'
'Big brain,' he said. 'Big thought capability.'
'It's about Germany.'
'I've forgiven them. The Baltic is very forgiving.'
'They have a policy of return for Jews.'
'A little late. I'm happy where I am.'
'It's too late for you. Didn't we have property in Berlin?'
'*We?*'

Slava went back to the kitchen to throw handfuls of coffee into a pot of boiling water. She stayed longer than necessary.

'Didn't that psychiatrist uncle of yours have an office?'

'Uncle Henryk Sternfeld? He was Polish, but he had offices in Berlin. And Vienna.'

'Forget Vienna. Did he own it?'

Slava returned with coffee, and a plate of Swedish cookies.

'He might have. He was very successful. It would have been like him to own his office just to show that a Polish Jew could buy up a bit of Germany and analyse German patients. Of course, he would have gotten pleasure by renting it and taking their money and not investing in Germany at all.'

Slava turned to Tewfiqa. 'You say *gotten?* It sounds funny.'

'He would have *got* pleasure,' said Lander. 'He would especially have got pleasure owning a bit of Vienna. On Berggasse, near Freud. What are you driving at?'

'You're still my friend, Daddy? You'll still do anything?'

'I'm Daddy. Friend is a subset of Daddy.'

And then came the favour. The German government would restore ownership of private property to the survivor families of Jews uprooted – ('You mean rooted,' said Lander) – by the Nazis. The Poles would do the same for bourgeois families uncompensated by Communist seizures of property. Unfortunately, the Sternfelds had all been killed, but for Lander's mother, by the time the Communists took over. That left only Germany.

'Here is a copy of the deed, Dr Lander,' said Slava, in a mixture of German, which he understood, and French, which he found elusive. 'You see, we have done research. It is in the East Berlin, near the main synagogue. Near Prenzlauerstraße, with all the whores and artists. A third-floor flat. Three rooms, high ceilings, balcony overlooking enclosed courtyard. Very nice. It can be yours.'

'It can be ours, Daddy,' said Tewfiqa.

Ours? he thought. *Ours?* In the name of all history, what exactly did 'ours' mean? The words slipped out like a grunt, as though he'd been kicked or slapped. *No* way. 'You want Great-uncle Henryk's old place? I can't.' *Don't be foolish,* he wanted to add. Have you no shame? Does history mean nothing to you? How can you even think such a thing? It was shocking, a chutzpah-update for the nineties. He thanked them for the dinner. He wished them luck with Australia.

As he was leaving, his daughter said, 'You have always been very fair to me. You gave me a good education. I played along with everything you wanted me to do.'

'And I hope to continue,' said Lander.

'But you never told me you love me. The only person who ever loved me was my mama, and I never even saw her.'

'I love you, Tewfiqa,' said Slava.

'We all love in our different ways,' said Lander. *Look at your fingers, for God's sake, she took your fingers, the spots on your ears, she abandoned you in a Dumpster!*

And then he walked out of his daughter's life. Lander had loved his mother, who'd taken Rachel on her lap in their dry-cleaner's shop, who'd wheeled her stroller in the park and said to the dubious and inquisitive, 'Isn't she smart?' It was in witnessing his mother's final Alzheimer's years that he'd developed his theories of the mind and language, the retention of personality, of humanity, despite appearances. Everything he stood for, in a way, was a monument to her.

Now it was in her name that the Germans were empowering him to act. History in its clumsy circuit had turned a brief spotlight on him. Is this what history had in mind? Restitution to adopted daughters? To *this* daughter, who makes a mockery of blood? Germany's blood myth admitted to citizenship any refugee with German blood, any displaced Volga or Paraguayan Mueller, any Vladimir or Carlos Schmidt, but denied it to Turks born and raised in their country. Is entitlement carried through blood alone? What would it do with Amber-Rachel-Tewfiqa Lander-Shvartz-Niggadyke?

No, he thought, it's absurd, a betrayal. History should die completely, his family should disappear entirely from this wretched continent, rather than give their killers the comfort of a generous apology. He wanted to keep faith with something clean and pure, a sharp break, not this salt-pillar of regret, this what-if, this second chance.

Lander strolled down the darkened, downward-sloping main street of Sopot towards the long, lighted wooden pier jutting into the Baltic, to the station to catch the last train into Gdansk. Gangs of young men in leather jackets, punk hair and chains shouted insults at him, made gestures, followed him a few feet cursing him in German. Some nights the thought of a good beating, at least a good fight, seemed restorative, an arbitrary end to rumination. A beer bottle was thrown, wide of the mark.

In the station, he waited with groups of teenagers, picnickers with water bottles and guitars, for the last train into Gdansk. It was Sunday night, their fair skins, the complexions of Ingeborg Holm and Hans Hansen, were pink from the sun. They sang, they joked, they'd be at work in the morning, bank clerks and salesmen and students, their peaceful bourgeois lives resumed after sixty years. No one knew him or noticed him. Maybe he seemed just Polish, which, in a sense, he was.

The memory kept returning. His mother would put Rachel on her lap and allow her to punch the numbers on the customers' tickets. His mother pushed the stroller. 'What are you looking at? She's my granddaughter,' she'd say. 'Isn't she smart?' Loyalty to the greatness of his mother, that was the reason he was on this tour, why he could eat pyeroguies in his daughter's and her lover's rhubarb kitchen. It would be a hard case to make, the rich absurdity. The Germans won't get it. Do you apologize only to blood?

This is my daughter, isn't she smart? Her great-great-uncle was Henryk Sternfeld. Send the papers to my office.

A truth had been rising: When you meddle in fate for even the best of reasons, you force a realignment that implicates the universe. When the whole world screws you up, it takes even more of the world's resources to straighten you out. Rachel's case was dramatic, but so had Judy's been in the final years of their marriage, with her law degree, her suburban divorce-and-abuse practice, the repressed-memory cases, her conviction that the world she'd known had been a lie, that it was an evil and sinister place full of molesters, husbands and abusive mothers' boyfriends. The world had turned monstrous. She'd gone through madness before coming out the other end.

He'd been spared. His mother had saved him, his training had saved him, his professors, his colleagues. He'd clothed himself in virtue, like his great-uncle Henryk, seeing patients, listening to Mozart, until the border, all the borders, were sealed. The train arrived. Who knows, given a different history, he'd be a Polish psychiatrist like Uncle Henryk, going back to work in Gdansk from a weekend outing in the countryside. He had the face for it, the ancestry. He was one of the few men he'd ever met who could say after fifty years I'm leading the life I always wanted, I'm doing what I always intended, and what I have prepared myself for single-mindedly, still free to discover who I am and what I am capable of, and I'm not displeased. Is that not the modern definition of a monster?

White Children

I WAS BORN IN BROOKLYN in 1936. My earliest memory must be of the invasion of Poland, with my mother and our whole building screaming when they heard the names of bombed-out cities and overrun villages. Probably it left an impression because I was frightened for my own safety from bombs and Nazis in our own little extended Polish village off Flatbush Avenue. Adrenalin is a powerful memory-fixative.

I have vivid memories of Pearl Harbor Sunday, of FDR's death, and the dropping of the atomic bomb. Growing up, I saw all the war movies, especially the Pacific ones. In the fifties we made fun of cheap, copycat Japanese products. The Japanese could handle repetitive tasks competently enough, we were told, but we needn't fear their creativity. 'Usa' was a factory-city in central Japan created so they could stamp 'Made in USA' on the back of their flimsy tin toys held together with half-bent metal tabs. I was a twenty-seven-year-old assistant professor holding a white rat in the basement of the old lab on 166th Street with Kenji Wakamatsu, a postdoc fellow – I injecting a protein in the rat's brain and Kenji preparing to administer a shock – when a technician ran in shouting that Kennedy had been shot. It was Kenji who broke down and cried. We didn't think they did that.

Now I'm the visitor to Kenji's lab at Tokyo Neurolinguistic, and he's arranged a small apartment for me in a university-owned building across from Kanishikawa Park. Everything is miniaturized: The television, the refrigerator, the stove; the ceilings are low, the tables graze the rug, my knees come up to my shoulders when I sit on the sofa, and my sleeping mattress is on the floor. I can't cook or store more than one meal ahead; half a watermelon would engulf the kitchen. It's perfect for the *bonsai* life I lead. A friend once described the absurdity of his parents' lives, slow-moving and growing witless, brutalized by an oversized house, unable to get to a ringing phone in time, bullied by the family range (*cook, cook!*), the cavernous refrigerator (*cram, cram!*). The sheer dimension and convenience of their house had become an intimate bully. If only space could grow smaller, to match our disappearing mass in the universe and the fleeting time remaining to us.

I'm here, really, beyond the research and my friendship with Kenji and atonement for my ancient bigotries, to see my son, the Buddhist monk.

Meditating on ice last winter, Sammy froze four toes and had to have them amputated. Kenji told me to come quickly, we would try to save him. What kind of father allows his son to starve in robes and walk with a limp? My daughter is now a Polish lesbian, my ex-wife a recovered pill-addict. Sammy's former girlfriend, an Australian named Melanie, my potential daughter-in-law, mother of my fantasy grandchildren, told me he'd surrendered his toes graciously, even ecstatically. The monastery, according to Kenji, is known for its piety. Its monks hobble proudly, like lepers, on a fraction of their digits. They do not encourage visitors. To meet his fleshy father, his coincidental progenitor, to be reminded of a specific bodyshell, they say, would disrupt his meditation. And so I spend my days in Tokyo doing research in Kenji's lab, waiting for my son's *sensei* to give his permission for me to board the Bullet, then a bus, then to walk up the mountains to the monastery.

My daughter smokes. Of all the incongruities in my life, advice ignored, examples set, I sometimes think that's the most inexplicable of all.

In the post-dawn jogging cool-down every morning when I'm making my way back through Kanishikawa Park, I have to cut like a halfback through rows of old folks, mostly women, trudging silently to the park to do their exercises to piped-in music and recorded commands. They crouch like imaginary archers pulling back invisible strings. I am the youngest person among hundreds. Some mornings, it seems like quintessential warfare between mythical antagonists, my sweaty, against-the-current, personal exertion versus their flowing-downstream collective choreography. They stare at me, some mutter to their friends. I don't think they're saying, 'Look at this marvel of human engineering.'

In the park at five o'clock every afternoon an old man in khaki shorts and a Colorado Rockies baseball cap plays – without mood or inflection, and with recurrent flaws – one stanza of 'Stardust' on a dented trumpet. Men normally avoid exposing the sour slide of their fallibility in public (I've spent most of my fifty-nine years hiding even a hint); his tactless insouciance seems to me – perhaps I'm being sentimental – Japanese loneliness, the other side of so much community and public virtue.

WHITE CHILDREN

We used to believe (and guys like me taught it) that you can never start training your children too early for a happy, productive life. By the age of two or three, they're already intact genetic and psychological entities. Nothing but a few social nuances can be added or subtracted. And so we read to our little entities, Rachel and Sam, we took them to plays and gallery openings, political rallies and poetry readings. We wanted them to share our irony and our passion, and all the discomforts of consciousness in a contingent universe. We wanted them to be stronger than we had been and to resist what we'd surrendered to. And of course, we wanted to be admired for all of it. We were the kind of parents any normal person despises.

(Now, when I hear young children coughing or crying at a concert, at a lecture or in a theatre, I want to shout: *If you can afford these prices, you can damn well afford a babysitter!* Spare me conversation during the opening credits of a movie, don't even ruin the Coke and popcorn ads, the trailers, don't destroy the atmosphere of surrender).

I remember those lecturers and their rhetorical questions from the podium: *Is this thing working?* (how I copied all their mannerisms! I knew I'd be a featured lecturer one day and that the witty, casually informative introductions I was labouring over would someday be another assistant professor's rehearsed ad-libs for me; great halls would fill, *for me*, and I'd have to practise the proper modest attitude, the solicitous concern for acoustics): *How about the back, can you hear me?* And Sam, who was four, would shout back, *I can hear you, Mister Beard!* Such a bright, confident, unselfconscious little guy, people would say. Once, at a great poet's last public reading, Sam started crying. I thought he'd developed a tummy-ache. *He's so sad,* little Sam explained. Such a kind, empathetic, tenderhearted child, well ahead of the pace of Piaget's theories. We were raising a genius of compassion and we didn't know how to deal with it.

This little boy of ours was an unfailing delight. Judy had had three miscarriages, then we'd adopted Rachel and she was a chore to manage, to bring back to life. She'd been abandoned in a Harlem Dumpster, she'd lost a finger, part of her ears, she had congenital heroin dependency. Then Sam, the miracle child, an uneventful pregnancy, and easy delivery – anxious to please even as a baby. Son-challenged at the *seder,* he was always our wise son, sometimes our simple son; Rachel always played the wicked child.

I loved him without limit or reservation. I woke him up if I came home late, I put him on my shoulders when we shopped. I ran up and down the aisles, along the sidewalks, down the office hallways, and he giggled (he had that easy laugh that I'd never mastered – my father would have discouraged it anyway); I held him in my lap, nibbled on his precious ears, blew on his neck, caressed that babysoft hair, God! that new baby smell, like a puppy or a kitten that we didn't want to have grow up too fast, but he stayed adorable at every age. I thrilled to his perfect little body running, always running, through the apartment. I wanted him running, eternally. I wanted to be his protector, forever.

And now he limps, walks with a stick. His ribs show, I'm told, though I'm not allowed to see him. His balding scalp is shaved. They've taken away his glasses.

He responded with love. He loved strangers, he was never shy, he trusted everyone and everything, a babysitter's delight. When bedtime came he'd sneak down the hall to his room, trailing his blanket, blowing a kiss and saying only, '*Me go pleep now*,' without our having to settle him down. Rachel, we practically had to dope, to tie down, to visit a dozen times in the night.

Sam rewrote all the manuals: No teething problems, no Terrible Twos, no jealousy, no selfishness. *Me go pleep now* still makes me smile, sometimes cry. He brought out the best in everyone, even his sister. She'd push his carriage, change him, answer back to Blacks in the park who'd demand an explanation for a little black girl attending a white boy.

'He's my brother, you fool!' I never loved her more. She called him Sam Lander the Salamander, not unkindly. She still calls him Sal.

I'm at a loss. He was untroubled and precocious. People used to say when he was eight years old, that little boy has *soul*. I can't believe that it's just my ego insisting that I'm somehow at the centre of everything, somehow to blame. I must have done something shattering. How did I let him down? I can't remember. He's lost, I can't find him, he's what my father called *a minyan in Minot*, a needle in a haystack. Rachel blames me for everything in her life, as did Judy, so I feel entitled to claim just a little responsibility for his russet robes, his mutilated feet and his ribs sticking out. I think back to that perfect little body running down our narrow hallway. I wait for 'Stardust', and I cry.

When Sam was nine or ten, he would go into Manhattan with me on the train and head to the museums with just a sketchbook and pencils. We didn't worry about security in those days. What could be safer for a boy than a day in the museum with a sketchpad, then joining his father for lunch? It was a delight to sit with such an attentive little boy who couldn't wait to get back to the Natural History or the New York State Museum in order to sit in front of the cases and sketch. He had that omnivorous attention to the world that all bright children have at some time, before age and education dim it, the ability to rattle off facts learned from plaques about Indian encampments, mastodon hunts, old subway cars, reconstructed interiors of immigrant tenements.

He was good at all of it, his drawings plastered my office doors and corkboards. I remember the diorama of *Cold Water Flat, Brooklyn, 1889*, from the New York City Historical Museum. 'That's the way we lived,' I told him, 'your great-grandparents lived just like this.' Even in the Brooklyn of my childhood, I'd lived six or seven years like that, those first memories of Poland and Pearl Harbor came from bathing in the kitchen sink and looking out the window onto the street, and I remembered the clothes hanging out the back, the ice deliveries, the shouts and crying from other apartments sharing our airshaft, and I'd quickly add happy stories of my mother heating the water on the gas rings for my bath in the kitchen sink, the cut-rate Elijahs rented from large families who timed their doorknocking to add drama to the *seder*. Otherwise, even the poverty of my childhood made him sad. I'd take him through the labs to the faculty lunchroom and introduce him to my colleagues.

Kenji remembered him, when he was two. In a roundabout way it's the reason I was invited to Tokyo Neurolinguistic, thirty years later. Sam called on Kenji when he came to Tokyo just three years ago. Back then, Sam was a different sort of person, worldly and fun-loving, looking up my friends, taking strangeness in stride.

After college Sam left to see the world and to learn off-beat languages, for which he had a knack. Two years stretched to seven. He became a DJ in Thailand, started English schools in Korea and Indonesia, and finally landed an advertising job among lively expats in Tokyo. He had an apartment in Roppongi, he learned Japanese, he had Japanese girlfriends, then Melanie, and then everything stopped. No letters, no calls, mail returned. Now, Melanie says, he's lost sixty pounds and he looks like Woody Allen playing Yul Brynner.

I worried that we'd deprived him of a normal childhood, the very reason we'd moved out to Chappaqua. No Little League, no Scouts, no music lessons or summer camps – that was Rachel's business, at which she excelled. He didn't want to give up his precious summers with me and the museums in the city. Neither did I.

Did I set him up to become a Buddhist when we took him to Australia for a year, putting the kids in an Adelaide suburban junior high? Australia to me was just another lab with friendly colleagues and a chance to interview Aborigines and study their language acquisition, aging and language loss, a pleasant house on a river where kids trapped platypuses, and kangaroos nibbled the hedges, but a city and country, for Judy and me, of no great consequence. But for Sam and Rachel, Australia was a full new society, a city to explore, new sports to learn, a set of new models and standards, where their accents set them apart. Six months in a strange place when you're an adolescent, compared to ten years when you're an adult, and the consequences are like a meteor slamming to earth instead of a light spring shower. He came back from Australia sounding like a perfect Oz, knowing the cricket and rugby stars, the local music. Perhaps settling down even in that most American of countries doomed my children to lives of permanent exile. Not just exile; transformation.

In Tokyo, I've learned to turn abstinence into a kind of hedonism. It pleases me to shop at the neighbourhood Co-op like an elderly pensioner, to weigh out spotty apples and woody carrots, to select a dehydrated dinner from well-stocked shelves. Every selection is a total surprise, no English on any package, no instructions I can follow, no taste I can expect. Sweet or salty, meat or fruit, I won't know till I take a bite. Clear plastic bottles filled with liquid; shampoo or cooking oil? I don't know the language, but I feel I can read the faces, the body language. It's reassuring to be surrounded by elaborate signs, knowing none of them apply to me. The opposite of Alzheimer's must be Kafka's disease, where everything points to you, but lacks all meaning. The steak house at the top of the street features a two-hundred-dollar dinner of *matsuzaka* beef, not just prime Kobe, but eating in Tokyo for under two dollars – that's adventure. Tokyo has rendered me slightly Alzheimered, unable to read, to respond, to learn from context. I've become an abstinence junkie.

I wonder if Sam went through any of this. He always had a native woman with him, he mastered languages from local dialects, he learned to cook the local cuisine. He knew the most specialized words, things a professor would have to look up, because he started with the fruits and vegetables, birds and trees, the cuts of meat, the fish, the sexual moves, the grammar of seamless belonging.

I like to think I have an appreciation for mysticism. In other centuries, science and mysticism were not so far apart. Then, ten years ago, quite literally, I dreamed my future. Faces started entering my dreams, my brain went on a kind of untethered voyage. At first, the faces frightened me, like circulating malignancies looking for a host organ. Other nights I would rush to bed, monitoring diverse populations trying to escape my brain, or gain admission. My brain was just a mediator between past and future.

(Now, I spend my nights in guilty dreams. I seem to have crossed wires with remorseless villains. Murderer! Liar! Disfigurer! The first hour of every morning is a long waking from nighttime dread. Thank God it was only a dream! But I used to trust my dreams, they contained visions and good advice.)

Ten years ago, I said yes to a challenge, or what I interpreted as a challenge. I was married, the children were grown. I'd served on the school board, done my bit for Democrats when even old friends were turning Reaganite, pushed for recycling and better race relations. I had a lawn to manage, dogs to walk, tickets to sports and cultural events, cars in the driveway, parties to give and to go to. I had a mother, failing in her mind, to visit. At times, like everyone, I felt like an unclaimed suitcase going round and round on a baggage carousel. Mislabelled? Abandoned? My face and body had begun to sag, like an underpacked, soft-sided suitcase after a long trip, revealing the outlines of something vague and resistant inside. I didn't know it was a bomb. I looked into the mirror and thought: It's not so bad today, but I don't want this process to go any further. Standard midlife crisis stuff. All in all, a good life, proper for a man turning fifty.

If an informed choice had been offered (maybe it's never a choice, more a Bargain with the Cosmic Prompter) to persist in the comforting life of exercise bikes, educational and slightly risky vacations (Cuba, Egypt, China, South Africa), fruit-tree pruning and dog breeding, investment tracking, harmless flirtations, or something more dangerous: surrendering to your dreams – literally, entering the landscape of your nightly release – exploring the power of your brain's own programming (is it Microsoft that asks, 'Where do you want to go today?' My advice is, unplug, don't answer), I would never have picked up the option. I would have stayed in Chappaqua.

By yielding to the challenge, I set in motion a series of events that implicated the world. I was given access to a population inside my head. It was a mystic's vision – that I might just be a drop of blood in the universe, but that drop was a diagnostic motherlode containing the whole world, everything ever written or known, every life ever lived, every landscape ever explored – but I was a scientist and it's very inconvenient for a scientist to receive such a prompt. Better to treat it as a symptom of something repressed. Buy a red Miata, have an affair, stay in Chappaqua.

Somehow, like a child picking berries who sees a bat flying from the hillside, or who feels a rush of cold air from a cleft in the rocks, I had stumbled into a fissure. But that fissure was in my head, a pathway of hyper-speech that should have been closed by normal speech, by social training, by the protocols of science itself. Those faces, those dreams, were the bats pouring from the hillside, and I entered (or it entered me, I was asleep), and I found inside my skull a lightless crystal palace, prehistoric bones, lampblack sketches, colourless fish and the agency of bats. A harder, more contingent universe than I ever suspected. The brain's software is infinite, Master Bill. I have been living in that cave for the past ten years.

I remember a moment from Erasmus Hall, my dear old school in Brooklyn, when the majesty of algebra dawned in my life, its appropriateness to every thought in the universe. I know that waking dream of my fourteen-year-old self as a precursor to nighttime dreams of fifty; I know that everything in my life between fifteen and fifty was, essentially, a diversion from truth. I heard music that day, the room went dark purple, the other students disappeared. The beauty of the numbers was overwhelming, like the night sky in the planetarium. Everything in the world can be made equal to something else! There's a formula to balance everything! The universe is composed of equivalents! The world is a balance of push and pull, light and dark, action and reaction. Every single term, every figure, every expression, can be balanced by something else. It seemed more powerful than antibiotics; algebra was a kind of purely mental penicillin. That's what all the great minds were doing: Applying algebra, finding the equation for neutralizing evil or suffering or poverty.

I say *this* equals *that* because I've put an equal sign between them; all I have to do now is solve the equation for *x*.

Is that what made him a Buddhist monk, Sam's equivalent *satori*, an early attachment to staged interiors, to the presumed purity of the diorama, to looming silent forms permanently caught with spears in their hands against a staggering mastodon, their women permanently pounding meal and flax, that, and discovering a cache of platypus eggs and accidentally destroying them from too much love, the taunts of a black sister and crying over Holocaust poetry at the age of four?

2.

'You cod-sperm jockeys are all alike,' says Kenji in mock anger. 'Yesterday *shirako* was on the menu. Today it's out of season.' We're on our weekly pub-crawl and restaurant-binge. He writes out *shirako* – cod sperm – for me in Chinese characters: 'white'/'children'. I spend the week on ramen noodles and dried dinners, proud of a perverse frugality that takes me through Tokyo on five dollars a day. I break free on Friday nights. I've been in Tokyo for the night of luminous dwarf squid, when the plates are served in the dark and you can follow the twinkling lights of a hundred chopsticks. I've eaten my way through sardine runs and the spawning of transparent shrimp. I've consumed the guts and brains and eyes of everything that sinks or swims or floats in Japanese water. In the place of cod-sperm he whips up a plate of salted squid gut.

'You want it fresh, don't you?' leers the *sashimi* chef as he carves bouquets, like unfolding roses, of beet-red tuna. 'Just like the lady cod. She likes her *shirako* real fresh.'

'*Seku hara,* too!' I interject, and the chef throws up his hands. How Japanese, to have learned the word for sexual harassment in a sashimi bar. It doesn't matter where I pick up words, contexts don't count. At nearly sixty, I'm a two-year-old in Japanese, grabbing at fleeting objects, unable to read or to express my needs and ideas. Thank God for baseball, a familiar, transferable attachment; thank God for sumo, something new to appreciate. Thank God for the beautiful logic of Japanese.

If I were a small, polite man in a black business suit, mindful of every step I took, observing the painful intricacies of a ritualized society, I too would dream sumo dreams, buffing up to a quarter ton, stripping down to an orange breechclout, planting one foot on Honshu, another on Kyushu, and gut-butting an opponent all the way to Okinawa.

'Sumo – lose it, or use it!' Kenji had joked. He led me through the tournament. Sumo stables like baseball clubs, colours like racing silks.

Maybe once a week I get the urge for company and restaurant food, and I call Kenji. Hence the cod-sperm bars with televised baseball, the salted squid guts, the weekly trip to our favourite *yakitoria* at Yurukucho, tucked among the girders under the Hibiya El. Waiters rush from table to table taking orders by cellphone in the smoky gloom. There was a time when languages fired my brain, like walking in an unfamiliar city long enough to gain comfort, make friends, find love. The years are gone when I could do a city on my own, when the streets and monuments, the smattering of new words, the growing familiarity that comes with a week of walking, taking subways and buses, when the magnificence of alien anonymity is enough to satisfy me. I need Kenji.

Kenji Wakamatsu and I are the same age, although I think of him as younger. He's trim and dark-haired (although he dyes it); I'm plump despite the running. I think of the matted grey hairs on the top of my head as a personal web-site. He'd been my student and he'd already published more than I had but he'd needed American certification for possible immigration purposes, and so he had placed himself in my class. A college teacher, I'd decided in shame, should be older than his students, wiser if not smarter, and more published. Kenji's presence helped me retire from teaching and to stay in research.

'If you could train your crows to eat cigarette butts, Tokyo would be the cleanest city in the world,' I tell him. We're walking at night along my morning running route, avoiding the restaurants I know by the fragrance of their overnight garbage. He's looking for a *mukokuseki* restaurant, something new to show me from Tokyo's 'bubble' days in the eighties when Japan felt it could afford to take the best from the rest of the world, mix them up, Korean and French, Mexican and Chinese, Italian and Thai, with a Japanese spin.

Without Kenji, Tokyo would be a meaningless maze. He tells me I did the same for him in those New York years, but I can't remember walks we took, or meals, only lists of suggested readings. He remembers baseball games, and where else could he have learned the Dodger lineups of the fifties, Yankee games of the sixties, except from me? He swears we watched

WHITE CHILDREN

Mantle and Maris together; now we watch Matsui, the young stud of the Yomiuri Giants, and the six-hundred-pounders of Sumo. He remembers my mother, meals I took him to in Brooklyn. Perhaps Kenji's New York was like Sam's Adelaide, a time of accelerated growth that left him forever dissatisfied with Japan and exquisitely tuned to America. He travels as much I do, we move over the surface of the world like touring pros, hitting the opens, shmoozing with the sponsors.

'Try the *patapata-gyoza*,' he suggests, and I check the English menu: *meat-stuffed boned chicken wings*. Other entrees seem jauntily existential: 'Let's roll wild duck meat and vegetables together by lettuce and see what happens!' He takes the squid and corn lasagna.

'Boned and deboned mean the same thing, don't they?' he asks. 'What's a foreigner to do?'

'Gutted and degutted. Seeded and seedless.'

'It suggests a certain deft but elusive logic,' he says. 'What is empty? Is it empty, or is it air-stuffed?'

'Sammy used to say I had a lot of baldness.'

'*Going to bat for someone* – means standing up for him, no? But if you literally go to bat for someone, you are removing him from the game, right?'

'How about recover?' I say. 'It should mean re-burial, but it means to restore. How can you recover and still get out of bed?'

'We're in trouble, my friend. Japanese, on the other hand, is so logical. Think of the white children.'

'*Second to none*. Supposed to be a compliment – think about it.'

'We get less Alzheimer's, too,' he said.

In his spare time, drawing on his American years, Kenji translates American writers, from self-help books to serious novels. If he had not been a Japanese male of his generation with parents and a family to support and a society to rebuild, he would have been a writer. He feels it his personal mission to rid Japanese culture of its mysterious anti-Semitism. It must not be easy, translating Dr Ruth and Cynthia Ozick, among others, into Japanese.

'I'm a child of the restaurant business,' he'd confided to me on other evenings, if only to apologize for certain pedantic asides that I always found fascinating. But this evening I want to talk of Sam; Kenji's culinary history doesn't seem appropriate. I fear that his monastery will be forever closed to me, that he's suffering and I will never see him. Kenji has been handling my petitions.

'This society calls itself Confucian, but we inherited Confucianism from China,' he says. 'Getting imported concepts slightly wrong is our saving national virtue, I feel. What you're up against is monks who think they are very good Confucianists and very good Zen Buddhists. They can therefore be hard and inflexible, then just as suddenly, enigmatic and compliant.'

'I'm waiting for some flexibility.'

'Unfortunately, they have no concept of waiting.'

And then he lights a cigarette, leans back, and smiles at me. Another chapter in the bright book of Japanese life, Kenji's personal history, is about to unfold. 'This is, in a way, about waiting,' he says. 'Your grandfather came to New York from –'

'Riga,' I say.

'Yes, beautiful Riga. Well, Riga in a sense came to my grandfather. It was 1884. He was five years old, and so far as he ever knew, an orphan. That is, he remembers no life before the arrival of Germans in Edo harbour. He remembers speaking no language but German, no food, no clothes, but German. A German boat came to Edo to establish a German embassy, and he eventually became a German cook. He never learned to cook Japanese. Even his wife was only a German cook. Pork, sauerkraut, sausages, beer, white wine. He learned to make all of it.

'Their son, my father, learned the art of German cooking inside the embassy. When they became our enemy in the First War, my grandfather quit and started a German restaurant. Even during the war, German officers used to eat at the Goldener Adler.

'Between the wars, it was the most popular restaurant in Tokyo. My first memories are of peeling potatoes in the back of the restaurant. I think we'd already bombed Pearl Harbor – sorry, my friend. It was an exciting time to be Japanese. A wonderful time! You can't imagine the entertainers we had, the German singers, the Chinese acrobats, the slave labour from Korea and the Philippines! Oh, the artwork from Bali, the birds from New Guinea! My father was a young man, and feeling very imperial. We had an unlimited food supply from all the countries we'd conquered. The clientele were all diplomats and navy brass and their girlfriends. We were the very centre of Tokyo society. The whole German

Asian fleet ate at our restaurant every night. My father decorated the place in swastikas.

'And then, you can guess. The fortunes of war started turning. We lost the lands, we lost the trade, and gradually we lost the diplomats and the admirals. We couldn't get fresh meat or vegetables and the commercial fishing boats were taken over by the navy to camouflage their equipment against air attacks.

'I remember every night running a thick black line through another menu item. *Unavailable.* Finally, there was nothing left, not fish soup, not even German beer. He refused to serve *miso* soup, and even our Korean help offered to make *kimchi*, but he would not serve anything Asian, because he was a German chef and we were a German restaurant. Then the American firebombing came and wiped out our house and killed my brother.'

"*Thirty Seconds Over Tokyo*," I said. 'I remember it well.' Even fondly.

'A week after the fire, my father went to the restaurant, took out a boning knife, or was it a deboning knife, wrapped himself in the German flag and committed *seppuku* in the kitchen. I was nine or so, and I had to extract the blade. It was a small blade, he did not perform the ritual as he should have. He was not sufficiently Japanese, consequently he must have died in agony over many, many hours. You see, *Wurst* and *Schnitzel* and *Kartoffelsalat* were the only things he knew. He had this fierce, inflexible dedication. He had an almost inherited sense of honour, but nothing to apply it to. He was fulfilling a destiny. I think of him as prototypical of my culture, at its most vulnerable. Personally, I'd always wished my grandfather had at least been picked up by a French boat.'

'It's a great novel, Kenji. It's a beautiful film. But is it about waiting?'

'It's about not-waiting,' he smiled. 'A deft and elusive form of waiting, and a little bit about getting foreign messages just a little wrong.' He twirled a bit of squid lasagna on his fork. 'No one should die over sauerkraut,' he said.

3.

Melanie is dark-haired and tending to flesh. She seems Mediterranean, though her last name is Scottish. She came to Tokyo to temp in an

English-language office and gradually drifted to English duties in a Japanese business. She'd met Sam at an Australian party; he'd arrived with a Japanese girl and left with her. They just hit it off, she said. She'd never met anyone with his spirituality.

The first time she visited me, she dropped off pictures of Sammy, the Sammy I knew, smiling, a little fleshy himself. Melanie in those pictures was slender, and quite the beauty. I gathered from her use of the past tense that she did not expect to see him again.

When I opened the door the first time, early in my Tokyo stay, her greeting went: 'Hello, Dr Lander, I believe we've met before.'

I thought, as I always do, yes, of course, analogically speaking, we've met. My son, our mutual loss, our near father-daughter relationship. 'I feel like we have,' I said.

'Many times,' she pushed.

I frowned, affably. 'Many letters, many calls, indeed.'

'Many billions, perhaps trillions of times,' she said, but tossing it off with a giggle. This, I thought, was excessive, even on the molecular level. Easy profundity; it happens to westerners in Asia. 'I've been in this room many billions of times,' she said, patting the low table, 'Do you know how many times Japan has risen from the sea?'

'I'm afraid I don't.'

'Never mind. The Enlightened Ones know. Sam knows. Sam is spiritually awake.'

When she says spiritually, she doesn't mean it lightly. She means incense and vegetarianism, aligning her foods and mattress and who knows what with heavenly and earthly forces, invisible to us but known to the ancients, to devotees, to the awakened. She leads her life under a spell of taboos which she calls mantras of freedom.

That first Sunday she took me out to Harajuko, where, she said, she and her friends were performing. She wasn't dressed for performance unless she was in a Shaker band.

On the subway, we talked. She had taken the subway a trillion-trillion times. We'd had this conversation an infinite number of times, of course – didn't I remember any of it?

Sammy was beginning to remember his past lives, she said. We had to get him away from all his distractions. The Enlightened One remembers a million lives, which is like, maybe, thirty seconds in a lifetime.

Are we talking about the Buddha? I finally asked.

The Buddha is an aspect of the Enlightened One. So is Christ, and the Prophet. Isn't it amazing how all the great men of vision are blind? They have the inner light.

Darwin? Freud? Ramanujan? I asked.

Aspects of the Enlightened One, she answered, smiling. Homer, Tiresias, Milton. Sheik Omar Rahman. And of course the Perfect Master. Her face made a slight contortion, ending in radiance.

Ray Charles? Stevie Wonder? I almost asked. I finally demanded to know, Who is this Perfect Master?

He has an earthly name for this transit, of course. He was born blind to human parents. But his name is the Enlightened One, she said.

And what constitutes his perfect wisdom? I asked.

Everything we see, everything we do or think has happened trillions of times before. We have had this very same conversation a trillion times before. Japan has risen from the oceans, man has evolved from germs and bacteria, someone has invented subways, America and Japan are destined to annihilate each other, all of this has happened and is happening and will happen again. It is not just astronomy that deals in big numbers, Dr Lander, it's little things like subway tickets and sex and children playing soccer in that field over there. Everything is déjà vu a million-million times. So everything we do or say has only a million-millionth of the importance we think it does.

Pardon my objection, but that is easy profundity, I said. But I was thinking, ... isn't this the stuff of poetry, too, Tennyson or was it Blake? ... *flower in the crannied wall* ... I was thinking of my adolescent self in the world of equations. I could see Sammy standing in my place, on this subway, looking down on this plump, serene face and body, and suddenly I felt terror, I could see him taking the next step. I could see myself, not so many years ago, taking the same step.

You and I have had this misunderstanding before, she said, and we've settled it with sex before – yes, that too is ordained – I know we'll meet again but we may be billions of years older, so we won't know it.

Yes, I thought, sex had entered the dialogue. I quickly changed the subject. We're talking stellar collapse, is that it? The universe pulsing like a hummingbird's heart, in-out, two hundred beats a minute, each beat a forty-billion-year cycle? So nothing that happens in this heartbeat has any significance, no meaning should be attached to anything … I shouldn't care about my son – is that it?

Sam would want you to be happy, she said.

Sexually?

In every way, like the other times.

A button had come undone. We were standing in a Tokyo subway, I was staring into cleavage and a warm zombie had just propositioned me.

She smiled. Geniuses in every discipline are given a vision of the unity of all things, don't you reckon, Dr Lander?

I said I reckoned they were.

The Enlightened One was given such a vision.

And what exactly is his vision?

We've risen from germs and bacteria to becoming me and you and Sammy a trillion-trillion times before. Japan has risen from the ocean and sunk below it a trillion-trillion times. America and Japan have destroyed each other trillions of times. Liberation comes from realizing that everything that will happen has already happened. But you see, he remembers a million transits, that is why he knows everything a million times better than the unawakened. You have written your books a trillion times and their tapes have been played to him at least a million times – that is why he is so interested in Sammy. You and Sammy have already joined us, in other transits. This time, we're going to break the cycle for everyone. The Enlightened One has secret plans.

Tell me about them.

Naughty, naughty, then they wouldn't be secret, would they? She clung to the pole in the middle of the subway car, a fetching pose. Sammy and me, we knew each other before, you know?

A trillion times, I'm sure, I said.

No, not that way! In *this* transit, in Adelaide. We were in school together in seventh grade! He was this American bloke. He remembered me, right off. Said he had a crush on me, can you imagine? Came to a party with a girl named Keiko, left with me. Fate, I'd call it.

He didn't have a chance, did he? I tried to smile.

I can remember twelve … no, thirteen, other transits and Sammy never came to Adelaide in any of them. So the Enlightened One is right, this transit is different.

* * *

We came to the station, the crowd surged, I could barely keep up. Thousands of us filled the pedestrian skyways and off in the distance, lining a closed-off parkway were the parked vans and portable stages of at least fifty bands. Live music, as far as the eye could see. Tens of thousands of Sunday strollers walked through the woods, stopping at food kiosks.

It's not just old American ballplayers who go to Japan to die – so do the fifties, sixties, seventies and eighties. Each band specialized in a style, and the style was perfectly reproduced: Heavy metal, glitter, punk, grunge, country and western, classic rock 'n' roll. Kool Kizz, Loft, Vanity, Vanishing Point. There were Alice Cooper and David Bowie look-alikes, Elvis clones, Beach Boys and Beatles, even some religious cults in their Hawaiian shirts and white pants, whumping tambourines and smiling beatifically.

As I feared, Melanie was one of the tambourine girls behind a threesome of toothy, bleached blond boys lip-synching Christian lyrics to feather-light rock. I stood in the middle of the roadway as long as I could bear it, thinking: My Sammy, his love and credulity, all his empathy and sketching; he had found a different father. My son was dead, and I had killed him.

I wanted to get away, not from the Japanese imitators, not from the packs of stylized dancers twisting away to elaborate choreography in tight jeans, boots, and T-shirts, fifties greased rhino-heads with foot-high do's, with air-guitar, combswiping and breakdancing routines, unlit cigarettes dangling at James Dean angles, the Marlboro packs twisted in the T-shirts over the tattooed biceps, the practised Elvis snarl; it was the sweet harmonies, the fake-Hawaiian hipswaying invitation to come inside, take the literature, meet the counsellors. It was Melanie, whacking a tambourine high over her head, a third my age from the land down under who represented that day the face of an evil I thought had vanished from my world.

4.

One morning, my subway train was halted and boarded. Policemen ordered us to abandon everything, and whisked us up staircase and emergency ladders to the street. No one complained, no one questioned. The procedure went calmly, as one might expect in a country where policemen wear white gloves. Just a few minutes later, we knew the reason. If I'd been on an earlier train, I might be dead. People on that train had been struck by a mysterious illness.

'Now you know. Our dirty little secret is out,' said Kenji that same evening. By most reckoning, it was the darkest night in modern Japanese history. Nothing had changed since the cult of emperor-worship, the bombing of Shanghai, the Japanese enslavement of the rest of Asia. Kenji had spent the day in tears. Modern Japan was a fraud, every bit of progress of the past fifty years had been wiped out. 'I warned you,' he said, 'we are an astonishingly crude country. We're all presentation.'

'Kenji, it's just a lone madman.'

Nothing had yet been announced, but Kenji had his suspicions. It was a religious cult led by a blind man. He didn't trust the telephone; we met in his favourite loud and smoky retro-future yakitoria, under the girders of Hibiya station. The country had already entered the traumazone. Everyone was looking over his shoulder for fear he was not seen denouncing it loudly and publicly enough – random killing of Japanese by Japanese – the fear that someone, in years to come, might sort through pictures of that evening and find a crease of merriment on anyone's face. It was Kabuki, the painted-on grimace. 'This is an evil greater than any we have known,' Kenji said. His hair was uncombed, white at its roots; I had never noticed the unruly, almost corrugated thickness of his eyebrows. 'It's home-grown pollution. It's the corruption of our collective soul.'

I wanted to touch him, to offer some measure of inclusion in the American century. Welcome to the millennium. Men in the standard young executive 'salaryman' black suits and white shirts, like a convention of Jehovah's Witnesses, were crying. Nothing the Japanese could do, no crime, based on my four months' residency, placed them beneath the plunging standards of world behaviour. You're not innocents! I wanted to cry out, Shit happens! This isn't Sweden after Palme's assassination. But the Japanese persisted. The country had sinned, its elites had betrayed a misguided, materialist society. The same country that refused to apologize for wartime atrocities, that denied well-documented massacres of Asian civilian populations, had turned its arrogance inward.

'That's it,' said Kenji. 'We never accepted our wartime guilt. We took punishment without ever acknowledging guilt.'

Patterns were emerging. The blind leader, the blind enthusiasm, the religious appeal, the enrolment of foreigners in a Japanese cause. Sammy, unfortunately, would know about it.

I asked him about my son, this time for the whole truth.

'He's in Hokkaido. I keep writing.'

'I think you're trying to hide him. I think he's involved.'

He made a shushing sound, held a finger to lips. 'He had no involvement. Maybe a little prior knowledge. He wanted to escape, but they wouldn't let him.'

'I have to see him. Where is he?' I had visions of dark cellars, safe houses, jail cells, mental hospitals.

'He didn't want you to see him,' said Kenji. 'He wanted to regain his strength. I thought it would be a simple thing, bringing you here, getting him out –'

'– and then she showed up?'

'They were using her to get to you, to get to him.' Ah, the fatal button. 'They kill anyone who tries to leave. They have agents at the airports, in the visa offices, their computers tap into everything. If he showed up anywhere, they'd get to him. I call it protection, but I've been lying to you every day about your son.

'What do you know of the Ainu people?' he asked.

Back in my student days, some linguists and anthropologists thought the Ainu, animist, tattooed, hunter-gatherers, heavily bearded, bear-worshippers of Hokkaido, Sakhalin and the Kuriles, were the aboriginal Japanese. They appeared to be Caucasian, or at least, non-Asian in features. They had no written language, just a rich set of oral histories, mainly explaining how the natural world came to be.

'I thought they were extinct,' I said.

'All but a few hundred. They are a pure people,' he said. 'Their hearts are noble. When I was still in high school I volunteered to work with the Ainu for the summer, like an American going to an Indian reserve.'

We were off on another Kenji story, this time more urgently, and, I sensed, intimately involved with Sammy.

'They believe everything has a soul. Earth, sky, mountains, animals, fish. They live a very brutal life, but they are the most spiritual people in

Japan. Before I die, the last pure-blooded Ainu will probably also be gone.'

What I had learned of the Ainu came from linguists and anthropologists thirty-five years ago. Back then it was said the unwritten, nearly extinct Ainu language was possibly linked to the Altaic tongues of central Siberia, with their connections to Estonian and Finnish. Others said no, there were Malayo-Polynesian remnants in the speech, indicating a link to south Asia, New Guinea, Australia, and the Dravidians of India. Either the Ainu had worked their way eastward from Siberia, onto Sakhalin and down to Hokkaido, or northward from the Malay peninsula, through the Philippines, Okinawa, Kyushu and Honshu, pushed by wars and landgrabs all the way to coastal Hokkaido. Both possibilities were exciting to a young linguistics scholar in the early sixties, attempting to arrive at a universal linguistic paradigm. Ainu was one of those link languages, the people one of those inexplicable genotypes, an undeciphered Rosetta stone.

Nowadays, the romance is gone. The language has been judged an isolate, a kind of far-east Basque. The people appear to be related to the Australian Aborigines, and are not even especially ancient, or particularly pure. Over the millennia they'd intermarried with every Asian tribe in their path.

But all I said to Kenji was, 'The one thing I remember about the Ainu was a line in one of the early reference books. "Their women are exceptionally ugly."' That passed for scholarship, a generation or two before our own.

'You'll have a chance to see for yourself,' he said.

Many years ago, when the Soviet Union was breaking up, I met a woman named Ainu, in Estonia. I joked about her name, the hairy, aboriginal people it called to mind, although the note on ugliness did not apply to her. Like most Estonians, she knew all about the Ainu. During the Russian occupation, Estonia might have been the *samizdat* Ainu research centre of the world. She was proud of her name. In those white summer nights she lectured me on Estonia's link to Japan. Estonians don't have European blood, literally; despite appearances, they are Asian. Their myths are not Greek or Roman, not of Nordic or Celtic gods; they have legends of a small, hairy, bear-worshipping people and of the struggle in the forests between dark bear-worshippers and the blond, invading hockey players we know today. Their blood and myths were absorbed.

In those years, the Estonians were desperate to find any link to any non-Russian, non-German past. Japan was the only world power not taken. A giant boulder in the east of Estonia had been proclaimed the oldest rock in the world, a space relic from the origins of the universe, perhaps even bearing the first molecules of life itself. Three weeks free of Russia and they were quietly forging the algebra of a new identity. Estonia, my temporary Ainu, was the link between space and earth, eternity and the present, speech, blood, myth, DNA, east and west, everything but the Garden of Eden, and on a molecular level, perhaps even that.

I thought suddenly, it all applied to Japan as well. Not so nakedly, not so plaintively, but far more dangerously.

'I received word from your son's *sensei*,' he said. 'It's good news. We can leave tomorrow.'

Much can be forgiven a society that invents and uses the bullet train. Riding the bullet brings back that pre-interstate, pre-jumbo jet promise of magneto-trains that were going to take us from New York to Chicago in an hour, with stops. Not so much distance travel as time travel, geography as time-lapse photography. Tokyo peels away, the suburbs fall, jewelled gardens glitter like lacquered boxes, hundreds of kilometres pass and we're never out of sight of clustered houses and multi-storied buildings, with their city-block squares of rice paddies and tended orchards in between, vegetable patches, greenhouses, and more rice paddies carpet the flatlands, orchards bloom on hillsides, mountains rise, until giant pine forests block the sun. 'Look, a monastery up there,' Kenji would point out with delight, and I'd think, hopefully, *Sammy?* but, no, it was just the overlay of time and cultures, like castles on the Rhine, and Kenji gave no signs. Watching the landscape transform itself is like a vision of successive creations, this folding and smoothing of the Japanese islands, all the way to Sapporo. Thank God I'm an atheist.

For hours we skimmed the coast, past fishing villages untouched by this century. Salmon ladders climbed into the forested mists. Suddenly those villages, the rocky shores, the mountain backdrop seemed the most appealing places in the world. Stop, old man, I thought. Get off here. Your son is nearby, you can live anywhere, you need to get off the circuit. Find a wife, learn a language, take up calligraphy. Meditate. This life will kill you.

'Two old neurolinguists on a train to Ainu country, looking for a crippled Buddhist boy,' I said.

'Some might call it a very Jewish story,' he said.

'I'll make your father an honorary Jew, wrapped in his swastika shawl.'

'You'd be a better son than I was,' he said.

Sammy wasn't in a monastery. To push an analogy, Sammy was in an attic behind a false wall, hidden and fed by strangers while agents scoured the streets looking to pick him up. He was in an old Ainu village near Sapporo, where a bearded man in robes didn't stand out so much. The monastery story was given out to save his life, because they were after him. 'Forgive me,' said Kenji. 'They were watching us.'

What about the toes, I asked. His suffering, the weight-loss, the meditation?

You might not recognize him. The body of your son is alive. The physical body endures. The primary objective was to get him out of Tokyo away from people who were trying to kill him. And to get you here, my friend. The research and lecture invitation offered a cover.

Did he ever say ... Why? I asked. How they got to him?

Cults are opportunistic feeders, said Kenji. Some of our best young people followed him. Don't blame him.

I don't, I said.

Don't blame yourself, he said.

In all the years I'd known Kenji, and in our daily contact, he never spoke to me of his wife, nor did he invite me to his house, wherever it was, for a home-cooked dinner. He had children, slightly younger than mine, of whom he spoke neither in praise nor despair. One was at home in law school, another in California getting an MBA. If he suffered on their account, if they fulfilled his dreams or haunted his nightmares, I have no idea. So far as I know, he devoted all his fatherly concerns on Sammy.

It is hard, he said, to imagine a child not wanting to have more than a father. It is hard for a father not to want to give more than he had to his child. But how can our children have more than us? How can we give them but a fraction of what we've got? I pulled the knife from my father's gut! I saw Tokyo in ashes, I buried my family, put my mother in an asylum! I promised myself to be a scientist; only science was rooted in truth, only science proceeded by hard, verifiable evidence. If I stayed with science, I would always be free. I promised my father I would learn from his blindness. I would learn from the war never to accept orders I did not personally approve – but that was easy for people like us. What of the children of fathers like you and me, who have been everywhere, seen everything, what is left that we haven't done? We can only give them scraps. Our lovely children, we showed them everything, we miniaturized the world for them, and they couldn't keep up. We should ask their forgiveness.

I clutched his hand. You've been a better father to Sammy than I have.

My country was to blame, he said.

A few minutes later he put down a book he'd been reading and asked, 'What about *in the know?* You don't say *in the feel, in the touch* ... isn't it odd?'

'In the groove, perhaps?'

'I always thought *in the nude* was a particularly regal expression,' said Kenji. 'In the Know, In the Nude. Knowledge and Nudity carry the article. It would be very interesting if English were written in Chinese characters and you had to make certain fundamental decisions about the properties of words, not just their sounds.'

'We must compare language acquisition and language retention in contrasting linguistic systems,' I said.

'So little time remains.'

There's winter-Olympics Sapporo, all Aspen glamour, and a few miles away, skidrow Sapporo, along the docks where Chinese and Koreans are smuggled in, where the tankers unload, and, if you're Kenji, you know places where the down and out, the Ainu and the *buraku* drink and find their daily labour. There is nothing strikingly different in appearance about the men knotting their nets or drinking in the harsh northern light: Japanese, Asian, lean, unkempt – in America we're so used to thinking of difference only in terms of race, or of alienation only as violence, that we're dulled to divisions that don't spit in our face or come wrapped in colour – I'm only beginning to read faces like a cop, to see in the headbands and moustaches and untrimmed beards, tattoos, the rough language, badges of identity as defiant as any gang marker on an American street. These are desperate people, my healthy respect is rooted in fear which I try not to betray, and I would not want to fall among them at night or on their terms. Sammy, I know, could be one of them, the dozing drunk, the druggie, the dull, suspicious eyes inside a darkened hut. It's been four years; I might not even recognize my own son.

Kenji speaks the language of the Ainu, or enough of it to show respect. I remember the Aborigines in Australia, the tall blond ones, the fair-skinned ones, the short, black and bearded ones – appearance doesn't matter. If you say you belong, whether you speak the language or look aboriginal or not, they take you in. The universal aboriginal brotherhood. Old men nod, and yes, they are shorter, huskier, hairier, they point us down the dockside, past dozing inebriates, the insane, the beggars. No one looks at me, or cares, I belong as much as anyone.

A long, dark warehouse of tin-topped tables squirming with squid. Faster than baskets and buckets and trolleys can dump them, teams of hunched-over, silent men and women slice and gut, steam and salt, and toss them onto conveyor belts. Many of the workers are hidden under elaborate hats, some of straw; others wear baseball caps, old hardhats. Only one is bald, with glasses, his thin, pale arms tattooed like a prisoner's. The others have all looked up, checked us out, returned to their work.

A foreman strolls over, bows to Kenji. After a few words, he departs.

'He says Sammy's his best worker. Always there, doesn't drink, doesn't use drugs, doesn't talk. No one's ever heard him talk.'

I could remember his voice, the breathless excitement after every museum visit, the endless questions. *I can hear you, Mister Beard!*

'At least he's safe here.'

'Salting squid guts. Merciful God.'

'Perhaps he'll leave with you.'

Me go pleep now.

He's still not raised his head, upon which he wears a baseball cap cocked to one side. Strike me dead on this spot, I pray, and I will praise Your justice, and Your mercy, for all eternity.

Doggystan

ONCE UPON A TIME Lander had a wife, a son, a daughter, a dog, a teaching position and a private practice, and, so far as he thought about it, the love of his family, the respect of his neighbours and the esteem of his colleagues. If he'd defined himself in terms of descending value he might have said: husband, father, researcher, citizen.

Now, on insomniac nights between beads of sleep, he replayed his confusions, the origin of his genius, the unravelling of his life. In a cluster of years on either side of fifty, too many strangers in Lander's life had begun claiming intimacy, too many intimacies were denied connection. Some nights, impaled on that razor-wire of insomnia, he would lie awake in strange hotels, not always alone, and not remember the country he was in, the time zone or climate, or even the language. His world had become universalized to familiar hotels with CNN, universal foods and even the same sympathetic women who would hang around after a lecture on the pretence of discussing a parent's decline. He would make his way to the breakfast table, praying for skim milk and Raisin Bran but rarely finding it. Skim meant anything that would pour and raisins were embedded in a müsli-mush with the density of a collapsed star. His driver would arrive and the lectures would begin, the lab-tours, the hospital rounds, listening to Alzheimer's patients in all the world's languages, studying transcripts of the translations – if his theories were provable they had to hold up in every language – drinks and a dinner, interviews, public lectures, acolytes, women. And so he travelled.

Lander was riding a tiger, sliding from conference to conference, continent to continent, in interchangeable hotels called Ambassador or President or Intercontinental, collecting toilet kits and sleeping masks, pockets full of business cards, soaps and shampoos in small plastic bottles, as badges of his new celebrity. He used to think it was pretentious when people spoke only of airport names instead of cities, until he realized he'd become one of them, going to Logan and Laguardia, LAX or Charles de Gaulle and never into the low warehouse sprawl that radiated from them. He wanted it to end but he could not end it alone. Each flight blended into all other flights – airplane time was generic – the clock stopped when he entered the waiting room and didn't start until he had got in a taxi at the other end. Airborne existence was a wormhole connecting hundreds of calming flights, a separate existence through all his confusions. When he got back to his new Chicago high-rise he'd lay out the little bottles of soapy booty and feel that they were the only tangible benefits in his new life.

Asia – the deep and mystical Asia behind the Pacific Rim – was a foreign concept to him and a little frightening. He'd always resisted those Hindu and Buddhist and Muslim countries where psychoanalytic theories were considered degenerate, hysterical, or immoral parts of a neocolonialist plot. Psychology doesn't apply to us, they'd say, we are invulnerable to your diseases of the mind: ancient wisdom combined with extended families, our faith and our natural diets make us superior to your rampant materialism, food additives and uncommitted sex. He thought of them as hypocrites, hoarders of *Playboys* worth their weight in gold in nightly rental fees back home.

This was his first trip to India. He'd avoided India in his teaching years because of encounters with skeptical students and colleagues, men (they were all men) committed to spiritual interpretations of mental disorder or some potent ayurvedic cure known only to their family's traditional quack. Freud and Jung, they were quick to remind him, had both insulted Asia, deeming it psychologically savage or infantile. The only way of remedying his mentor's ancient wrong was for him – Freud's direct intellectual descendant, according to popular belief – to do them the courtesy of proving they were as sick, and for the same reasons, as everyone else. And so at last and with nothing to fear he had agreed on this brief lecture and demonstration tour of India squeezed between residencies in Japan and Israel.

Mangy dogs lay like piles of oily rags, fused as tight and still as roadkill to the pavement. Dr Dalal slalomed between them to his gate. Perhaps, Lander thought, since the street dogs of India were no longer bred for human vanity this was the way all dogs would choose to look: grungy patches of dun and white somewhere between jackal and retriever. Hell, thought Lander, it's the way I would choose to look.

Lander, a lifelong dog-man, shopper at dog pounds, adopter of lost causes, defender of mongrels, found these dogs threatening and unappealing – even the bandy-legged pups still sucking on a bitch's teat just inches from his feet as he got out of Dalal's car. She growled. As in all things he'd observed in his first few days in India, fertility was raw and naked, neither maternity nor infancy having a thing to do with benevolence or play or cuteness, no respite from mange and filth.

Two weeks in India, however – to give the dogs credit – and he'd not seen a street dog, whatever its deprivation, attack a child, a kid-goat, calf or piglet, despite their mutual unsupervised foraging through the same stacks of gutter refuse. He could not say the same about Westchester purebreds, where Judy had raised showdogs before the breakup. Street dogs belonged to no one yet they were partially looked after and partially loyal, beneficiaries of indifferent scraps of shade, water and tolerance, attached loosely to houses or shops. They responded not with gratitude but aggressive territoriality, the poor man's watchdog. This was Gujarat, a meatless state, and the dogs had adjusted to a vegetarian diet.

'Protective, not aggressive,' said Dr Dalal, president of the All-India Psychological Association, as he stepped over a dog and slid open the metallic latch to his front gate. Dalal was fifty, an august name in Indian research though not exactly on Lander's wavelength. Dalal had spent too many years in the Freudian trenches proselytizing for broad classical psychiatry. He had become too committed to the classic outlines to tolerate much revision. His three-piece-silk-suit orthodoxy, his trimmed moustache and dyed black hair had made Lander yearn for stubble-chinned, henna-dyed, wild-eyed ayurvedic practitioners in stained dhotis crying out as they had at his first lecture in Calcutta: Forget genes. Forget APO-E4. Study the true cure, *Ashwagandha.* Study *Bramhi, Shankhapushpi, Vacha.*

On the distant front porch behind rose bushes, across a patchy, browning lawn, he noticed a tall slim woman in a white sari holding the leashes of two large howling white dogs. She was too far away for Lander to note her appearance, only that he didn't have to. She was clad, or wrapped, in a white sari that for all its modesty might have been unblemished Grecian nudity. She seemed part of a master's miniature painting rendered in delicate strokes by a single camel's hair. Even at a distance he could count the stones of her necklace, the gold carving on her bangle. He knew she would be as beautiful as her husband was ordinary. Her voice and manner and accent would charm as much as his had irritated. He knew it because of her profile as she turned to go back inside before dropping the dogs' chains. He was staring. It was a mythic moment.

'Dr Lander, bringing her into my life, at my age, you understand, has undermined everything I believed. That's why I became attracted to your work, sir. It somehow ennobled what I had done, even while I was feeling the deepest shame. You cannot know how I ... well, the suffering I have caused. I was a married man with children. I had many of the things I had worked for. Bringing her into my life was like bringing in the future, or maybe the past, discovering the superhuman ... well, I cannot explain it.'

In an instant Lander was ripped from a timeless world of the woman on the porch, the confessor at his side, to an explosion of dust as the two dogs leaped the rose bushes and propelled themselves, jaws foaming, tongues flapping, eyes pinpointed with hate, to a snapping, snarling halt inches in front of Lander's shoes.

Dr Dalal reached out his hand perhaps to be licked, or snatched away.

'Crude, but lovable,' he said.

Old scabs and fresh scratches laced his forearm more like an indulgent cat-owner's than a dog-fancier's. 'We took them from the street when their eyes were still closed. You saw their sister just outside the gate. Such dogs are blessed with sweet natures, you'll find, despite appearances. My wife says we should not call them dogs at all.'

What then? Lander wondered. Jackals, pariahs?

Dalal laughed, reading his confusion. 'Canines, Dr Lander. Dogs are domesticated canines. Canines are immigrants into the country of dogs.'

Whatever they were, they were large and strong, front legs and shoulders bunched with muscle, faces broad and intelligent with long, overdeveloped muzzles and powerful jaws rehearsing a full repertoire of Alsatian, Labrador and Dobermann ancestry – they could pull sleds, or carts, or tear burglars into small pieces – while their sloping, apologetic hindquarters with fluffy tails curled along their backs betrayed generations of back-alley encounters with wild and degenerate breeds. The whole mixture struck Lander as heroic and unfortunate, the abject, sexually excited tail-wagging, the foamy-jawed growling, the ferocious timidity of a confused enthusiasm.

'Loyal, but untrainable,' said Dr Dalal.

* * *

After the tea and fresh fruit juices served at the landscaped border of a pond and waterfall, after the tour of the house, the work of a foreign-trained local architect, with its panelled walls of modern Indian paintings, its CD-trees of American rock, Indian ragas and Western classics, at the dinner table, Lata Dalal asked Lander, 'What do you know about zebra mussels?' They were nearly finished with dinner, an elaborate and elegant vegetarian spread attended by the dogs whom both Dalals fed rice balls, chapattis, and bits of peas and potato samosa. Lander had finally asked her, now that he could face her beauty directly and not hide his enchantment, what exactly she was researching.

'Ah, biology,' he said.

'I'm a sociologist,' she said, 'so I am very interested in zebra mussels. They've nearly turned San Francisco Bay into the Dead Sea.'

'Lata did her doctorate at Berkeley,' explained Dr Dalal.

'Forgive my confusion –' said Lander, '– but mussels and sociology?'

'Prakash rescued me from marriage,' she said.

'No, my dear. I rescued you from divorce.'

'From the endless round of fucking and being fucked. Prakash is my third. The usual story – ambitious girl from good family is stuck with an arranged marriage, goes through with it, tries suicide, gets divorced, goes to America, falls in love with the first American she sleeps with, marries him. All the usual boring details, finds out he's the usual –'

'– cheating mussel?' asked Lander.

'– mussels are actually rather noble in a good-of-the-race, self-sacrificing way – no, it was more the armed robbery and drug-dealing. There is such a thing as too much America. So, she divorces and rebounds and rebounds, a boring story, no? Loving and being loved is so much better, isn't it, Dr Lander?' Her voice was hoarse and throaty, her accent a complicated confection, rather like a cuisine that offered no familiar openings. Her hand had risen to his arm, the flesh cool, silky, but the wrists scabbed like her husband's. A jagged white scar was barely covered by a watch and gold bangles.

'You've had some rough times, haven't you?'

She glanced to her wrist, and smiled. 'From my first night in jail.'

'Dalal means middleman,' said the doctor. 'We are all traders by caste, not professionals. My father and brother think I should be running an import business in Flushing or Southall.'

'Lander just means farmer, or a person from a particular place.'

'On the street, Dalal means pimp,' said Lata. 'You can't escape your calling.'

'Lata is very direct, you'll notice.'

'What about those zebra mussels?' he asked.

'I am writing on the transformation of Indian society by the presence of millions of what we call NRIs – non-resident Indians – either returning to India from years abroad, remitting money, or visiting. Every smuggled computer is a zebra mussel. Every child who disobeys his parents is a mussel. Every daughter who marries for love. Every VCR, every western adult film is a mussel, every labour-saving device, every vacuum cleaner, every coffee-maker, is a servant-killing mussel. The servants respond, poor things, and become treacherous thieves and vandals, or worse. In Berkeley I studied the Indian community in America. Isn't it interesting that men without two rupees to rub together in India become millionaires in Texas? Do you know there are villages not ten miles from here where ninety percent of the able-bodied population is in England, Canada or the United States? It's people from here who own your motels and 7-11s. I don't think you'll meet a person in India who doesn't have intimate family living abroad, or who hasn't studied there or isn't planning to send his children to Harvard and Stanford – zebra mussels are very adaptable. They were sucked into the ballast tanks of the big oil tankers in Japan and their larvae got expelled at the Oakland docks. They have no natural enemies.'

The only question would be, Lander thought, how to spend two nights in the Dalal house without obsessing over Lata Dalal, wherever she might be at any moment, where she slept, what she thought of him.

'We are intermediate life forms, Dr Lander,' she said. 'What would you call this house with all its comforts and conveniences – India? And yet where else do we belong? What else do you call us?'

'Like these creatures,' said Dr Dalal. 'Are they dogs? They are enacting in just one or two years the whole history of their species' domestication.'

'They are immigrants to Doggystan,' said Lata Dalal. 'A brand new country. Just like all of us.'

The male had begun climbing, cat-like, up Lata's ladderback chair, laying his head on the top rung where he licked her neck and softly moaned while humping the scroll-work at the back of the seat, the sloping hindquarters marvellously fluid in their piston-like pumping, the bright pink glistening member erupting with each thrust to brush against the pleats of her sari. It seemed like a frieze out of Khajuraho. The bitch at Dr Dalal's feet had manoeuvred herself to take full advantage of his naked toes.

'Shoo-shoo,' she cooed, kissing his muzzle. 'Don't make a nuisance.'
'Knock knock,' said Lander.
'I beg your pardon?' asked Dr Dalal.
'Ah ... who's there?' said Lata.
'Ayurvedic,' said Lander.
'Ayurvedic who?' she asked.
'Ayurvedic for the doctah?' he giggled.

They had drained the bottles of imported wine and local brandy. The dogs had retired to the porch, Lata and Dr Dalal shared the couch, Lander sat in a leather chair. American music had given way to distant ragas. Indian languages, closer to the origin of western speech than any others, were discussed: perhaps Sanskritic roots, thought Dr Dalal – pre-industrial, pre-literate, with compound nouns and heavily inflected verbs – supported Lander's theories. In his current state, tipsy and infatuated and living inside an erotic sculpture, all theories made equal sense. If civilization now permitted us to live longer than our bodies' programmes, if we accepted the toll in cancer and heart disease, diabetes and bad eyesight, weight and arthritis as inevitable, why shouldn't our brains outlive their language programme? If there is less Alzheimer's in India – and there is, Dr Lander – it is not because of food and ancient wisdom; perhaps it is only the languages we speak and lack of overload. We don't have to process as much. Perhaps, who knows, we will find that one picture is worth a thousand words and that thirty years of television exhausts the brain, destroys its linguistic capacity. Crashes its RAM, so to speak. Dalal was coming alive, Lata was drowsing, the dogs were scratching the door, and Lander was as close to non-existence as he had ever felt.

The language of Alzheimer's patients appears to share common traits, he heard himself agreeing. The so-called Lander grammar. Yes, cried Dalal, clapping his hands and startling his wife: There are tribal languages in India, older than Sanskrit, that anticipate all the rules of

Alzheimer's speech. Pronouns of attribute not of persona, verbs of recent position not movement. You sit on a stool in front of a man and he calls you Broad-Shouldered Friend with One Eye. He says, Broad-Shouldered Man with One Eye brings fish to Fat Woman's table. But those people aren't there and there is no fish, no woman and no table. You are fully sighted and slope-shouldered, see, Dr Lander? Languages whose present can only be expressed as the past, self that has no grammatical marker at all.

Ontogeny recapitulates philology, thought Lander, filing it away. His brain was softening, turning to mush, he could sleep for a week.

Lata Dalal stood, and held her arms out to him. He rose, took her by the tips of her fingers. 'My room is just across from yours,' she said. 'I am a bit unsteady. Please take me.'

'I'll be along directly, Lata,' called her husband.

Outside his door she delivered a kiss and a cool hand on the back of his neck. He could imagine their bodies flowing together, like rubble from collapsed walls. 'Please feel free to call if there's anything you need.'

'Dr Dalal?'

'I sleep alone.'

'Then perhaps – I know this is bold – you will feel free to call on me.'

At first she smiled, considering her options. 'And which of us is the mussel, Dr Lander? And who is the bay?'

He felt a dog slither past him in the hall.

For his first thirty-five years, his innocent and luminous years, he had missed a great deal by not seeing everything as sexual, every woman as a potential partner. In his next twenty, he had thought of little else. It had ruined his good name, his dignity, his pride. It had brought no peace. These feelings at his age were unseemly. Lata turned, raised a hand in half a wave, her bangles jangling, and disappeared inside the darkened room.

Lander began undressing. Early in his travels a Russian woman had told him, we have killed what it means to have humanity. Jews had it and we killed them. Christians had it and we killed them. Old-style Russian peasants had it and we killed them, too. Now all we have are half-men and half-women who never knew what it was to be human.

We used to know, Lander had said. We're losing it, too.

Poor you, she'd said.

I want to be whole.

In the darkest night of his life in a room so still and black that he couldn't tell if his eyes were closed or open he awoke to the rustle of bedclothes, the white body assuming her place on the adjacent pillow, folding her legs, crossing her arms, eyes imploring. The proof of all his theories was upon him. It was one of those nights when he could believe there was no madness, no disease in the world, only new languages to discover. And so that way they spent the night, his stiffened cock up the bitch's cunt, her jaw clamped firmly on his wrist.

Dark Matter

A NORMAL LIFE OF EIGHTY YEARS can be expressed as a parabola, like the equations you graphed on little blue squares in ninth-grade algebra when you had no idea that the points you plotted and the lines connecting them, peaking at forty and falling away, were the picture of your life.

Lander's current coördinates placed him at midpoint on the downslope. As a man of sixty with strong genes for the heart, dubious ones for long-term consciousness, he could bet on ten more years of research and adventure followed by a decade of confusion and decline. Playing the back nine, as it were, midway through the thirteenth hole, bunkers and sandtraps, doglegs right and left, clubhouse in view, but when he got there this time, there'd be no nineteenth hole, no gin and tonic on the deck.

'Do you like pears, Dr Lander?' his escort, David Fisher, asked. Fisher, a publicist from the American embassy, had been assigned to Lander for the conference. Fisher cultivated the local look: orchestra conductor on a summer break, white shirt hanging out, sandals, sleeves rolled up, bushy grey hair in need of grooming. They were waiting in the crowded, smoky lobby of a fancy hotel in the middle of Tel Aviv for the arrival of a childhood friend of Lander's whom he could not have recognized or avoided. Fisher was there to see that Lander didn't get lost, bored or bothered. Fisher flashed a chrome-plated switchblade and carved a dainty sliver of glistening pear which he balanced on the blade.

'I grew it myself,' he said.

Halfway between forty and death, Lander mused, matches a point halfway between birth and apogee. Lander at sixty, in Israel for a conference on 'The Human Language, Economics to Theology,' was staring directly through a time-tunnel at his twenty-year-old self, the boy he'd been when he'd visited the Promised Land for the first time.

Yoo-hoo, kid!

'We lease twenty hectares from a kibbutz up on the Golan,' Fisher continued. 'I'm taking early retirement and staying here.' He plopped a knit yarmulke over his convenient bald spot, then pocketed it just as quickly, with a wink. 'I tell them I've got a place in Beth Ezra and they hear it as Bethesda. It's better that way.'

'*Aliyah* at our age? You're a brave man.'

'Pears belong in Eretz, don't you think?'

This time, Lander took the proffered pear. Sweet, firm, a Chosen Fruit. Fisher's own patented Sabra-sounding cross-breed, green-flecked, golden-skinned with overtones of red.

'I really despise oranges, those greedy little sun-suckers. Remember Jaffas?'

'I do indeed,' said Lander.

'Pears get firm in the wind and sweet in the cold. Pears need the Golan, Dr Lander.'

'A regular foreign policy fruit.'

'Precisely. When you finish eating an orange what have you got? Skin, seeds, pulp and all that disgusting white matter – am I right, or am I right? What's left after you eat a pear, Dr Lander?'

'Evidently very little, Mr Fisher.'

He suddenly remembered his mother bathing him in the old Brooklyn kitchen. The radio was on, she singing. Crosby, Andrews Sisters, or was that too early? Before the war. She rolled back the wrinkled skin at the tip of his tiny penis: *Wash here, sweetie, learn to do it yourself. See the white matter that sticks in there. You don't want to get an infection.* Belly-button, too. White matter. Earwells. Eyegunk. Your comb, curls of old toilet paper up your butt.

'My point exactly. Sweet and firm, packs well, ships anywhere. I even eat the seeds.' He made an eloquent throat-clearing noise that Lander had not heard in forty years. 'Oranges and bananas, they were Russian dream fruits. *Venn ve're free, den ve plant orange trees!* Oranges are diaspora. They should have stayed in Florida.'

'So all the fruits are political?'

'Why shouldn't they be?' Fisher answered.

And is every question answered with a question? He didn't ask.

Little did you think, Jerry, or Gershy as they called you in that heroic *Exodus* summer of '56, that every twenty-year-old is spied on by his inner old man. Little did I think, looking at those rugged old kibbutzniks, that every sixty-year-old is still the kid inside. It's the opposite of nostalgia. As though memory were a function of youth, not old age. What you plant is what you remember. It was Lander's basic thesis: Nothing is lost, no gesture in the universe goes unretained.

'More pear? I brought plenty.'

When he was twenty and Israel eight, Lander spent a summer packing oranges in an English-speaking kibbutz near the Lebanon border with mostly New York and Montréal kids whose grandparents wintered in the same Florida ghettos – affirming identity, defending the land, falling in love and nearly staying. But Davia Appelbaum, his first great love, who could roll cigarettes with one hand while strumming chords with the other and still lead folksongs in African click-languages, reckless lovemaker on any lumpy horizontal surface and against quite a few vertical ones, behind, or on top of packing boxes where the fragrance of just-picked Jaffas and the memory of stolen passion would kickstart his mornings for the next forty years – that Davia Appelbaum had giant ambitions.

She, *dear boy*, was only passing through, from Jo'burg to London. Israel's sinewy farmers and citizen-soldiers reminded her of back-country Boers, pistol on hip, trussed with bandoleers; they would never create an urban culture. She'd left South Africa at sixteen with no intention of waiting for majority rule and the inevitable slaughter of whites and Indians. Constant preparedness was the enemy of all creation.

Lander returned to his junior year at Chicago. They wrote for a few months. He cherished her letters, the only tangible sign, to that time, that he'd had a life. He found himself going to small theatres and jazz clubs and was freshly drawn to a folk-scene he'd always ignored. She was singing, acting, discarding identities and lovers. Not to be outdone, he declared a psychology major. That appeared to be the great legacy of Israel in his life; a taste for performance, a premature embrace of the sixties, an appreciation for Joan Baez, a weakened strain of the Appelbaum virus.

And now he couldn't remember enough Hebrew even to sound out the street signs. You'd think, after all these centuries of careful inbreeding, a mutant gene for reading Hebrew would arise. Of course, it's a different Hebrew, Fisher had reminded him, Torah piety crossed with army profanity. He'd even come to Israel without a hat.

All Lander could remember from his attempts at mastering the sacred language was the panic of memorizing passages in an unheated annex to the temple library where he and three other boys, Marty Fogelman, whose father paid for the *melamed,* Arnie Zucker, and a strange boy named Anatol, sat after school with a glyptodon from Lublin, a distant relative of the Fogelmans. Even in that cold room he wore short-sleeved white shirts, better to expose the tattoos with the European barred sevens on the underside of his frail white arms. *See what happens?* those numbers said.

He'd been Gershy in temple, and it was as Gersh that he'd received a note on impressive stationery from (now) Ari Zucker. *Dear Gersh: Saw the write-up in the paper, fancy company! Nobel Prizes and all, a guy I went to school with, I'm impressed, really. I came to Eretz in '72.* Married Leah here, three kids, all smart like their mother. You remember what an ox I was. Let me show you the family, the stores. Life's been good. Maybe I didn't make it as big in Brooklyn as I said I would, but try to buy an appliance in Tel Aviv without me.

Back in Brooklyn, Arnie Zucker's only ambition had been to capitalize on his A to Z initials. He'd been a throwback to the peddler-era, no law school, no medicine, no teaching in his family or his future. A to Z Hardware, Radio Repair, Shirts and Suits.

Lander was not a Nobel laureate, could never be, given the nature of his work. He was often introduced as a Nobel Prize winner, a mistake nearly impossible to rectify once it was made. He wanted to print it on his card: *Gerald Lander, Clinical Psychologist. No Prizes Worth Mentioning.* The other conference participants, natural scientists, economists, writers, were nearly all Nobel winners. Witty, modest, cultured people. He wondered if they were as lost as he.

According to the conference brochure, disciplines may start out modestly, corrections and footnotes to prevailing opinion, but as they mature they begin to offer totalizing explanations of their own. The interaction and conditioning of social groups, the inherent patterning of myth, the exchange value of productive labour, sociobiology; call it language-making, brain chemistry or the subconscious, they all point feebly at times, insistently at others, toward a god, or away from it. Since moving between disciplines opens an intellectual to charges of dilettantism, it was thought that the conference itself could serve as the forum. Let the audience make the connections.

So why not Israel, home of dispute, where everyone's an expert, where intellectuals strike public poses, where ideas have immediacy, in a city where gods and language came together and split apart? It was time for him to find out. An assimilated, diasporic Jew – on which word does the emphasis fall? Israel was either the purest and most concentrated form of his experience, or its total denial.

A fawn-coloured Cadillac pulled into the portico.

'Your ride,' said Fisher, pocketing the switchblade and dropping a slim pear core inside a napkin into the ashtray. 'Shall we say after the conference next Sunday at Beth Ezra? I'll pick you up in Jerusalem. My wife's anxious to meet you, too.'

'That would be fine.'

'We'll send you all the tapes of the conference. Anything you need, the embassy will provide.'

'Thank you, Mr Fisher.'

'Dovid,' he said.

The bigger the car the smaller the driver had been Lander's observation on trips to Florida, and Ari Zucker was no exception. Lander immediately remembered him, unchanged from half a century: a wiry little guy with thick arms, shirt out, knit yarmulke, shooing the valet-parker away, ignoring the doorman's salute. Lander rose to meet him, this boy from Brooklyn who'd meant absolutely nothing to him fifty years ago but who'd suddenly thrust himself back in his life. The second time as tragedy, was that the formula, third time as farce? Everything in his life was gently folding over, everything a replay.

'Gershy!'

Arnie had a still-young face, less weathered than many he'd seen. He'd kept his hair, unlike Lander, and all but the temples was suspiciously black. His forearms were a real kibbutznik's, stretching the links of a gold watchband. Lander was embraced, pawed, thumped, lifted, he felt loved and tribal, desert and Mediterranean all at once, plucked from the polite company of the conference and into the companionship of something all-forgiving, all-demanding, Mafia-like, direct and earthy.

Ignoring the horns and shouts of drivers he'd blocked, Zucker took him to the street outside the hotel, pointing out the storefront just across, its frontage loud with sheets of fluorescent tubing, turning half the block studio-bright on a Sunday afternoon.

'All my stores get the same treatment, Gershy. It's a Japanese technique. Brighter than a thousand suns. Hop in, I'll tell you a story.'

Zucker was determined to show him the city, and to take him past as many Zuckerlands as he could. After a while, Lander could sense their approach, something hot and glowing in the distance. 'Mossad came to me two years ago. Very serious guys, Mossad. Said the American spy satellite told them we were conducting some kind of laser-testing. All this heat, all this light in Tel Aviv and Jerusalem. So they lay out a city-grid, plot the so-called sites and guess what: Twenty-two Zuckerlands! I'm in space, who needs a web-site?' Then his expression soured. 'If I could write "Fuck you, Hafez al-Clinton" in the biggest lights in the world, I would.'

He wheeled down a narrow, market-lined street, glaring at the vision of Arab stalls, piles of vegetables, breads and clothing spilling out into the street. 'They won't be happy till they turn us into another Third World country,' he muttered, honking away the Arabs, cursing their slowness, their sheer numbers. 'They'd slit your throat for a shekel. You can smell them!' Lander winced, trapped in his golden, air-conditioned cage of a Cadillac which had never seemed so uselessly large, wishing he could lose himself in the swirl of street life.

'Did you read about the bomb on the bus? My accountant lost his wife in it. Twenty-five years old, just married, or does Jewish blood make the papers in America?'

'I read, I saw,' said Lander.

'So, it sells.'

Arnie Zucker's American life had been a failure so vast he'd even enlisted in the Vietnam War, waiving deferments, pulling strings, hoping to die. So what happened? They made him a procurement officer. He prospered, saw opportunities, tapped the possibilities. 'I was thirty-two years old, you'd probably won your Nobel Prize by then, and what was I doing? Well, actually, ashamed to say but I'm making out pretty good. Had my own apartment in Saigon, selling air-conditioners right off the ship. Then I woke up one morning and it hit me: I'm fighting *their* war. Simple as that.'

'Whose war?'

'Exactly. Westmoreland, some redneck from Carolina. McNamara? Johnson? Nixon? Those were teachers' names for God's sake! They could have been Japanese.' He leaned across the wide front seat. 'I tell you this, Gersh, it's America that's killing us. They'll sacrifice us for oil. What America's doing to us makes Hitler a drop in the bucket.'

'Don't get crazy on me, Arnie.'

'Ari.'

When he came out he packed his bags for Israel, arrived in time for the '72 war, rose to captain and met the money men from Buenos Aires who initially set him up. He saw himself as a nation-builder, wiring the desert, if only for cable TV.

'Here, at least wear this,' he said, pressing a knit yarmulke into Lander's hands. 'Bet you haven't worn one in... what, twenty years?'

'You call me Hitler one minute then you give me this?'

'When, Holy Days? Bar-mitzvahs? Shivah?'

'Don't turn Forty-seventh Street on me, Ari.'

'What, now you feel ashamed? Typical diaspora reaction. Wear it, okay?'

'I'm bald, it slides – you got the same model in Velcro?'

Could one live in Israel with a sliding yarmulke, with ambivalence? The most precious thing in the world to Lander was his belonging to a place that subtly excluded him – or was it his right to reject a place that subtly included him? Israel was a club he wished would reject him.

Ari kept up a steady commentary. Lander was accustomed to being the object of questions; Ari Zucker was as unimpressed by intellectual accomplishment as he'd ever been. No questions about his work, about his life, family, loves, travels. Only one trip counted, and that was the passage to Israel.

'What, our facilities are bad? Students aren't smart?'

'No complaints, Arnie.'

'Ari – if you don't mind. So, come. You're never too old. Get an apartment somewhere. What, didn't your parents teach you a Jew should always keep a bag packed?'

These fierce old parents that everyone quotes, where do they come from? Lander suspected that most people, himself included, were in the parent-manufacturing business. He remembered Arnie Zucker's parents and his own as the ultimate get-along types, New Dealers, benignly liberal in the abstract, a little jumpy after the first robberies, the graffiti, the name-calling. But giving up America, packing a bag, making *aliyah*? That was for the relatives left behind, the second and third choice after America and maybe Canada. Down there with South Africa and Argentina. Australia wasn't bad for Jews who surfed.

'Christ, Arnie, Ari, I'd sit around like those *alte kockers* in Brighton Beach, sipping *glayzl chai* and moaning about Odessa.'

'What, you're more the beer and schnapps type? *Hey, Germans love me, this Hitler guy's a joke*.'

'Get something straight, Ari. History isn't a recording.'

'What, for Jews it's one big loop, Gershy, you get that straight. For you, what, history's a laugh track? America loves you, gives you all these prizes? Anyway, why should you worry, they'll never come for you, will they? You're too valuable.'

'I resent your tone.'

'What, my tone? We're an abrasive people. We don't back down, get that straight. Russia backed down. Israel never. I'll do anything it takes to get through to you. Or do you want to go quietly?'

They cruised in silence through suburban streets that could have been not quite California, maybe Florida if Florida had slopes. They corkscrewed up the hills, the houses clinging like California chalets for purchase on a bit of grass and flowers, a stone wall, sudden views of the Mediterranean. Every stone was biblical, every old tree had borne witness, withstood the Ottomans, the Mandate, and welcomed the ancient owners back. It was in the blood, even Lander could feel it, be caught up in it, the mystical attachment, the martyrdoms, the ritualized landscape.

Nothing disruptive in these elevations, no Arabs, less noise, more strollers and baby carriages, more children out, more men in hats. Lander had avoided Israel for forty years for the same reason he avoided moral knuckle-rappers and religious authority. The right wing, wherever he encountered it, made his skin crawl. But if he were a debater, he'd rather argue the side of human depravity, the inevitability of catastrophe, the genetic hostility of disparate ethnicities, than any accommodationist position.

'By the way, did you see the Million Man March? A million black men hate your sorry ass.'

'I was travelling.'

'Very nice. So, how long you think you've got before they come for you?'

'They?'

'How many blacks in America now, how many Spanish, how many of those *meshugge* Christians? Fifteen, twenty, twenty-five per cent – you got over half of your countrymen *that want you dead*. You ran the slave ships, you were Christopher Columbus, you nailed up their Messiah. That Million Man March scared the shit out of me, and I've been in three wars.'

'Lighten up, Ari.'

'I've made my money, I looked after the family, I brought my parents over and buried them here. I've fought for two countries. Now, only the survival of my people matters to me. I can meet any price. Even if *you* don't care, I do.'

Arnie's home was a low, California-style ranch occupying the top of a steep hill. No neon, no flags, nothing showy or unusual. An artful tangle of semi-desert plants, bright flowers, low trees, rocks and sand gave the illusion of more space than it actually occupied.

A stooped old woman in a babushka and buttoned sweater kept up a sullen sweeping of the stepping stones. A man, short and thick, her husband perhaps, clipped roses along a trellis. Their deeply lined faces suggested peasantry, the Balkans, those faces of the ethnically cleansed.

'Shalom, Figs.'

' 'lom,' he muttered.

Wraparound windows commanded a three-sided view of the sea and the blocks of houses and switchback roads rising from the city to the south, and to the north the long sweep of the ocean studded with developments as far as vision permitted. No English magazines on the coffee table, no English books in the bookcases. Ari poured out two small glasses of a dark fluid; Israeli cognac perhaps.

'We owe those people out there, Gershy,' said Zucker. 'Bosnians. They're suffering for us.'

'Agreed.'

'I'm glad you do. The Jews of Europe.'

'Bosnian Jews?'

'*Real* Jews, Gershy, the only real Jews left in Europe. What's a real Jew, tell me that?'

'I don't need this, Arnie. You're not my rabbi.' The cognac was dry, surprisingly good.

'What, need? We're just two old friends debating a serious question.

Rationally, God forbid we should be emotional. What is a real Jew and how do you know him? It's simple. A real Jew is known by his enemies.'

These Old Testament types, always right, never in doubt, was it something in the water? He saw where it was going, even as Ari bulled ahead.

'So, who hates that poor old couple out there the most? Germans, naturally, since they back the Croats. Americans and the *New* OPEC *Times* and Khomeini News Network since they all back the Muslims. There's the Afghans and the Turks and the Iranians and Arafat's boys and don't forget Muhammed Clintonov, who bombs them. Who's defending Europe against the Iranians? Who, Gershy, who?'

My enemy's enemy.

'Serbs,' he sighed.

'Serbs. I'd bring the whole Bosnian Serb army over here if I could. A little ethnic cleansing is what we need. Instead, you're cleansing us – America! Moving Jews off our land! I never thought I'd see the day, America and Syria against Israel. Old Figs – that's all he eats now, figs stewed in condensed milk – old Figs was a company commander. Lost his sons, lost his house, his daughter was raped by Muslims in front of her mother. The old lady hasn't said a word in two years. Bet you don't read that in the OPEC *Times* – Arab oil money buys them off.'

And just as his neck cords were popping, his voice rising, Leah Haddad, fresh from her shower, entered the room. Ari sat, smiled, and seemed to shrink. She was petite and dark-eyed, Tunisian. The rest of the Haddads had moved to Paris and Montréal; she'd been the only one to move east to the maternal bosom. She took him on a tour of the house, her study, their paintings and manuscripts. She was a theatre and gallery patron, a collector and preserver. Nothing in Israel lacked a story, a history, its own private suffering. In her presence, Ari was a man of few and mild opinions, respectful of Lander's books, which Leah had been reading in their French editions.

'Such an honour having you here, even so briefly,' Ari declared, as Figs served platters of cakes and tea, the hectoring gone. In its place, the familiar tone of respect that Lander had come to expect, and distrust, in the world.

'When Ari said he knew you, I almost doubted him. *Almost*,' she flirted, 'didn't I?'

'It's strange, you gotta admit,' said Ari. 'A *zhlub* like me knowing a *kopf* like him – it really don't figure.'

'That was Brooklyn in those days,' said Lander.

'Remember Anatol Kirshbaum?' Ari suddenly interjected, 'the guy who went to Hollywood?'

'Yeah, right, I've been trying to remember that name. What ever happened?'

'Don't you know?' Leah jumped in. 'Andy Kirkwood?'

'Andy Kirkwood, Jesus,' and now for the first time in the day Lander could laugh. What a tribe, what a community. Andy Kirkwood was the runty little guy who'd made neurosis sexy.

'He came over to open our new civic theatre,' said Leah. 'Ari's contact.'

'And a new Zuckerland. Cut the ribbon on that store I first showed you. Stayed in your hotel, came up here, sat right there. He's a serious guy in real life. Said he thinks of settling here all the time.'

'With his problems, I might too.'

'He misses the old language. Misses the sun. He buried his parents here, their request.'

So what can you say? If Marty Fogelman, king of the bypass, had lived – lung cancer took him out twenty years ago, a brilliant doctor who should have known better – that little Hebrew class had paid some heavy debts, given some pleasure, kept the faith in different ways.

'It's been good,' said Lander.

'What? This afternoon, this life, what?'

At the conference that began in Jerusalem the next day, Lander found himself grouped with the linguists and brain-mappers, but more attracted to the writers and economists. Five years after his work on the recovery of meaning in severe dementia, he was still the Alzheimer's man, though his new concerns were elsewhere.

What is meant by memory? Memory had always been considered involuntary, a kind of passive default position. You can't *not* have memory, even, if you accept Lander's hypothesis, in all but the final stage of Alzheimer's. But what if memory were a construction, or at least constructable, and not just a residue of past experience? Certain cultures still had it, certain languages still embodied it. Songlines, sweat-lodges, dream-quests. Bar-mitzvahs, he was tempted to say, without the shmaltzy songs and tables of pastrami. What if one were to have vivid memories of future events? So vivid even the young could be guided by them? His speculations were drawing him dangerously close to mysticism, a fact he was not ready to share with his colleagues and audience.

In the spirit of the conference, he too was edging towards a unified vision. If he had stated it boldly it would have caused headlines: Man at one time had clairvoyance. There are languages, cultures, that draw no distinctions between future, past and present. Of course we call them primitive. We have evolved, retaining at best a vestige of ancient memory called merely anticipation. We wait for the pleasure of making memories of the future.

Anticipation and memory. Is what we anticipate also what we remember? Are they matching points on the same parabola? His mother had died, essentially, of starvation, unable to remember the taste or texture of food, unable to anticipate its arrival. Just a hot or a cold object thrust into her mouth; no wonder she let it dribble away. If nothing else, Lander's talk elevated anticipation to new heights of seriousness. He heard it referred to the next day as *anticipationality*. It was even called *anticipation theory*, which aroused the interest of certain economists.

There was, in the world of macroeconomics, a ratio known as Kaminsky's constant, which had earned Joel Kaminsky a Nobel in the first years that they had been awarded to economists. In the profession, Kaminsky was called the Prince of Darkness for his interest in the utility of waste, corruption, and other unsavoury elements of economic activity. *In Praise of Corruption* was a kind of dark shadow of Galbraith's *Affluent Society*, or even, some said, a direct descendant of Machiavelli. Kaminsky by now was well over eighty, luxuriantly eyebrowed, stooped and lean, travelling with a much younger Asian woman called 'Kaminsky's second constant'. It was Kaminsky who sought out Lander, sending a message to meet him for coffee.

He liked to call himself a simple gardener, though he still consulted for governments wishing to ascertain the magnitude of their hidden economies. When he and Lander compared travel notes, it became apparent that Lander was the stay-at-home. The world he travelled was comparatively safe and well-lit, the comforts of home nearly replicated. Kaminsky's world, by choice, took him to villages, through squalid back alleys, to the loading docks and train stations of the Third World. He was the Mahatma Gandhi of self-imposed discomfort.

Kaminsky's lecture had been 'Towards a Theory of Economic Dark Matter'. In astronomy, we subtract the visible and known weight of the universe from what – according to all our theories of light and gravity and motion – our calculations tell us must still be out there, unseen. You start with a huge number, you subtract a huge number, and you come up with a huge number for what must be the invisible weight of the universe. The so-called dark matter, the stuff that's as heavy as everything we can see, only we have to take even its existence on a kind of theoretical faith.

Well, the economy is a little like celestial mechanics. It yields some astonishing numbers. There appear to be mysterious forces that bind an economy together ('I called them *feygelehs* once, and it popped up in very sober Japanese journal, so I'm careful about giving names to anything,' he said), and there are forces that fling it apart. As in all things great and small, no? Marriages, families, even the human mind, if I understand your work, Dr Lander. The older I get, the more I see the universe working its same Manichean magic everywhere. Light and Dark. Everywhere, there's dark matter. Without it, we'd just sail into infinity. Is an economy capable of infinite expansion like the universe? Or does it reach a point when all coherence is lost, when market laws are no longer operable? Will we crunch up into a little ball?

Is that a workable model for the mind, for memory, as well, Dr Lander? I leave it to you.

Kaminsky discounted the difficulty of his theory. 'Like calculating the existence of Pluto by studying the orbit of Neptune. It's all trigonometry,' said the Prince of Darkness. 'That's where it started, Brooklyn Tech, trying to work out sines and cosines for something more interesting than ladders against the sides of buildings. I didn't count on the military interest, but that's another story.

'I anticipate your next question, Dr Lander. The cleanest real country in the world is Iceland, after dear old Singapore, of course, which isn't real at all. Angela's Singaporean,' he said, causing his ex-student to blush. 'Singapore gives us the baseline. We know everything's accounted for, nothing's wasted or diverted. There are no jaywalkers, economically speaking. But no dark matter is a perfectly wretched way to live, in my opinion. We need our darkness, don't we? Shadows make us human. Norway's good, all the usual Scandinavian virtues. New Zealand, too. Is a pattern emerging? I hope so. The U.S., Mexico and China have much higher corruption rates. Nigeria's off-scale. At some level one might say being too human is an enormous burden.

'One might legitimately ask, what level of dark matter is beneficial to a society? I'm devoting the rest of my life to that question and I have no doubt I'll carry it unanswered to my grave. I only know it's always been with us, it's part of the dynamic of human culture. The Phoenicians had their thumbs on the scale.'

'Israel?' Lander had asked.

'Military spending distorts the model,' said Kaminsky. 'Also, so much unearned overseas remittance. I'd say Israel's pretty healthy. Good balance, dark and light matter. Personally, I'm heavily invested in Israeli stocks.'

The week droned on. The human languages multiplied. He heard himself quoted, also mocked. Some brain-mappers couldn't find any evidence of any retained consciousness even in mid-stage Alzheimer's patients, suggesting that Lander's life work was something of a fraud. Some linguists couldn't interpret Alzheimer's word-salad as anything but gibberish, thank you, Dr Lander. ('Wait'll they get hold of Kaminsky's constant in a few years,' the economist had whispered during one long, sustained attack). When the conference ended, Lander counted himself dented at the edges but basically untarnished, with important new allies.

The question that was forming was simpler than all the others: could I be happy here? Not that he feared American fascists of any colour; merely, did these cantankerous countrymen of Ari Zucker offer the completion his life had been missing? It was a question he'd never posed, could not have imagined asking at any time in his life, right up to a week before.

'Avivas?' Lander asked on the drive up to Kiryat Shimona, the last major town before the Golan. They were back to the pears. 'Aren't you afraid college kids will say "check out the Avivas on her!"?'

'I love it,' said Fisher. 'No more melons, no more hooters. Avivas!'

Lander had known these northern hills and the distant mountains forty years before, when the country was wild. You could take a gun into the hills and come back with gazelle, wild goat, even lions, some said. It was a frontier community back then with bad roads and no services, the housing was wretched, the bodies squat and faces rugged from tilling arid land between kibbutzes.

'Actually, Aviva approves. She's no prude,' said Fisher. He was a man in love, just two years into his marriage with a film-maker named Aviva Golan. The drive up from Jerusalem had begun to humanize Fisher in Lander's eyes. He was more than his pears; it's hard to begrudge a man so obviously in love. Lander's views across the board were softening. He was receptive to the dark matter within himself, within Israelis, the harshness of their views, the splits in their society that seemed only more developed than those in the States.

There had been two failed Fisher marriages, the second to a foreign service officer who'd risen more rapidly than he, got choicer postings, heavier responsibilities, a Russian specialist who saw her future in Washington and not in the field. 'You see the list of promotions and there's twenty-three women and two men – one Hispanic and one Indian, I might add – and if you squint real hard you can make out the handwriting on the wall. They offered some kind of desk job for me in Washington, but I wouldn't take it. Israel came up, I knew the language, I was interested, I looked very secular on paper which really means slightly anti-Semitic and it was just the sort of dead end job that an older man takes before retirement.'

There had been a much earlier marriage, one of those sixties things, he called it, to a Nicaraguan civilian, a Jew, back in the days when it required security checks and approval all the way up the line. By the time permission came through, he'd fallen out of love, the girl and her family were lining up for favours and immigration and he'd learned that community alone is no guarantee of compatibility.

'My then-wife and I also did a sixties thing,' said Lander. 'We adopted a black baby.'

'So now she hates you?'

'She hates men and Jews and the American government in no particular order. Loves Germans, though. Calls herself Tewfiqa Niggadyke.'

'Go figure.'

'I'm giving her the title to some old family property in Berlin if she'll just change that goddamn name. We'll die out where we started, my daughter and her girlfriend. Only the colour changes.'

'No other children?'

'A catatonic monk in Japan.'

'You're really spreading the wealth.'

'You have to jab him with needles to get his attention. If a man's judged by his children, I did something wrong.'

'When I think back over my so-called career at State, I know I blew it in Nicaragua. I thought the whole Jewish Latina number was so sexy. I took a risk, it failed, it caused repercussions. Somewhere, in someone's eyes, I'm a bad risk.'

'Hello, Jonathan Pollard,' said Lander.

'Don't remind me. That *chazer* hurt us all.'

And in this way, weaving stories, establishing their expertise – for Fisher, Spanish, Russian, Hebrew and Arabic – the two drew closer, the kilometres clicked by, the land rose, the mountains drew closer, and soon they'd come to the settlement called Beth Ezra. The orchards were just beyond the fences. The Fishers' modest three rooms were inside the kibbutz, kitchen and dining were shared.

Aviva was worth waiting a lifetime for, Fisher declared in an outburst of sudden passion. The short walk from the parking space to their door was taken up in reverence for Aviva of the Pears, Aviva of the Films, Aviva of Aliyah. She too had survived bad marriages, she too had thought the time for romance in her life was over. 'What she sees in me, I don't know. You know her films, of course,' to which Lander nodded.

She was waiting at the door, a trim, indistinct, grey-haired figure with the light behind and above her. 'Hello, Gershon,' she said, the voice familiar, British. 'It's been a long time, hasn't it?'

Walls were collapsing, trees breaking with incredulity, lions, jackals, hummingbirds, 'Davia, my God!' and he melted into her arms without the consciousness of movement, two charged particles cutting through static. There were fragrances, Jaffas, tobacco, cedars and sandalwood, unlocked in an instant. Her breasts rested against him in a place untouched for forty years that unleashed tears he didn't know he had, or that anything could release. It was Lander hugging, lifting, pawing, thumping, kissing, Lander the demonstrative one, Lander the Old-World embarrassment.

'My God, dear God, oh, my God!'

* * *

She'd prepared lamb in the kibbutz kitchen with pear cobbler for dessert, good wines, fresh green beans, just-picked corn, sweet butter churned from Beth Ezra's herd of dairy cattle. Lander was shown around, no one knew him, none responded beyond the nod to America, where most had been and many had worked. It was not an English-speaking kibbutz; Lander was at a welcome disadvantage. Then they retired to the Fisher-Golan bungalow.

'My two grooms! I can't believe Dovid kept the secret!'

'Exceptionally easy, love, considering I didn't know.'

'Dovy, I told you all about Gershon. When was it, God! forty years ago?'

'A princess in '56. A queen today,' said Lander.

'I kept up with your books, you know. I was in England till about eight years ago.'

'Her husband died.'

'My third. I'm getting much better with practice.'

Practice was never her problem, Lander thought, smiling, and he could see Davia's dimples begin to flutter (he'd forgotten the dimples that made her seem so innocent, and then he remembered how she hated her dimples, who could be a serious actress with dimples?) Lander had no interest in bringing up the past, particularly if it clouded the innocence of their marriage and the earnestness David Fisher had brought to it. But, given the warmth of the greeting, the body language, how could he not know, not guess something even worse?

'Still married? Judy, isn't it?'

'You've got the name right.'

'How long?'

'Going on ten years.'

'Anyone else?'

'Not at the moment.'

'It's time to settle down, don't you think?'

'I've thought it for a long time.' Find me a Singapore economist, he thought. Find me another you.

'You don't want to face old age alone.'

'I'm facing.'

'Love, Gershon is thinking of settling. We talked about it on the ride.'

'Oh, smashing, jolly good!' she exclaimed in her best West End manner. 'You can back my films!'

'I don't know what I'd do. Keep a bag packed, get a foothold in Israel, I suppose. Seems like good advice.'

'Beware of the older women. I think they all left Miami Beach and came to Tel Aviv. There's lots of blond widows, lots of blond divorcees out there. Get a dog.'

'No dogs,' said Lander.

'Aviva thinks Jewish women get blonder as they get older.'

'It's a fact. They think it's closer to natural. Closer to white. Black would be cheating, like covering up. Blond is just ... emphasizing it. So they think. I know, I've been there.'

She wasn't blond now, she was silver. She could have posed for a vitamin ad, a denture commercial, any kind of upbeat older-woman-on-a-cruise with a fit, tanned, grey-haired husband who'd looked after their investments, golfers in paradise, sailors waving to grandchildren at the dock. Not the type to make you think, however briefly, God, the cocks that had been inside her, the legions of men, the casting couches, the crews, the casts, the backers. And then himself, the boy in Israel stunned by a girl, the researcher, the young husband and father, and then the women, bodies piling up, like buses rear-ending in the fog.

'That's a complicated look, just now,' said Davia. 'If I were filming, I'd try to capture that.'

'Good thing you're not.'

The dimples fluttered.

'I think this is a miracle,' said David. 'The only word. Figure the odds.'

'I used to. Now I expect it,' said Lander. 'There are only five billion people in the world, maybe in a lifetime we see a million faces. Maybe we get to know about five thousand and we all go to the same places, hang out in the same way. I know I'll see friends in a bookstore. It would be a miracle if old friends didn't meet. Distance is no longer a factor.'

'So logical, my deah, deah boy.'

'I didn't mean a miracle-miracle.'

'Understood.'

'How about this for a miracle? You said you had a black daughter, right? I was a kind of wandering rabbi for the embassy when I was posted in Moscow. All the Jews were trying to get out, you know. Also a lot of non-Jews were trying to take advantage. I'm the guy that had to test them. So I wait till we get three or four visa applications from any given city, and I then take a visit. You know Tashkent?'

'My dau –' Lander began.

'Nasty, dry, hot place in the summer. Typical Soviet destruction of a foreign culture. So there's this guy named Shvartz, classic name, married to an American. I go, he's gone. Wife's there.'

'Black,' said Lander.

'Did I already tell this? Yeah, *shvartz* was a redundancy. No sign of him, but in perfect Russian she tells me she's an American, takes out pictures, recites –'

'– the *haftara*.'

'This is too weird.'

'Darling,' said Davia, 'I think Gershon is trying to tell you something.'

'Well, when the Soviet Union was starting to break up, you had a lot of desperate characters trapped in some pretty strange places. Somalis, Zaireans. They had forged passports, they had bribe-money, they had knives. This lady was very good –'

'Missing a finger? Spots on her hand?'

'May have. Really good English, too.'

'Coffee?' asked Davia.

'A miracle is probably a black Russian woman reciting the *haftara* in Tashkent,' said Fisher. 'Imagine the desperation of those people.'

'I'm going out for a cigarette,' she said.

'And there's the lesser miracle that she's my daughter.'

'But you said –'

'She wasn't then.'

'What about the miracle that we met? The miracle of Davia?'

'Those were just the odds, love,' she said, heading outside.

'I know,' she said. She still rolled her own. 'He's a dear, sweet man and I don't want to hear any disrespect. I will not say anything disrespectful about my husband. He was following orders. Doing his duty, that's all. What happened happened.'

'Good.'

'So she met a good woman and moved to Poland and then to

Germany and lived happily ever after. But what about you?'

'I'm a survivor. I do what I have to. Don't tell him, he thinks I'm English. I've had some successes, Gershon. It makes him proud.' She stubbed her cigarette, and rolled another. All around them, outside other doors, women were standing and smoking. 'You say Jews should keep a bag packed? Think about South African Jews.'

'Too many things are collapsing, partitions are suddenly coming down.'

'It only means age, dear. The pendulous *tristesse* of breasts. Same with you, no? Cock, tummy, chin wattles, old man's earlobes...'

'It means Judgement Day, the Messiah coming, Moloch, Armageddon, something big.'

'Dear boy. Dear, dear boy.'

The door opened.

'Catching up on old times? Look, I've been thinking. I'm sorry, I'm terribly, terribly sorry. Consular work is nine-tenths stoneheartedness, suspiciousness, saying no.'

'And being just a little bit anti-Semitic,' said Lander pleasantly. He debated saying it, and finally did. 'It's the one-tenth that judges us.' He could feel Davia's withdrawal, Fisher stiffen. 'I brought some pear brandy,' he said. 'We can have it under the trees.'

Back to Tel Aviv, the same hotel, the same sheet of white Zuckerland lights, new conferencees arriving, the old ones packing up. Lander had crammed fifty years in a week, he felt exhausted and exhilarated. Israel was so concentrated, so opinionated, so raw and so sophisticated that he felt himself returned to helpless childhood and clueless adolescence, then flung outward, into the widest reaches of maturity, weightless around a familiar planet. Only as he packed did he realize this had been a celibate conference, his first in years. Had age finally caught up with him, or did the writers clean the pool? Where were these blond divorcees, and did he really care? Perhaps he had passed out of a phase, a long destructive one that gave back less than he put into it. If that's it, so be it.

What country do you give for a man who has everything? He longed for Ari Zucker's clarity of motive, of mission. Save my people. Lander had become a citizen of the world, Chicago more convenient than most stops, but not a burial site.

His departure was set for late the next night, time still to debate the options. In the coffee shop, where he'd least expected to find them, sat Joel Kaminsky and Angela, sharing ice cream from a silver goblet. Lander felt himself becoming the third wheel in some very strange relationships.

'My life,' he sighed, when asked his problem.

Kaminsky was reading a Hebrew newspaper, eyes darting right to left. 'What about your life, Dr Lander?' asked Angela.

'Lonely, confused, bizarre.'

'You should find a woman, before one finds you.'

'That's very sound advice,' he said.

'Not too young, however,' she went on.

'Aviva Golan's a lovely woman,' said Kaminsky. 'She told me you'd met, after many years.'

'I knew her under a different name. A different life.'

'I knew Davia when I taught at LSE. A remarkable woman. Your life's been blessed with many good friends, Gerald.'

'You probably know Ari Zucker, too.'

'I knew him as Arnie, but yes, I advised some friends of his a long time ago. It turned out well for everybody.'

'This country's one family, isn't it?'

'On our level, yes. I don't know the new Russians, I don't know many north Africans. The Yemenis are a mystery.'

'Could I be happy here?'

'Why not stay back a day or two? Make inquiries. I can give you names. They have a saying here. An Israeli should keep his bag packed. Don't give up your Chicago place.'

And so it happened two days later that Lander didn't take his ticketed flight. He wondered, as he often did, if by ditching the flight he'd reshuffled his diminishing deck, brought the fatal card closer to the top, or buried it deeper. Tomorrow would he wake to the news of a terrible crash, or would the fated crash now be his, whenever he took it? His son, the Enlightened One, would have something to say, if prodded, about destiny and the afterlife, about ego, the futility of attachment to the flesh, the mind, the career.

One more book, one more decade, anticipation and memory, all the binaries, all the plays and novels and poems that fed into it, all the religious texts, the dark and light matter of the universe, the solitary pleasure of writing. He had already wasted so much of his life, spent so much energy in pursuit of ... ego, the flesh, ambition. He walked to the lobby, glad to be unrecognized, picking his way through mounds of luggage, groups of Americans and Japanese, a few local businessmen in untucked shirts and pocket calculators meeting with dark-suited Japanese, a sign in Hebrew which, miraculously, he could read. 'Cohens May Enter,' it said, meaning safe for priests, whatever food or services lay behind it.

Things coming back. The tide washing in. A man lowered a Hebrew newspaper, slowly, as though afraid of what he might see, and Lander recognized him as well, his ancient double, the man in a dream of so many years. What to do now but smile, and make the hands-out, palms-up gesture familiar to them both? But the man panicked and bolted from the chair, dropping the newspaper. The front of the hotel was blocked by baggage; the double took the side-entrance, nearly running through the glass door. 'It's all right,' Lander wanted to cry out, 'it's just the odds, nothing more.'

He thought of himself suddenly as a zebra in the short grass of the African *veldt,* one among an identical many. He thought of lionesses, of hyenas, the leap of an enormous weight upon his back, teeth clamped about his neck. He couldn't breathe, the air was turning purple. The purple of his algebra vision so many years before, the purple light of discovery when his mother's words became explicable. He was surprised he could even stagger under such a weight, that no one in the registration line had turned in astonishment at such a sight, a zebra in sandals and a loose white shirt, in the lobby of a fancy hotel, attacked by lions.

And then the shadow he'd been pursuing these past ten years suddenly took on substance. It was all so simple, really, the beautiful vision, the unified field theory. It was the lion. His life's work wasn't the final thing; it was only the beginning. The brain is wired for thousands of applications, not just for speech and spotty recall, but for clairvoyance and telepathy and a thousand other higher powers. Our tragedy is profound – we've lost the access codes. We've invented excuses, like time, to symbolize the unknown. Language is our pale compensation, porpoise calls and wolf howls, for the loss of our true humanity. Language is fax instead of e-mail, an electric typewriter instead of a word processor. The embedded syntactical structures of our brain are too complex for mere language. Language is a primitive lung, an evolutionary stage.

What chemical, stored in the deepest fold of the primitive brain was being released at just that moment, what protein of recognition allowed the zebra, the wildebeest, the house cat slinking to the basement corner, to enter his final moments convinced of the futility of escape? The dominance of our species has been purchased with the capital of our brains' own wiring.

They live in the moment, we say of animals and of people we depict as primitive, of Alzheimer's patients. It seemed an exquisite profundity. What does it mean, *to live in the moment?*

This would be his work, in the time remaining.

He went outside, across the portico to the corner to stare at the wall of Zuckerland's cold white light, brighter than a thousand suns. He did not notice – no one did – a gleaming Mercedes parked in front. But a man walking past did look in, did stoop, and then began to run. Others coming out of Zuckerland carrying appliances, Lander at the corner about to go back inside, the kids flipping through CDs, the bus honking and then unloading around the illegally parked car, the tourists in the lobby, none of them noticed, none of them heard the warnings of one crazy man running and shouting hysterically. No one had a chance when the car mysteriously hiccuped and a fireball erupted. Its windows blew out and the fireball expanded. The street shook, shards of fluorescent tubing lifted and propelled themselves, light as balloons in every direction, to radiate in a pattern like a glittering fence around the crater, the bodies, the luggage, the bus and the front half of the hotel.

It was all caught on satellite footage, the calm day, the city far below, '... and now,' announcers around the world intoned, 'watch for a bright light in the lower left. Keep watching, and you'll see the wave of destruction.'

Many commentators picked up on the irony that if one small shred of hope can be gleaned from such a catastrophe it might be this: that had the bomb gone off just thirty-six hours earlier, it would have eliminated the greatest collection of minds ever assembled in one place in the past half century.

Dear Gershon, the letter read, opened by a postal clerk and sold to investigators many months later. *I cannot rest tonight, not after the way we behaved. You were a gentleman to me always, my knight as the years wore on and it seemed there were no heroes left. Seeing you again, not being able to hold you, to be held by you, has broken my heart in ways I did not think possible in one so old, and presumably, so accustomed to heartbreak (and, you're probably thinking because I can read your face, heart breaking). You were going to stay in Israel, but after our behaviour how could we expect you to? How could I? This morning we awoke to the terrible news of the bomb that went off in front of your hotel; if you'd stayed, you surely would be no more. I take the smallest satisfaction possible that something started in Tashkent and revealed in Beth Ezra may have, in some bizarre twist, saved your life. For that, I thank G__D. All my love, Davia.*

Migraine Morning

> Indeed, it is not unusual for the memory to condense into a single mythic moment the contingencies and perpetual rebeginnings of an individual human history. – Sartre, *Saint Genet*

FORTY-TWO YEARS LATER, at about the time of his sixty-sixth birthday, Gerald Lander's life would end in a bomb-blast on a Tel Aviv street. For a week or two, Palestinian and Jew would belabour each other's guilt. The world would mourn. In time, an urban myth would evolve. Some felt he had not died – his messages were immortal – but had chosen to slip away for a higher, instructive purpose. His was not an untypical face; credible sightings on five continents could not be dismissed out of hand.

Today, however, an overcast late autumn Boston Tuesday in 1963, deep in the stacks of Widener Library, Lander was, or had been until five minutes earlier, a healthy, even lusty, twenty-seven-year-old linguistics graduate student. He would remember till his dying day – even, in fact, in the final split-second of his dying day – the book he was holding: István Gotlieb's *Language and Capital: an Inquiry into Acquisition and Accumulation*. Those wily, cultured Europeans made him feel inadequate, weaving Marx and Freud and a myriad of cultural references into language study, extending the reach of linguistics into brain structure and history. Language as cultural DNA was a vivid idea for a young American in 1963. He had no way of knowing that Gotlieb was pointing in the direction his own research would take, that in time it would be Lander who pushed linguistics beyond its historical limits.

For his doctoral thesis, he would do the expected thing. He found a language, a coastal dialect of Highland Malagasy, itself an ancient form of Malayo-Polynesian brought by Javanese sailors west and south to Madagascar instead of eastward towards the Pacific islands. By then, four years in his future, he'd fairly well have mastered the Germanic, Slavic and Latin languages. The thrill of studying language was their inexhaustible supply; there was always something new and surprising in the infinite expressiveness of the human soul. After proving himself in Madagascar, the linguistic world awaited him: the expanses of New World aboriginal tongues, the undeveloped tree of African languages, oceans of Chinese and all its derivatives, the Semitic deserts, the Himalayan heights of Indo-European ... and the paleo-languages, the dead, the dying, the evolving. His early study would lead – 'inevitably', they wrote in his obituaries – to his crowning achievement, the paradox of living, but imaginary languages, the languages of schizophrenia, paranoia, humour, politics and finally, Alzheimer's. Nothing ever devised by humans, according to Lander, was ever lost.

It is the nature of all inquiry to turn speculative, and of speculation to fold in on itself, he would answer: the unmappable *géographies de la nuit*, imaginary languages, metafictions, string theory, logical positivism, the quanta. None of the advances of the modern world concern the visible, the audible, or the comprehensible.

His first excursion into the field of imaginary languages would occur in Madagascar. Why did certain coastal dialects incorporate many Arab/Swahili words, but retain paleo-Malay syntax, while others did not? It was a simple question, really, easily answered by conventional language-acquisition theory (vocabulary 'borrowings' in no way affect the deep structure of a language) – or by neo-Marxists (what were the value and nature of the goods being traded? Why were fishing communities more adaptable than agricultural settlements?). But the young Lander pointed the discussion elsewhere, to the possibility of, and then the describing in detail, of a temporary, mediating language, a creole, that must have formed to buffer the collision of disparate syntactical structures. A creole flexible enough to allow for simple transactions; a language of the night, a language of silence. Critics accused him of inventing a language. Where is it now, why didn't it evolve? Not all creations evolve, he replied. Language is both durable, and fragile. Linguistic extinctions outnumber survivals.

But that so-called extinct creole lived on in traces, he answered, in certain anomalies (and as a careful researcher, like an archaeologist brushing clay from a shard of pottery, he found them); he called them 'language shadows'. But even an ingenious creole could not bridge the gap. The creole turned chaotic, literally unspeakable. Can you imagine that tragedy, to be trapped inside a language that couldn't express clear thought or meaning? Like schizophrenic voices, like Alzheimer's.

He sensed from the beginning the presence of shadow languages. As he studied the extant, he imagined their dead parents, their missing siblings, the quirks that survived, and the elegant solutions that did not.

On that Boston morning in the Widener stacks he could not have imagined himself in thirty years as anything but senior faculty in a respectable college, tape-recording vowel shifts in tribal backwaters. He would find a dying language somewhere in the deep bush, tundra or desert and become its sole non-native speaker. He could not have imagined a time in Frankfurt thirty years in the future when he would sit on the first 'Imaginary Languages' panel with the elderly Hungarian exile, István Gotlieb. When they met – or, when they *will* meet in thirty years – Lander would break into tears, smacked by the sudden confluence of memories. He will see himself as a young man in the midst of his first passionate love affair with the sexiest woman alive, his losing marriage, his children gone missing, and the memory of holding Gotlieb's book on the morning of his first migraine and the events surrounding it. On that day at the German conference, it seemed to Lander that István Gotlieb had somehow presided over his last innocent moment. Before that day was over, he would lose everything.

For someone later identified with Jewish causes, or at least, the possibility of peace in the Middle East through mutual effort, it's remarkable how indifferent he had been, in his youth, to his own origins, how oblivious he was to religion or community. The only 'community' he recognized was his own language group. He was a typical young man of the early '60s. Vietnam had not yet risen to a level of national concern. Kennedy would be president for another five years, as far as anyone knew. The world admired America and envied Americans as never before, but the president would be dead in another ten days.

Being American would never again be that easy. Confidence would vanish. America would be playing intellectual catch-up for the rest of Lander's life.

On that autumn morning, the sky a harsh, uniform Boston gray, and the fluorescent lights dancing off the page, he looked up and his eyes failed to compensate. All the light of the universe, one gigantic flashbulb, imprinted itself directly on his brain. The blank white page followed wherever he stared. Squiggly lines of print turned purple and yellow, resolving themselves into saw-toothed patterns. The stacks, the ceiling, the floor, the windows, were ribbed by dancing lights. He lost perspective and depth perception. He bumped into stacks, he was afraid to take a step. His hands were numb, his wrist sagged, the book fell and dizziness made him sick to his stomach. He could feel his head shrinking, being squeezed and crushed, as though the air itself had become miles of dense liquid pressing down. He vomited on Gotlieb's book, his knees buckled and he fell into a puddle of his own making. He thought he'd suffered a stroke.

Let's flash back three hours. Back in his Beacon Hill apartment, he'd made love for the fourth time that long night and morning, and said his reluctant good-byes to his girlfriend of three months. The six-room apartment was shared with a teaching assistant, who kept a back bedroom on the rare nights he was home. Lander took the noisy front. Good Will furnished the living room and dining room. His mother had donated the basic plates, skillets and silver. Lower Irving Street was a slum (in true Boston fashion, with the golden dome of the state capitol looking down upon them) and the six rooms went for a hundred and twenty dollars a month.

Her name was Nancy Landis, and she had a body to make a young man whimper. 'You're the linguist,' she said, 'Landis and Lander, would it be bad if we were related or something?' she asked, which had launched him on an impromptu lecture about false cognates in general and cognominal *faux amis* in particular. 'I meant about having monsters,' she said, twenty minutes after meeting him.

It had been late summer; he was working in a bookstore. She'd asked for an obscure text on the history of dance. On that morning, he just happened to be the world's leading expert on that particular book. Store policy forced each of its five salespeople to pitch new books to the rest of the staff, as though to sell them. He was the store's serious academic; the others were poets, novelists, or children's specialists. Lander had read the dance history and found ways of making it palatable. Nancy was so impressed that she indicated she would not frown upon a lunch at the Bick, and asked if they were related.

That's how the first great dangerous love affair of Lander's life began. She was sexy, available, and Jewish, any two of which, in his upbringing, failed to comport with any third. She did some modelling to pay for dance and acting lessons and to put herself through BU at night, and she had an eighteen-inch waist. Remembering his high school algebra, $C=\pi D$, he figured Nancy Landis had less than a six-inch diameter, or less than a three-inch radius. To continue with the algebra: if x stands for her waist circumference of eighteen inches, then 2x stood for her other vital statistics. When she walked, she seemed like two halves of a person held together by an invisible force field.

No, sexy is wrong. She was sex. She deserved the noun, not the adjective.

He knew she was bad for him. She was slutty and ignorant and would ruin him in academic company. She hated cigarettes, so consumed Baggies of pot. How and where she got it, he never knew. The men who hung around her in Beacon Hill or Harvard Square could have been attracted to her for any number of reasons. *And he didn't care.* He felt sorry for any Harvard junior fellow who didn't have a slutty, ignorant girlfriend with bad habits and improbable contours. He learned something from Nancy Landis that he'd never suspected, and that was that Gerald Lander, junior fellow, had an almost self-destructive sexual side, that he would cut lectures for the promise of something new and daring. Together, they explored the varieties of prepositional positioning: in, out, up, down, over, under, beside, inside. She showed no interest in his work and very little tolerance for anything that took his attention away from her. He couldn't study in the apartment – she was all over him for sex the minute he opened the door. She threw his students' papers out the window. She hid his books and notes. She threatened to erase his tapes. He should have stayed till midnight in the Linguistics common room to study and grade his papers, but the thought of Nancy in his bathrobe with wet hair, arms outstretched as the robe opened, would drive him back just minutes after his final class. She was ruining him, and he didn't care.

And now, this: wallowing in his own puke in Widener Library, and when two students rushed to him, drawn by the pistol-loud thwack of Gotlieb's book falling, he found he couldn't speak. His tongue was slow and thick. Epilepsy, he thought, almost with relief. I'm not dying; I'm just about to enter a new, uncertain and painful phase. The students backed away. He heard one: 'Drunk as a skunk, that's all.' He pulled himself up, grabbing the book ledges, and groped his way to the stairwell, leaning his forehead against the cold handrail, grateful for its relief. The headache that gripped him now was almost orchestral; every vein in his head throbbed at a different pitch.

For twenty-five years he would suffer migraines, at least once a month, sometimes five or six. It became his shorthand self-definition: 'I'm migrainous, you know. There will be days when I'm out of commission.' It seemed an appropriate affliction in some way, the veins in his brain expanding, pressing on nerves, the quickening of every response in his body, the brain daring to announce: *Don't take me for granted.* He tried every medicine, but found the need to carry pills in a little Anacin tin with a sliding top, rattling as he walked, an unwelcome reminder of his vulnerability. He preferred to get through the three-day pain by reciting a mantra: *It reminds me I'm alive. I'm more alive than others. I must make the most of my good days.*

He would be sitting at his desk or walking on a summer or winter day and he'd casually look up at the sky or at a white page, and he'd know: it was coming. Only three or four times did it recur with the fury of that first day, and never with all its disclosures. His mouth would fill with saliva, his hand grow numb, and the nausea would rise. He'd close his book, pull the blinds and go to bed. That's it for the day. If his wife or a woman were near, they knew to avoid him, or to sit with him in a darkened room, or if he gave a sign, climb into bed to lie beside him.

On the lecture circuit it was said, 'Lander gets migraines, you know.' 'Poor man.' 'Poor dear, he suffers so.' Then one day in his late forties, he got the aura and waited for the headache, but it never came. A few days later it happened again. He was spontaneously cured.

Till his dying day he was prone to the migraine aura, sometimes so wincingly bright he would wrap a moist towel over his eyes, but he never got another headache.

He practically crawled to the MTA that first time, keeping his eyes closed until he felt leaves underfoot or bumped into a bench. He couldn't stop the dry heaves, but every strain, even the slightest bend, tightened the vise around his head. His shoes were pasty, his pants cuffs warm and wet with sour curds. Somehow, he made his way down the stairs to the MTA, felt for change in his pocket and dropped it in the slot, feeling nothing with his fingers. He couldn't sit. Passengers moved away from the stench. He clung to a centre pole, leaning his forehead against the cool chrome.

At the first Boston stop there was a high pedestrian overpass, something he'd been dreading ever since getting on. He would have to open his eyes, he would have to descend one leg at a time, like a cripple, and use the handrail for his head and hands. He was making his way down the stairs when he bumped into a man, forcing him to open his eyes.

'Where you think you're going, man?' It was a high school boy in a basketball jacket. In his thickened voice, Lander said, 'I'm sick. Not drunk. Can't see. Gotta get home.'

'You ain't sick. You smell! You drunk!'

'Sick. Dying. So cold.'

'You right there. Gimme your money, sick man. Gimme your smelly money or I throw you off the bridge.'

'Can't reach, can't let go ... rail. SICK! I'm ...' He thought: I voted for Kennedy.

He felt the boy-man's hands on his shoulders and the slight wrenching that pulled his hands off the rail and then the push down the final stairs to the sidewalk where for the first time in an hour he felt comfortable, curled on the concrete, his legs and ribs now contributing to the burden of pain, evening it out, and even the one, two, three sharp kicks to his back were welcome and the tearing of his hip pocket and pulling out of his wallet, welcome, welcome, welcome.

Just a few blocks now. He knew the path so well, the Chinese cleaners, the small grocery, the corner cafeteria for old Italian men. All the smells equally foul, but the brick walls welcomed his hand. No more streets to cross, just slither around the corner like a cat, holding to the walls, just five doors up Irving, and three floors up.

On the day of his death, in the split second he looked down and saw his shoes and pants on fire, his hands black, his glasses melted to his cheeks, he remembered all this, one giant clot of memory shifting like a great ice floe breaking up, like a calving glacier falling free. I have been an explorer, I apologize to all the natives I've disrupted, I forgive them their trespasses, I forgive that boy I offended, I forgive Nancy, running from his roommate's embrace in the back bedroom, covering her nakedness, I forgive, I forgive, I apologize to my wife, my children, the lovers...

I am Icarus, I got too close to the blinding light.

Yahrzeit

From our correspondent in Tel Aviv, June 24, 1997. Affiliates please copy...

As Israel prepares to mourn more than six hundred deaths one year after the Black Tuesday bombing, speculation deepens over the whereabouts of renowned psycholinguist Gerald Lander, last seen in public just minutes before the blast.

Lander is best known for his groundbreaking work on Alzheimer's disease, and for applications of his theories to the treatment of schizophrenia, autism and other brain disorders.

The Black Tuesday bombing of downtown Tel Aviv is the bloodiest terrorist act of modern times, exceeding in carnage the 331 deaths in the bombing of two Air India 747s, allegedly by Sikh terrorists, some dozen years ago.

No linkage, however, has been established between Lander's disappearance and the bombing. Local intelligence authorities have discounted the possibility of foul play or political abduction, despite claims of his captivity and demands for the release of prisoners by Muslim groups under Iranian control. Such claims have been labelled fantasies by Israeli intelligence.

Nevertheless, even well-connected authorities in Israel and the United States agree that the situation is far from resolution. Dr Lander has missed lectures, appointments and travel dates, including major addresses in Paris, Berlin, Tokyo and New York. More disturbing to investigators, his apartment rent has not been paid, his piled-up mail occupies a 'Lander room' in the Chicago post office, bills are unpaid, cheques uncashed and personal letters unopened.

'It's like he died,' said the building superintendant who still faithfully waters plants and does minimal dusting. The police are in agreement, after APBs and Interpol failed to turn up a trace of his whereabouts.

'I'd feel better about this if he'd taken some simple precautions,' said a high-ranking official of the Chicago Police Department. 'He's an adult, we can't go looking for him without cause. But no rent cheques, no mail pickup, no cancellations – this has the earmarks of foul play.'

He is, apparently, a man who has lived a year without using his credit cards or cashing a traveller's cheque. New York attorney Judy Miller, his former wife, is as shocked as anyone. 'It's not like him,' she said, citing his social habits, and their own frequent contact which she states has been broken. 'The man's everywhere. He has friends all over the world, he's a restless traveller. I can't imagine him going underground and settling somewhere. He even drops in on friends at their public lectures, anywhere in the world. It gets to where people leave tickets for Lander the way they do for Elvis. It breaks my heart to say this, but I fear,' she concluded.

'It would be harder to hide him than Salman Rushdie,' added his editor in New York, who has had long experience with both Lander and the India-born Rushdie, still under death threat for 'blasphemy'. 'A Thomas Pynchon or J. D. Salinger [authors well-known for their reclusiveness] he's not.'

Two eyewitnesses, a married couple from New York who wish to remain anonymous, affirm that they saw Gerald Lander, a famous face, after all, flee to safety. 'He jumped out of his chair as though he'd had a vision,' claims one witness, who was nearly knocked over by the man now the subject of worldwide concern. Other witnesses, part of a late-arriving Canadian group who left the lobby discouraged by long check-in lines, swear he stayed behind. 'I saw him sitting there big as life and wanted to get his autograph,' said Mrs Betty Nicholson of Montreal.

Credible reports of other sightings are abundant in Tel Aviv, where the nature of this state, and society, makes anonymity next to impossible.

Positioning at ground zero is all important; there are no known survivors from the hotel lobby, its street-facing rooms, or from adjacent buildings.

Further, to urban dailies...

Latest speculation centres on the possibility that Dr Lander, world-famous for his inquiries into the languages of mental disorder and deterioration, has absented himself deliberately and even changed his name as a prelude to immigration to Israel. Security, privacy and perhaps a deep personality change are cited as possible motivations. He is known to have been working on new applications to his theories, elaborated in a talk delivered in Jerusalem the same week of his disappearance, that hinted broadly at the possibility of tapping linguistic potential, or, as he had put it, 'a unified theory of language de-acquisition, and what it might suggest of older, but still powerful brain structures.'

Fellow researchers have always acknowledged Lander's contributions to fundamental thinking about language and consciousness even as they divide over their strict application. 'He is the last of the great nineteenth-century rational humanists,' stated Dr Karen Toomey of the University of California at Berkeley, 'he never questioned that reason could unlock and decode any irrationality, or that the human soul, if I may use so quaint a nineteenth-century term, could ever be exterminated. And if I may add a personal note, he is a charming, even playful, always fearless researcher.'

In a recent publication of 'Lander Reassessments' (Harvard University Press, Dalal and Gordon, editors), Dr Kenji Wakamatsu of Tokyo Neurolinguistic Institute likened the 'Landerian brain's' untapped resources to ever more powerful computers, whose technical capacities may run ahead of their users' ingenuity. 'What programmes we input, the brain can run. Landerian theories support the notion that structures exist in the brain which are passed through language itself, as though language were the brain's DNA.' Pressed further on that point, Dr Wakamatsu suggested that the brain might indeed be 'wired' for telepathy and clairvoyance, in much the way it is for language acquisition and the storage of memory. 'We must ask, as Lander does, what language is. Words are like fibre optics, their carrying capacity has barely been explored.'

For that reason, others, like the leftist French social linguist Marcel Feininger, suggest, 'the corruption and coarsening of language, notably through mass-appeal television, can, over time, desensitize the transmission of the capacity for thought itself.'

Dr Prakash Dalal, co-editor of the Harvard University Press volume, states in his introduction, 'When we assess Gerald Lander, we clearly re-assess Freud, but less directly, we re-indebt ourselves to Einstein, to Darwin, to Ramanujan. It was the unaided human brain working nearly alone without basic calculators let alone computers that devised theories that our most advanced telescopes and microscopes are only now confirming; that hinted at the existence of such exotic and seemingly irrational concepts as black holes, binary systems and dark matter, or, as in the case of Darwin, that made sense of mad abundance, useless replication and mindless variation, that eventually broke down the rigid orthodoxy of time itself. Today we treat the universe in its incomprehensible scale as an evolutionary event. Tomorrow we may do the same for the brain and its link to consciousness.'

His friends even arranged a well-publicized Lander Roast this spring, thinking to lure him back into the spotlight, in which the biggest names in the field signed on for a 'Gerald Lander, Prophet or Fraud?' fifteen-year assessment of the so-called Lander Revolution. He did not appear. A lecture in Paris two weeks later was held open until the last minute, the crowd that was turned away that night at the Sorbonne is said to rival that mobilized for rare lectures by *les immortels* or the latest intellectual craze. Perhaps in Berlin, the cry went up, but Berlin was cancelled as well.

His daughter, Tewfiqa Lander, contacted at her home in Berlin, said the last communication from her father had been a card from Israel, which she agreed to share with reporters. *Dear Tewfie and S____; I am well, and much excited by a new project which must remain very hush-hush. Incidentally, I met the man who changed your life in Tashkent. On our behalf, and at some personal cost, I did not forgive him. Love, Daddy.* The references remain vague at this time and attempts to access Embassy files have been blocked at the highest level. The Landers have a son, last reported to be in a Buddhist retreat in Japan, who could not be contacted for this article.

The Nobel Prize-winning economist, Joel Kaminsky, who last saw Lander in Jerusalem at a Human Languages conference, and then later in Tel Aviv on the Sunday preceding the blast, confirmed the impression that Lander might still be in Israel, working in deep privacy on problems of a personal and professional nature.

'Gerry Lander is well connected in Israel,' said Kaminsky from his home in New York. 'There are people who would shield him if he wished to avoid the public'. Kaminsky's major work, *In Praise of Corruption*, was known to have influenced much of Lander's later thinking on so-called anticipation theory, which some regard as the 'disused pathway' (Kaminsky calls it 'the rabbit hole, like Alice's plunge into Wonderland') that could open up an unmapped neurolinguistic universe.

Asked if he had been given a hint of Lander's latest undertaking, the eighty-four-year-old economist said, 'It will be revolutionary. It will do for all of us, even functioning geriatrics such as myself, what his first book did for the so-called senile demented. He has discovered a power of the brain that was always there but never tapped. Something we left behind.'

There continues to be speculation, now hardening to firm belief in many circles, that Gerald Lander was one of the dozens of unidentified victims of the Black Tuesday blast. He could have left the hotel but circled back. 'Maybe he forgot something, maybe he wanted to make a phone call, whatever,' said an old Brooklyn friend, Ari Zucker, now a Tel Aviv resident. Zucker, owner of the appliance store directly at ground zero had himself been delayed at home that Tuesday morning. He says now, 'I torture myself. Maybe he was coming back to see me, have a coffee or something.'

A check of airline departures discloses that Lander had cancelled his original departure date, which would have placed him safely back in the U.S. at the time of the Tel Aviv tragedy. His personal and professional appointments on that last morning in Tel Aviv are all well-known and exhaustively documented. Dr Zvi Cohen, director of neurolinguistics at the Hebrew University of Jerusalem, acknowledged that Dr Lander had been in contact regarding the offer of a permanent research residency. But Israel immigration authorities have no record of his application for Israeli residence and citizenship. Diasporic American Jews, like Dr Lander, are routinely admitted to Israel and permitted dual citizenship by both countries.

The irony that Gerald Lander might have perished in a blast triggered by fringe elements in a tribal conflict that has nearly been resolved by political means would be grotesque, a tragedy for all who read his work and honour its lucidity, and who dare to think they had an ally in the highest reaches of science, someone who thought for them, lived for them, believed in them.

Plans are being laid in the United States and in Israel, with contributions from publishers, foundations and researchers in nearly every country where Gerald Lander lectured or counselled patients, to endow a permanent facility in neurolinguistics in his name should his death, the last of the Black Tuesday tragedies, ever be proven.

Meditations on Starch

POTATOES: Mr Spud opened at the local mall, and hired my high school boy for his first job. He was saving for a trip to Europe, where he has relatives.

He's been taught to do amazing things with potatoes. They're just a shell of their former selves. No longer prized for snowy yields, for understated contribution to stews, now they're just parka-like pockets waiting to be stuffed. It's the fate of blandness in the mall-managed world, I tell him, to be upscaled into glamour like pita bread and bagels, chicken and veal. Stuffed with yoghurt, sour cream and cottage cheese, spread with peppers, cheese and broccoli, topped with Thousand Islands dressing and bacon bits.

What wizard thought this up?

Mother!

I still like mashed potatoes. Even the name is honest and reassuring, after the *gepashket* concoctions with alfalfa sprouts and garbanzo beans. Butter-topped, cream-coloured bins of heroic self-indulgence, inviting a finger-dip the way a full can of white enamel compels a brush.

Is there a taste explosion in the world finer than the first lick of the Dairy Queen cone, the roughened vanilla from a freshly opened tub, the drowning in concentrated carbohydrate where fats and starches come together in snowy concupiscence?

CORN: My son never knew his grandmother, whose presence comes back to me as I stand at the Mr Spud toppings bar. She only exists in these sharpened moments, triggered by significant images that otherwise baffle me. 'Mother,' I murmur, 'what do you make of this?' Questions to my mother are questions to history, answers from her are brief parables of the twentieth century.

Don't you know? she tells me. The yearning for a clean, quick, anonymous bite is universal.

My mother found herself in Prague in 1933. Her art school in

Germany had just been closed down. One of her professors offered escape with him to Rio. Many went to Paris and Brussels. These weren't the Big-Time Bauhausers; New York and L.A. weren't in the cards. These were commercial designers ('but not designing enough,' my mother would joke). Shanghai, Istanbul, Alexandria, Stockholm, with the leaders taking off for Caracas and Rio. One got to Vera Cruz. Maybe eventually some of them made their way to America. My mother got to Montréal.

I was a stamp collector. I knew the tales behind those thick letters with the high-denomination stamps, the elegant handwriting in black ink turning to olive. Cancelled stamps are less valuable than mint, but I treasured them for the urgency of cancellation. My mother had known a time when the germ of genius was clustered in the back streets of Dresden and Weimar and Dessau, before the Big Bang flung it to tin shacks on the shores of Maracaibo.

The poles of her existence can move me to tears, the B. Traven world of artists from the heartland of order and austerity rotting in the rat-infested tropics. She showed me photos of an art college, hand-painted signs on a tin-roofed shack, Herr Professor in jodhpurs and bush shirt, teaching from a canvas deckchair.

'Poor old Dieter,' she'd say.

She'd wanted a career in fashion design. Her surviving portfolios from art school feature ice-skaters and ballerinas. She was the Degas of Dresden. But the faces of the skaters and dancers seem grafted on, dark and heavy, like hers. The eyes are shadowed, in the movie-fashion of the day. They stop just short of grotesquerie, for those girls will never soar, never leap. She could get the bodies, but not the faces. I can't tell if it's Expressionism, autobiography, or mild incompetence. I don't know if these were the drawings she kept out of fondness, or the ones that didn't sell. Others found their way into magazines. The idea of my mother influencing the Prague Spring Collection of 1934 fills me with wonder.

Or do I read too much into those drawings, too much into everything about her? Had she somehow, secretly, read Kafka? The idea of her Europe, of pre-war Central Europe, tugs at me, the continent I missed by the barest of margins.

There was no concept of Eastern or Western Europe in those days – Warsaw and Prague were as western as Paris. Russia and Spain, of course, didn't count; they were Asian, or African. Budapest and Bucharest had reputations for pervasive dishonesty, deriving perhaps from the perversity of their languages. So the stories I grew up with and passed on to my son were of an *idea* of Europe that hasn't existed in eighty years, a Holy Roman Empire in which a single language and a single passport dominated all others and the rest of the world suffered paroxysms of exclusion for not being European, and specifically, German.

When he was twelve, I asked my boy what he wanted to be when he grew up. 'A European,' he answered.

In Prague she got a job painting commercial signboards to hang over doorways, like British pub placards. One of the first signs she painted was for something called 'Indian Corn'. A corn café! Nothing but stubby ears of corn, cut in half, standing in pools of butter. In Prague, in 1933.

She had never eaten corn. Her parents considered it servants' food, part of a cuisine beneath serious cultivation. Nothing that required labour in the eating – and corn on the cob looked like work – was part of their diet. My grandparents, whom I of course never met, favoured pre-nouvelle cuisine French cooking, which meant soft, smothered, simmering things, the mashed potatoes of their day, short on fibre, low on spices, long on labour and quickly digested. Much favoured were compotes and warm puddings, since they detested anything cold as well as anything hot. Worst of all were the still-churning, molten messes that had become chic in Germany with the rise of Mussolini. Upscaling the lowly pasta. My grandfather's response to history is summarized in a single gastronomic grumble. 'Why couldn't *il Duce* have been a Frenchman! At least we would have eaten properly.' My grandmother, no less patrician, responded, 'Be grateful. He could have been Hungarian.'

Of all the stories I want to know, of all the things my mother told me of the secret lives of complicated people, I remember only these ridiculous little lines. So she painted her cob – half a cob, and the cobs weren't big in those days – standing up like a stubby candle in its pool of butter. Each kernel was treated like a window in an apartment tower, radiating a buttery light. It wasn't easy, before acrylics, before the conventions of Magic Realism, being a German artist, to devote herself to a humble corncob.

'I didn't know anything at first. Or maybe I discovered it as I worked. It was love for America,' is how she put it. 'A craving for Indian corn saved my life.'

Franz Kafka had been living a few blocks away just a decade earlier. He'd written *Amerika* under the same mysterious craving, though it didn't save his life. Maybe America-worship was in the air, at least among those who professed no longing for Germany. For my mother, Prague was just another provincial German city with an interesting Slavic component to be respected, but faintly pitied. She couldn't imagine civilized discourse in any language but German, with the possible exception of French in well-defined circumstances. French and German divided the dignified world between them, the spheres of pleasure and labour, though her French years were still in the future.

Her boss had a son, named Jürgen Jaeger – a good movie name, and he had dabbled in films like many German-speakers in the '20s. He still thought of himself as a set designer, a property man ('but not a man of property,' he joked, and the joke has survived them all because my mother jotted it down). He also identified strongly with Hitler's Sudeten policy, feeling himself mightily abused by the majority Czechs with their dirty, mongrel ways. I am making him sound unappealing – a Hitler of sorts, another expansionist sign painter with acting ambitions, born on the rim of Germany – but my mother never did. His attitudes were too common to be evil. I'm sure most Prague-born German-speakers yearned for enosis with the Fatherland, all other implications of Hitler-rule to be put aside, temporarily.

This, then, was my mother's situation in 1933. She was thirty and unmarried, talented, attractive, and stateless. She had an admirer whose rechannelled ambition was to join the political and if necessary military services of the greater German state. I have seen his picture, the suggestive swagger, as I interpret it, of one leg up on the running board, elbow on the windshield, body tight against the touring-car's flank. No monocle, no duelling scars, but a leather coat, a self-regarding little blond moustache, and a short, elegant cigarette that can only be carried in a theatrical gold case. He strikes the pose of a big-game hunter, even on a Carpathian picnic in the summer of 1934. This is the man who must be eliminated before I can be born.

Pictures of my mother show her always smoking, though I never saw her smoke, nor empty an ashtray without a show of disgust.

I came into her papers five years ago. That's when I unwrapped the first of many portfolios she'd been keeping under her bed. I had never seen them, and she had shared everything with me, I'd thought, the only child, the late-born son, the artistic and sensitive man in the family. Some of these I had seen – my grandparents sometime in the late twenties at a resort in the mountains. Taking the Cure. All those faces, relaxing, carefree, getting away from business and the city and the nameless sickness that seemed to stalk them.

I look like my grandfather – her genes won out. The gene for baldness, carried through the mother. The gene for Alzheimer's disease – who carries that? My mother maintained a saving fiction all the years that she was able, that her parents could have left Germany in time, just as she had, there was an uncle in Montréal who would sponsor them all, but her father lost first the will, then the sense of all urgency. It was, in his case, a medical, not political problem.

'Who is this man?' I asked her, and she pretended to look, and to smile. 'He's very handsome, mama. Like a movie star.' Still no response. The photo is sepia, faded, and extremely small. If only it could be blown up, Jaeger and the touring-car, the mountains and forest in the background, I might understand just a little more. There are other pictures, equally small, taken from upper windows, overlooking city squares. Brno? Bratislava? Carlsbad? Prague, perhaps, or the view from Carpathian resort hotel. Maybe Jürgen is standing at her side, whispering, '*Sehr schön*'.

'Jürgen Jaeger, mama, does it mean anything?'

She held her hand out to appease me, her fingers now blue-edged tines, but she didn't look.

I can read German, speak it enough. Her old-style handwriting is difficult. *I tell him he must do what he must do. His father has interests in Germany. They have relatives in Leipzig.*

I read it out loud, looking at its author's face, which gives back nothing. She probably jotted down these notes in ten seconds, sixty years ago. Now, the simplest resurrected fact of her life embraces the world. If I don't take these boxes now, they will be lost. She is going away and won't be coming back, and we have decided we must leave Canada.

He says, 'Der Führer may be a little crude for your tastes, but he's no fool! He knows who makes money for him. And with this Rosenfeld getting elected in America, well...'

There is another tiny, sepia street scene. It is the most precious picture in the box. For an artist, my mother took terrible pictures. A tram snakes off the top of the frame. Half of a bundled Frau crosses the street. Uniformed men – police, army, Czech, German? – fill the space at the corner, outside a coffee shop. There seems to be an *Apotheke* next door. Cold-looking children play a sidewalk game using chalk just outside its door. You would miss it if you weren't looking for it, the sign for *Korn* struggling for attention against much larger and fancier boards.

This is the picture to be enlarged, at any cost. I palm it and slip it away, knowing I am taking her soul, and fearing that something will slice through all the blown cells in her brain and reach out for it, and then destroy it.

Fly! Fly! Go west and don't stop. I tell you this as a friend, as someone who knows.

This on a worn sheet of airmail paper, initialled with what appears to be a double 'J' inside a crest, with a swastika hanging below it. So strange to see, as it were, a sincere swastika and not some gangland graffiti.

J. J., Visa Clerk, Leipzig.

RICE: In my wife's culture, Usha is called a 'cousin-sister' which means any female relative approximate in age. Actually she is Anu's first cousin, daughter of my father-in-law's oldest brother. In the ancestral long-ago, they had lived in the same Calcutta house, the *jethoo-bari*, part of a joint family numbering forty.

She is married to Pramod, and both are physicists. But instead of staying in the university world and settling down on some Big Ten campus, Pramod had taken a position in Holland, setting up a lab, and the Dutch government had recommended him for similar work in Indonesia and Surinam and before too many years, he had found himself sidetracked into sophisticated, high-level nuclear management, the protocols of which led, inevitably, to international agencies. He is now with the UN's nuclear-monitoring agency in Vienna, and Usha works as a researcher in physics for the University. They have been in Vienna for fifteen years, their children are European, they own an apartment in the city and a garden house in Wiener-Neustadt. It's a comfortable life in a country where immigration and assimilation as we know them are impossible.

We are all together this night in Vienna, enjoying a huge Bengali banquet, cooked from locally gathered fish and rice and vegetables, simmered in spices brought back from frequent trips to London and Bombay. My son and I have our Eurail passes, Anu will be with us only three days before going on to India to visit her mother and sister.

It's this life we lead, I silently explain to myself, and to the ghost of my mother. Vienna was another of her cities, briefly. The world has opened for us, no fears of the unknown. My mother shrank from the very idea of India, but tried to disguise it with images of Gandhi and respect for ancient wisdom.

How under-defined I feel, at fifty, compared to Pramod; a father who has written some books, who teaches when he must, who dabbles in cultures that have their hooks in him.

We are talking of Canada. 'They've become like the British,' Anu says, spooning out rice to our son. 'Hateful little people.'

The Sens had visited Niagara Falls last summer, and been turned away at the border for an afternoon's visit. For pleasure trips they use their Indian, not UN passports. 'He said things to us I wouldn't say to a servant,' says Usha Sen. "How do I know you will leave when you say? How do I know you own a house as you say?" They are very suspicious about Indians, I must say.'

'I told him to go to hell,' says Jyoti, the Harvard boy. 'Who needs the hassle? The Austrians are bad enough, but I always thought Canadians were better.'

I remember when it wasn't so, in our cosmopolitan refuge of Montréal, when my mother and I lived like Alexandrians in a large apartment in Outremont after my father's death. We had original paintings on our walls, French-Canadian artists only. My father was an old man even in my earliest memories, a lawyer nearing retirement, then dead two months after achieving it. I remember the visits of his grown-up children from an earlier marriage, of being the same age as his grandchildren, and of wondering what, exactly, to call our relationship. My son and Jyoti are, precisely, second cousins. Usha is his first-cousin-once-removed. He calls her *mashi*, aunt.

'Have more rice, please. There is plenty.'

'Mother, this isn't Calcutta,' says Tapati, the MIT daughter. Everything this evening is exquisite. There is no cuisine in the world that excites me like Indian, no painting that thrills me like Moghul miniatures, no city, for better or worse, like Calcutta. After India, Europe is a bore. I'm staying back for my son's sake, his ancient dream of being European.

Anu is explaining our move to the States. 'To be Indian in Canada was to be a second-class citizen no matter how good you were, no matter how Canadian you tried to be. At least if we're second-class in the States we know it's because we're just second-rate.' I wish I could sink into the rice, the dimple-topped pyramids of snowy rice scooped out for fish and vegetables. I want to grab handfuls of rice and smear them over my head and rub them in my face. I want to do something vulgar and extravagant in this apartment of excellence, among these diligent and exquisite people, out of my own shame, the accumulated guilt and incomprehensions of my life.

Tapati is asking our son, 'Is there anything special you want to see in Vienna? I can take you there.'

They are amazed that for who he is and what he represents to them – America, after all, the place and people they most admire – he speaks only English. Usha's children have been raised in Europe, but with Indian ways. Each of them speaks eight languages, but they have no country. Jyoti writes rock lyrics in German, plays in an Austrian band, studies economics at Harvard. Tapati has a Ph.D. and an MBA and now interns at the World Bank. Both are in America, but not of it – too exquisite for the mall-culture America I know.

'Anything,' he says. 'It doesn't matter.'

'No, there must be something.'

He looks to me for help. He wants Europe, he wants saturation, a way of entering. He's been studying German in high school, but it's the last thing in the world he'll admit here to his second cousins. He doesn't trust himself to understand a single word. He's heard Bengali all his life, but never thought it part of himself. He spent half his life in a French-speaking city and did his French exercises perfectly, like history. It's the legacy of the New World. Jyoti has already told him, he'd trade it all – the languages, the sophistication that dazzles his Harvard friends – for a simple work permit, for the chance to stay and work the summer at Mr Spud.

'And what about you, Uncle?'

'Berggasse 19,' I say.

'The Freud house?' Usha asks. 'Why that – there's nothing there, believe me.'

'Wasn't he a coke-head?' my son asks in all seriousness, and the question sails over the heads of all but Jyoti, who smiles and nods. A conspiratorial friendship is starting to grow.

'Berggasse is very near my lab,' says Usha. 'We can take the tram there tomorrow. But it's not what you think – it's just a couple of rooms with photos on the walls.'

'Bor-ring,' Jyoti hums, as my boy suppresses a grin. We're there at eleven o'clock the next morning, my son and I, and Jyoti who's brought his guitar along. He'll do Freud with us, and we'll do the music shops with him. He's promised us a tour of the lowlife dives of Vienna, the coffee shops where the punks hang out, the places where he spent his high school years avoiding expectations to be good and dutiful.

The first cousins have gone out for a proper Viennese lunch, *Kaffeeschlag mit Sachertorte*. Nothing that has to do with the man who once compared the ego – rational and altruistic – to Europe, and the libido – rapacious and murderous – to Asia, inspires my wife to sympathy. A foolish little man, racist and chauvinist, with bad science to justify it.

It is a sunny, summer day, cool but bright, sweater weather. Children are playing on the sidewalk of Berggasse, outside the corner *Apotheke*. Jyoti says to us, 'Watch this – you think the Austrians know anything?' He asks the oldest boy, 'Do you know the Freud house?'

'Did they just move in?' he asks.

'Get that?' he laughs, turning to us. My son translates it.

'You could ask anyone on this street. Old, young, it doesn't matter. One group wants to forget, and the other one never knew.' We cross over the narrow street, looking for brass plates outside the formal doors. Number 19 is just a flat, as it always was, squeezed between other flats and offices.

Usha was right, it's only an old doctor's office cluttered with photos. The second-cousins browse respectfully, faintly embarrassed by all the fuss. It's all Jyoti can do not to unzip his guitar case and start banging out something scandalous for the Freud Museum. I don't know what I expected to find.

This is the room where all of them came, I want to say. Princess Marie sat there. And the young Viennese Circle – see their pictures! – met here, in this room. In this room, someone challenged the incomprehensible with bad science and bad politics, in the name nevertheless of reason. The smallest facts had the deepest gravity, chance events were all connected, public events were the ritualized form of private projection.

Son! Are you listening?

Someone dared to say our dreams had a pattern, our dysfunctions a cause, our beliefs a pathology. On the walls, the Holy Roman Empire surrenders, and Freud stands on the dais, Vienna's most honoured, most famous citizen, as the Austrian Republic is declared. Here, Freud is welcoming the President of the Republic and his cabinet on the quarter-century anniversary of *The Interpretation of Dreams*. His birth-cottage is decked with bunting.

And it chokes me, suddenly, the realization that science and music and literature can be so advanced, and do nothing to influence a political culture in its infancy. Austrian democracy was younger than Ghana's when the Nazis crushed it. I want to turn to my son and remind him of the great despairing poems I've read to him, of Yeats, of Auden, and the vast literature of the Holocaust that radiates from this room and a thousand others in this city, and echoes off these grey, sunny streets. The tradition, however faintly, I belong to. Poems about the imbalance of what we are capable of feeling and thinking, and what we have inflicted.

They've gone.

'They heard music outside,' the ticket-seller tells me. 'They said for you to follow the music.'

At first I hear nothing. I watch the children across the street, and the old women slogging their way from shop to shop, carrying groceries in string bags.

Berggasse slopes downward, and I follow it a block, half-imagining a rhythm, a few high notes and a beat in the air. Turn right, twist left. People are in the streets now, following something.

Up ahead in a small square at the rim of a fountain I can see them, clowns juggling, and a small crowd clustered. The performers wear top hats and putty noses, their cheeks are reddened, and one of the boys is darker than all the others, in a borrowed top hat, crouched on one knee like Chuck Berry, cutting in front of the clowns and drummers, leading everyone in lyrics I can't understand. And at the edge of the fountain is my boy in a borrowed vest and putty nose, punching a tambourine and doing a snake-dance on the fountain's edge.

Did, Had, Was

1. IT WAS A COOL, gusty Belgian morning, the low human landscape dwarfed by billowing clouds under a sky of porcelain blue. Over the Channel, a storm was brewing. Picard shivered; he'd been working out of Asia for nearly thirty years. He thought of the masters of the Flemish School and how innocently this commerce had begun: under the fluted clouds of grey and gold, the stubble of ships' spars in the distance, black-clad burghers in buckled hats unfurled their trading maps, while old empires crumbled and new ones rose. Ugly, slate-purple clouds were on their way. Pike's-eye purple, he used to call them when he fished for *doré* in Lac Mégantic.

He'd passed a northern childhood in the mountains east of Montréal. Weather like this, pinched summer days of the purest light and morning frost, had meant the end of summer and time of the apple-harvest. His father would hold the ladder, while his mother and sisters arranged bushel baskets under the trees. Gaby and Maty picked from the lower branches and tried to sneak windfalls into their baskets. At treetop level the spits of rain coming at him 'slantindicular', as his father called it, lashed his face and knuckles raw.

He remembered it sharply, being fifteen, standing in the mudroom just off the garage. Gaby with popcorn going in an old wire popper over an open fire, apple fragrance surging through the house from three hundred bushels stored in the garage for the second *presse* of autumn cider. And he would be waxing his skis for the winter's first run.

He had to remind himself that this was Bruges nearly forty years later. Rather than the train direct from Amsterdam to Paris, he'd taken this brief, nostalgic detour. He'd spent the previous night in Amsterdam with two Indonesian whores whose names he'd already forgotten.

Paul Picard, called 'the dean of Asia correspondents' had decided to retire. A school of journalism had wooed him with a major commitment: The Picard Centre of International Communications. A trifle grandiose for a man who'd worked alone for nearly half his life out of a two-room apartment with a portable typewriter, a notebook, and his remembered file of secret contacts.

He was on his way back to Canada, slowly. In the past eight months he'd interviewed leaders in every country from China to Turkey. Being Canadian, he was thought to be inoffensive and objective. He'd compiled a monumental file of tapes. Student assistants, a new and welcome concept, were already transcribing them.

The founding fathers of the Third World, the proud products of Paris and London, were already in place when he'd arrived in the late fifties. They had seen in him a mirror of their own impotent worldliness. He'd moved ever eastward, establishing contacts with a less savoury generation of emerging leaders while they were still deeply wedged in their military and civil services. He had an eye for talent. Over the years, his level of access had risen with them.

He'd opened China and reported during the Cultural Revolution despite eight months of house arrest.

He'd been the first witness to the slaughter of the Chinese in Jakarta, scene of his most widely anthologized piece, 'On the Streets of Jakarta, a Reporter Begs for His Life'. He planned to discuss it in his first public lecture in the fall. He would reveal it all: *In Jakarta, a Reporter Is Caught in a Chinese Whore House. In Jakarta, a* Kris *Is Held to a Reporter's Scrotum Until He Begs.* In Jakarta he is forced to watch men, women and children being tortured and burned. It was, he felt, a paradigm of the reporter's art. Passion, contacts and luck into research and objectivity.

He'd covered the war in Bangladesh. And Vietnam. And Cambodia and India.

He'd personally carried diplomatic messages in Vietnam. He'd been barred from the United States.

He'd tracked the emergence of Japan and taken an early economic interest in Korea, Malaysia and Singapore.

He'd not neglected the arts and human interest, the film-makers, the painters, writers and traditional craftspeople. He'd lived with peasant farmers in India and Java, in China and the Philippines. He'd tracked a Thai physicist teaching quantum mechanics on a slate under a banyan tree. In thirty years he'd filed over ten thousand stories, four thousand in French, and written a dozen books.

He could walk into nearly any Asian capital and get an interview on short notice. Politicians have long memories; they owed him favours. He knew where their skeletons were buried. Since his next book would not be appearing for at least two years, an eternity in Third-World politics, normally guarded leaders had been generous with their time and revelations. *Adieu, Tiers Monde/Third World, Farewell* would be his autobiography, a reverse-Montesquieu laced with Henry Adams. It was in Asia that he came to understand the world, and where it began to elude him. His contacts were losing power, and dying. So was his memory.

One of his friends in Hong Kong used to joke, 'Picard, old man, the book you should be writing is the Erotic Atlas of Asia. Damned sight more useful.' There might have been a different woman for every story he'd filed. In a life that was otherwise monastic, women were his daily reward. Now that he was leaving the continent and its network of sexual convenience, he realized his dependence. On this final trip, he even found himself going to prostitutes before his interviews. It was a challenge. In the Ayatollah's Iran he'd found women within sight of the central Mosque, despite the threats of death by stoning.

In Bruges, he was remembering a town of almost perfect proportions. It seemed to him it must have been Bruges where he'd gone up from Paris to meet Daisy Lesser on one of her trips from Boston, and they'd had three days of walks and bicycling, perfect food and long conversations that had settled them in their lives. He'd just broken up with his girlfriend of two years. Daisy had grown tired of Harvard Square and decided to settle in Israel. He'd had one of his bad migraines and he remembered Daisy sitting with him and reading in his room as he tried to sleep it off and from that moment he realized how good a person she was. Some sort of higher friendship was possible between young men and women. He associated it all with Bruges and its perfect light.

The Bruges he remembered was a town glazed in highlights, brick homes with glistening doors and shutters, each brick pointed precisely, every leaf of every tree etched against a cloudless sky. The effect, like a Magritte, was surrealist in its perfection. *Ceci n'est pas une pipe.* He remembered the geese and swans, fish restaurants and the nutty sweetness of Belgian crepes. Even now he could conjure the lemony smell of tiny Belgian potatoes roasted in parsley butter. He remembered the peculiar green squiggles of goose droppings on the walking path, precisely the streaked colour of weathered copper, and he was back to his student days at McGill when all of Montréal was low and grey, with green streaked roofs. He remembered a passionate young couple at the table next to him discussing fine points in Thomas Mann. Only in Calcutta and Bruges did people care so much for books.

One of the agonies of spilling too much of one's life in the Orient, and learning to adjust to it, is to render Europe as too angular, too orderly. Civic neatness no longer inspired him. Bruges, this cold June morning, was cheap and vulgar. He spent a numbed morning walking along the dikes but feeling pushed out by the German tourist buses. He reboarded the first train for Brussels to pick up his bags and connect with the Paris express.

He was aware, from time to time, of his own faltering mind. He found himself all too frequently unable to finish a sentence, losing the clear conclusion before he could get there. He indulged the need to interrupt, for fear he wouldn't remember his own response. He remembered his mother in the years before her forced retirement. What he and his father had taken as irascibility, then paranoia, proved to be mental bankruptcy.

'No more deposits, no more withdrawals,' his father had said, tapping his head while his mother stared in space. They sold their newspapers and went to Florida.

Now, for Picard, the perfect words were refusing to yield themselves. He could picture – almost smell and almost hear – the word he wanted. He knew it by syllables, by first letter, but it would bury itself deeper in the folds of language whenever he tried to pull it out. Words were like the fat sluggish mountain carp that lolled at the end of their dock back in Lac Mégantic. Huge things that wouldn't take a hook, that wouldn't flinch even as he dived in above them, and would only twist away when he sounded their depth and tried to spear them.

You could catch them when they spawned. They thrashed around like otters in the shallow water.

He had to keep consulting the notes he'd made to himself: his suitcase receipt at the *consigne* in the Bruxelles-Nord station, the address, phone number and directions to Daisy Lesser's house far out in the Paris suburbs. Parisian addresses had been so easy, when he'd last lived there thirty years before. No one considered living outside the city gates. Rueil-Malmaison sounded like an address in New Jersey or Long Island, or parts of Montréal that had become chic in his absence.

He plodded through the Gare du Nord, as instructed by Daisy's letter, then caught a suburban train to downtown Rueil, then the Malmaison bus. He stood in a shelter with half a dozen Down's syndrome labourers, short, thick, profane men in caps and blue smocks, smoking their foul yellow cigarettes and carrying their lunch pails and rolled-up papers. It took him a while to understand their French, but it seemed they were talking about an American singer named Madonna.

2. To Picard's father, a self-defined 'Darwinian Catholic' and old-fashioned patriot, Canada was a genetic blunder. Man's biological imperatives were clearly thwarted by life in the sub-tundra. This explained Canada's lack of true accomplishment in the arts and sciences. *Homo sapiens* (his father invested his generalizations with ponderous Latinisms and obvious chemical formulae) was a creature of the savannahs. He stood peltless and erect. Catholic man, however (which was to say, moral man, enlightened man), does not abort his blunders. There was only one compelling reason for ever leaving Canada to go to the United States. The word was warmth; it took the shape of Florida.

A hundred miles east of Montréal, the family names and home languages were thoroughly confused. Hence his parents: Alastair Picard and Fabienne Dussault Meacham. For years, Picard Senior's paper, *Herald of the East*, and its French-language counterpart published by his wife, *L'Herald de l'est*, lamented Canada's 1949 annexation of Newfoundland. Imaginative negotiators should have picked up Barbados – a warm-weather port – instead. Readers of his mother's paper were invited to plaster the French West Indian islands of Martinique and Guadaloupe with referendum ballots to join Canada, clipped from the French edition. The French government eventually protested.

One other reason for leaving Canada was tolerated in the Picard house. Call it access to culture or education. A winter in New York, timed to the concert season, was not disgraceful. Neither was education if it went by the name of Harvard, Yale or Princeton.

He'd tried for the Ivy League coming out of boarding school, but failed. He'd gone to McGill, done well in English, classics and hockey, and edited the *Daily*. Life in Montréal in the mid-fifties was claustrophobic, relieved only by the presence of Leonard Cohen, the cheap bistros of the east end, and the coffee houses opened by the Hungarian refugees. Cold cherry soup was the very elixir of worldliness. All of Canada's writers lived in London or Paris.

Montréal's undeniable attraction was its complicated linguistic etiquette. For those who'd mastered it, or been born to it, every other city on the continent seemed simplistic. He graduated in 1958 and told his father he was off to Harvard for graduate school. Radcliffe ran a celebrated summer course in book-editing and publishing. He planned to get hired in Boston or New York, and become a famous editor. His great desire, then and always, was to be a Maxwell Perkins, a discoverer of talent.

He had some advantages over his editing classmates. He'd been raised with the French and British classics. Thanks to a boarding school that taught Latin and Greek, a home life that included French, a father who carried a copy-editor's special pedantry into every conversation, and a McGill arts curriculum that modelled itself on Oxford, he was far better educated than most Americans. He could spell, write fluently, and was sceptical where most Americans seemed enthusiastic by birthright. He was the only male in the class (in that distant, pre-feminist era) who'd read Virginia Woolf.

He remembered walking down Brattle Street that summer and feeling mildly envious of a typical Harvard Square product – a young man in work shirt and blue jeans, tweed jacket and tie – who was at that moment passing on his Lambretta scooter. He made a sudden U-turn and called out, 'Daisy!' so enthusiastically that Picard himself had turned, and stared in the face of Daisy Lesser, a woman from his editing class.

Until that moment, she'd seemed to him a perfect editor, quiet and studious with long earrings, lean and pale with thick black hair and large blue eyes behind black-rimmed glasses. The thought that she had friends like the man on the scooter, that she had a life at all beyond books, changed his perceptions immediately. She wasn't pale and retiring; she was witty and forward. 'Daisy' wasn't just a sunny name from mountain fields of grass and flowers; it was also slightly corrupt, like Daisy Miller and Daisy Buchanan. He wanted Daisys to stay Daisy-like – old-fashioned and smelling of salt spray and apple cider.

She recognized him, tapped him on the shoulder and said, 'Let's have coffee some day,' then ran over to the man on the scooter and hopped on the back.

Picard felt he was, momentarily, in Europe. It seemed Parisian, and for some strange reason, the memory of that moment condensed his future as well as his past. Daisy Lesser entered his life that day to become an emblem of his first freedom in Boston, and it seemed inevitable, once he got to know her, that their lives would run in rough parallel. She came to symbolize the life of Harvard Square in the late fifties: living arrangements out of *Jules and Jim*, in unheated apartments with the gas ovens on and blankets over the window; despite the poverty, frequent parties with crisp bread and red wine, pasta dinners that lingered in the memory as somehow perfect.

He thought of the scooter of Harvard Yard as a reaching out for Paris and Rome. Scooters were a pledge to trust and intimacy, a denial of the armoured and efficient American self. He'd had a scooter in his first year in Greenwich Village, but sold it when he moved uptown.

By then he was a very junior editor in the text acquisition department of a textbook publisher. He was involved with a woman in Boston – not Daisy, who'd gotten a job editing a Harvard physics publication. His girlfriend was a McGill classmate, now a resident internist at Mass Gen. Once in a while he'd call Daisy, catch up on gossip about their classmates and then, discreetly, about her current loves. She had the nearest thing to a Continental existence of anyone he'd ever met.

Marriage was on his mind, except that Mindy had applied for a two-year post-doc residency at the Pasteur Institute in tropical medicine. There were no jobs for junior text acquisition editors in Paris. He spoke to a friend at the *Times*. There was a chance, he said, if he took a cut even from his measly editorial salary, to get assigned to the Paris bureau for a couple of years, given his skills in the language. The work could be laborious, but the Paris setting might make up for it. For forty-two dollars a week, he took it.

After a year in Paris, Mindy was sent by the Pasteur to Madagascar, of all places, to study the transfer of certain viruses from lemurs, to monkeys, to humans. He applied for press credentials, in hope of writing it up.

Within two months, he had made contact with cells of communist guerrillas. He interviewed grizzled old French *colons* with attitudes that would have been reactionary even in Algeria. He found an outpost of Indonesian linguists, attempting to draw a linguistic map of Madagascar in hopes of finding the precise landfall of Indonesian mariners, and to match it with the precise point of departure from the Indonesian Archipelago. He heard the unmistakable accents of his own ancestral French and discovered that Catholic education on the island was historically the responsibility of Sacré-Coeur Fathers from Québec.

By the time Mindy went back to Paris, it was too late for Picard. He'd committed himself to instability, an article a day on a world around him that no one had ever seen before.

Mindy went back to Canada. Picard found a room on the Vaugirard in Montparnasse, a property that corresponded, accurately in those years, to Connecticut Avenue on the French Monopoly board. By then, he'd discovered the intoxication of a journalist's freedom: to lay out a new course of study every day; to turn from medicine to politics to film-making in a single week, to see a dozen articles taking shape, like auto bodies on an assembly line. Here, only the windshield wiper blades are missing. There, the bumpers, the doors, and far off, years away, the engines.

3. Daisy Lesser owed her married name, Famahaly, to her brief career as a physics editor, and to Picard's even shorter stay in Madagascar. She had gone to Israel for a few months but found it as loud and grating as Harvard Square. She'd shown up one day in Paris, calling him from Orly and wondering if she could stay a while to sort out her life.

Most of his Paris friends were radical *malgache* students at the Sorbonne. His closest friend was Louis Famahaly, a physics post-doc, Marxist pamphleteer and poet. Picard introduced them, and overnight Louis went from left-bank *poète maudit* revolutionary to pipe-smoking, wine-sipping Paris sophisticate. They were married before Picard left for Beirut and the beginning of his Asian career.

Only the Americans do suburbs well; only Americans believe suburbs to be a profound good. For everyone else, especially Europeans, suburbs are a consolation – and they look it – for not being able to afford a city. By the time Picard found Daisy's house on rue Emile-Augier, it was dark and cold and the Belgian rain had spread throughout the north of France. The houses were tiny, with the lawn area sacrificed for parking space. The last house on the street was Daisy Famahaly's. Characteristically, she was standing by the opened door.

'Only eight hours late, Picard. The soufflé has fallen. I've drunk the wine.' If anything, she was thinner than ever. No grey in her hair, and nearly his height. They embraced at the door, she led him inside.

'I went to Bruges,' he said. She poured them both some wine.

'Bruges,' she snorted. 'Whatever possessed you?'

'Was I wrong to remember it fondly?' He wanted to say: I needed clarity and perspective. I wanted to possess the perfect modesty of Bruges for just an hour or two.

They were sitting in armchairs in the *coin malgache,* under bright batiks and mounted funerary sculptures from a Madagascar grave. Louis was at CERN for the summer, accelerating particles. The son, Clovis, was in Boston visiting her parents. Siri, the daughter, was in Madagascar, visiting his. Daisy had settled into a career of writing: stories and poems and occasional reviews for British and American magazines. Twenty-eight years in France; what a strange set of classmates they'd become. She felt as strange in America as he did in Canada.

'That's right, Bruges used to be very pretty. Then the Germans and British discovered it. And we were there, weren't we? And you got sick somehow, I remember that.'

He tapped his head. 'Migraine. I don't get them any more.' He knocked on the wooden chair-arm. Now, just as frequently, he got the dancing lights and foreshortening, the whole migraine aura without the headache's following. One of the hidden benefits of ageing.

'You and your poor head. I remember sitting with you in Boston. Your hands got cold and you asked me to hold them and I thought, 'This is very novel.' But they were cold, so I made you some tea to hold. I used to ask myself: How is this man going to survive in the world?' She dropped her voice to a whisper. 'Would you like some tea now? Decaff?'

He was starting to feel uneasy.

'What I remember about Bruges,' she went on, 'is us sitting in some little restaurant having this very loud debate about the virtues of Thomas Mann. I was for him and you were against. You had these very set opinions about literature. It was all Flaubert and Balzac and Dickens and Thackeray. I liked the Russians and the Germans and even some of the Americans which you, of course, had never read.'

'I hadn't remembered. But I remember your sitting with me in Bruges when I had a headache.'

'Maybe so. You've had a lot of headaches. You've probably had headaches and someone to sit with you in every city in the world.'

She wanted to know about this deanship business, of which she strongly disapproved.

'I felt it was time. They told me what I knew and what I could pull in was worth a six-storey building with my name in marble.'

'Picard, what you know – even what you've forgotten – more than fills a six-storey library.' He kept quiet.

'But I feel mentally old,' he finally admitted.

She turned on the late television news. 'Who doesn't? Especially you. You're probably burned out from trying to understand the Japanese or whatever.'

It's what they all said. He'd gone to a doctor in Tokyo who prescribed more exercise and contemplation, then marriage to a simple young woman. After a certain age, chaos becomes exponential in a man's life and the brain rebels. Picard had thought the diagnosis excessively Zen. It was easy to admit that Picard looked and sounded tired; being *seriously* impaired was inadmissible.

'There's lots of American news these days. I like to get the French slant,' she said. She used it in her stories.

It seemed that the chief U.S. spy, a decrepit old man by the name of William Casey, had just been diagnosed with brain cancer. He'd had a seizure on his way to testify. The French arrange these things a little less obviously. Picard knew nothing of the case, which appeared to be about arms trading with the Ayatollah. It was practically impossible to understand how Americans operated in the world. From time to time over the years, Picard had asked American journalists about each new president, and gotten such grotesque responses he'd tried to ignore them. America was increasingly inscrutable to him.

'Listen, can you make out what they're saying?' she asked. The original American soundtrack was barely audible, under the running French translation. 'They don't know how to refer to him! "He was ... is, I mean ... He did, I mean does" ... that's really weird. Did, had, was.... Does, has, is.' She scribbled it down on a scrap of paper. 'I can use that,' she said.

He woke up in the night in a room so dark he thought his eyes were closed, and couldn't be opened. The girl was close tonight, as she often was. Suhan. Fifteen, she'd said. He'd been with her three times, a violation of his own principles, such as they were. All because he'd seen her one day holding on to a boy on the back of a scooter, and the boy had looked to Picard like a student, or at least studious, and that didn't tie in with him giving rides to very young whores.

There had been rumours for weeks of Mao's involvement in Indonesian politics, his influence over Indonesian communists. That night, he'd wandered through Suhan's place of employment. In a back room he'd paused in front of a coir curtain and seen the same young man again, drinking beer with friends. On the wall behind them was something Picard should not have seen – a portrait of Mao Tse-Tung.

Suddenly, things were clear, though hardly publishable. The whorehouses of Chinatown had been politicized. The Chinese of Jakarta were Maoist. That's when Suhan had been sent out to turn him away, and he'd been willing to be turned, like never before. She'd come out of the back room and stood in the dingy hall. Unlike every other woman in the house, she was dressed in sandals and a pleated skirt and a white cotton man's shirt buttoned to the throat. She simply raised her arms high and ran her fingers through her hair, and as her arms rose up, so did the untucked blouse, merely to the midriff and the lower line of her bra. In a continent like Asia and a city like Jakarta at the time of its most wretched crowding and ethnic violence, such sights were replicated on every corner. But Picard had followed her and in this nightmare he was still following her, after twenty-three years.

She'd gone from precocious confidence in all her charms, the smile of calm, perfected wickedness, to the universal innocence of her death in a matter, perhaps, of several seconds. In the nightmare, the two masks of her face were reversed, and he'd followed the death mask down the hall and confronted her sexiness in the moment of death. He felt like her murderer.

There'd been scrambling in the hall. The building was too flimsy for the noise of broken glass or splintering wood. There'd simply been Indonesian boys going from room to room with revolvers and machetes and Picard had grabbed Suhan's hand and she'd taken his shirt to put over herself. They headed for a back door, he pushed against it and they'd suddenly been outside in a screaming, fiery night. His car with its PRESS sticker was near and as they ran towards it he felt a lightening of her grip. He turned then and saw her arm fall from her body in one machete blow by a child younger than she, a boy wearing a T-shirt with an American sports team logo and a red headband.

It's the look on her face that only Picard has seen. It must be the look reserved for the executioner by the condemned. In her face he saw every woman he'd ever lusted after, every face he'd ever loved. She had only a split second to look at her stump of an elbow and then to look at the boy who brought the blade down across her face.

'You were shouting,' said Daisy, as she turned on the hall light. He was in a teenage girl's room with its Parisian maps and trophies, its school books.

Daisy was holding a glass of water. He could see the white roots of her hair, dry, puffy skin. She felt his forehead, and he realized he was shivering, though not from fever.

'What's really the matter?' she asked.

He remembered an old journalist he'd known in Calcutta. One day he'd come shivering into Picard's hotel room. He'd seen two tram cars linked together. Their four-digit identification numbers were those of his birth, 1918, and the current year. Picard had tried to reassure him that not everyone in Calcutta born in 1918 who saw that tram was going to die that night, that some emblems have to be mere coincidence.

'I'm living in the past,' he told Daisy.

'Bullshit, Picard.'

'My brain is sick. It's dying.'

'I said bullshit. You're our Orwell. If anything's wrong it's bad food and no rest and probably a lot of bought sex. You're worse than Louis. Watch out for that kind of stuff in the West, with AIDS.'

Another word he'd encountered in the American press, but hadn't bothered to understand. It hadn't penetrated Asia.

'Find a good woman back there in Canada who understands your work and let her help you. Don't be like the Trinidadians say, a "mutton playin' lamb". You're a mutton now, Picard, so take better care of yourself.'

He remembered driving his mother around North Hollywood, Florida, in the years after they'd retired. One day she'd turned to him and said, 'I know you're very familiar and I'm sure we've met.' She'd been sixty-two years old.

'All those tapes I've sent back – they're bullshit,' he said. 'I don't know these guys any more. I try to make out questions in advance and I end up looking for women instead.'

She gave him a European sleeping pill, something that knocked him out gently and dreamlessly. When he woke in the morning, he saw she'd left a nightlight on.

4. Mornings were his best time, especially the cool, wet mornings of Paris, life in the crisper-drawer, preserving every leaf and fruit, settling the dust, focusing the light through millions of tiny filters. The pill had left no side effects; he was downstairs by seven, alert and rested, and rummaging through the kitchen to find the coffee beans. He ground them up in an old hand-held *moulin*. He thought he'd surprise her with coffee and baguettes on a tray. By the time the coffee had brewed, Daisy burst in through the kitchen door in light gloves and a running outfit. She pulled off her sweatband and gave him a light, solemn kiss, the way French workers shake hands each morning.

'Better?' she asked.

'Much.' No one would think they'd been classmates: he was bald on top, grey on the sides, sallow-skinned and deeply wrinkled. A candidate for skin cancer, the young reporters always said. They had notions about hats and sunscreen. She had the hair and skin of a college girl.

'I don't suppose you run, do you, Picard?' He'd been astonished by the presence of runners in Hong Kong. He'd even seen them now in India. In Japan, of course, it was a rage. 'Everyone our age in the West is into running. Do it, the circulation is good for the brain.'

'The people I see running look like they don't need it. The people I see drinking diet colas look like it doesn't make any difference. From that I've concluded to lay off diet soft drinks.'

'I run three miles every morning. You can join me. I run for mental health, not physical.'

'I couldn't run fifty feet,' he said.

They each had business in Paris; he with the editors at AFP – he was hoping to arrange summer internships in future years for some of his bilingual students – and she to browse the English bookstores, the galleries, then take care of a hair appointment. There was a cousin of

Louis's she was meeting for lunch. She and Picard would go into the city together on the bus and train and Metro, then arrange a time and place for dinner.

She was planning a book on Madagascar, on the clash of Africa and Asia on a single island, in a single people. 'The Incredible Shrinking Island,' she called it, a culture the world had managed to mislay. The French Foreign Office had the necessary documentation, and she was probably the best-connected foreigner in the world, to tell the story. What India was to the British, Madagascar was to the French.

'A sobering thought,' he said. He remembered the imitation Parisian culture of Tananarive nearly thirty years before: sidewalk cafés, baguettes delivered in Renault vans, potable red wines and the most arrogant prostitutes outside of Sweden. To the French, a successful colonial enterprise.

He extracted a meaningless promise from the managing director of Agence France Presse to of course consider M Picard's personally recommended students, since it would cost them nothing. He dropped in on the editors at Hachette who'd brought out two of his books, and assured them that *Adieu, Tiers Monde* was proceeding valiantly to a provocative conclusion sure to win him a spot on *Apostrophes*. He spent several hours trying to find his favourite old museums, only to learn that modern paintings now hung in a loud architectural monstrosity known as the Pompidou Centre and that the Expressionists had been moved from L'Orangerie. He ended up communing with the Egyptian sarcophagi in the Louvre until it was time to meet Daisy for drinks at a bistro of her choosing, near the East African library of the Sorbonne.

He wanted to say, like Freud of America, it is all a mistake. This modern Paris, his life. He'd passed women during the day, especially a Vietnamese girl, obviously available, who would have given him the only calm he trusted. It would be unfair to say of Daisy she was twittering, but it sounded to him the way French women often sounded, only she was speaking English, bouncing from topic to topic like a mind on drugs. The bistro was loud and densely smoky. He wanted a dark, quiet room, moments alone and a chance to focus on just one thing.

'The restaurant is just around here,' she said, as they stepped out into a cool, moist evening, for which he was grateful. 'There's a lovely *lyonnais* place, simple country food that Louis and I adore – '

He knew this area, knew it intimately. He'd walked these streets for years and it brought him some moments of peace now, to be walking these streets with a woman, her arm lightly in his.

'There's a marvellous Hungarian place,' he said, 'just down that street. Basement, cheap, great cold cherry soup. You like cold cherry soup?'

'Of course. I didn't know you knew —'

'Know this place?' He turned around, getting his bearings one last time. The grey bulk of the university buildings, the narrow streets clogged with students, the cool air of a summer night in the northern latitudes. 'Of course I know it, didn't I go to McGill for four years?'

He felt one last tug from her arm, her touch on his shoulder. 'Picard,' she said. 'Whatever you say.'

Sweetness and Light

1. I HAVE LOOKED into the face of love, and it is black. Black as well are its hands and limbs, and the rest is uniform grey. Up close, there are scars. Tense and silent, tail erect, he paces the railing of my balcony, snapping the buds of the hibiscus that stud the vines stretching to the roof. Baring ferocious incisors, shocking as a bat's, he hisses, then seals his mouth and slowly blinks. I read into his closed, wrinkled eyes a weary tolerance of my presence. He cuffs a female half his size, upon whose back rides an indifferent child – what are his women called, cows? mares? sows? Those clinging little beasties – are they pups, kits, calves? I am out of my element here. My element is, or was, language.

I call him Boom-Boom, and not just for the avalanche of bodies and branches he unleashes on my tin roof at dawn. His harem tears fruit and vegetables from the garden I've tried to raise. Fierce Boom-Boom, liege and pillager, extracts his ten percent on a daily basis.

The flowers – hibiscus, azalea, roses, bougainvillaea – what are they for my Lord Boom-Boom? Appetizers, sherbet to clear his palate, a lozenge, dessert? None of his harem brings him blossoms; these he nips himself. He makes the buds of flowers seem the most extravagant pleasure in the universe. Pink lips unsheathe to surround the bud, tongue circumnavigates the boll, parting its tightly folded head which he licks at first like a delicate cone, then chops tight to the stalk where ants then rush to stanch its syrupy flow.

Boom-Boom surveys it all, regally, from my cool stone veranda. I've drawn up behind him, close enough to admire his battle scars, to watch the muscles twitching, to see the salt-and-pepper glint of his middle-aged muzzle. We're coevals, my liege and I. I stare down with him at my trees and rows of garden while his women patiently dig up my carrots, bend and break my beans. We're in this together, the harem-keeper and the bachelor bull. Once he whirled and swiped a sticky hibiscus blossom from my extended hand, breaking the skin.

Accidents will happen.

He's watching his women.

Despite everything, I think of monkeys as essentially playful, dolphins of the trees, not territorial scavengers. I wish I still had children to show them to. A wondrous thing, monkeys on your porch. 'See, Bayard,' I would say, rolling back the clock twenty years, 'he wants to play. He wants to be your friend.'

Two years ago my bride and I made a honeymoon visit to a ruined palace at the desert's edge. On the cracked and pitted parapets of the emperor's walk, an old guide had whispered, 'Now I am imparting erotic informations, saar. Maybe the lady should not be hearing...'

'She can take it,' I said.

We were staring at the maze of old *zenana* walls, Rajah Singh's stockyard for twenty-two brides and six hundred concubines.

'Seven feet tall, saar,' the old guide intoned, reaching above us to an imagined canopy. 'Four hundred pounds,' and his arms fluttered buoyantly over the hot stone railing. Then, sliding closer to me, dropping his voice, he giggled, 'Penile member, saar, twenty-four inches.'

My bride tittered.

'Jesus, Meena, two feet! How about that. If he couldn't slam-dunk, maybe he could pole-vault.'

My young bride's bosom strained that day against her sari, one breast pressed tight against the discoloured marble, the other flaring in profile from it. How like a painting she seemed, how eternally erotic, the scene enacted a thousand times in catalogues and collections: *'Maid on Parapet Awaits Her Lover.'* Elephants at a distance, camels against the dunes, and I, the would-be rajah, clutching his Sure-Shot, staring down at the empty breeding pens and wondering, which will it be tonight? One of my experienced courtesans who knows the hundred ways of drawing ecstasy like clear water from a dry well, or one of the shy and painted virgins borne on camel-back as tribute from the villages, who, in their ardent innocence, their exquisite accommodations, can kindle fire from a dampened old stick?

'Saar, a gratuity.' the guide tugged my sleeve.

They are gone by mid-morning, and I am alone with Baba, my father-in-law, under the fan in my private quarters where a serving woman brings me tea and a banana for breakfast and later, yoghurt and fruits sprinkled with coarse sugar. Twice a day an old gentleman in khaki carrying a jute sack tinkles his bicycle bell and drops mail in the wooden box. I can spot my bride's airmail letters from way up here on the veranda where I read and snooze the days away.

At night, after Boom-Boom and his harem make their evening appearance, I change into a clean devotional kurta and pyjamas and sniff about on all fours, thrusting my head into the thick bougainvillaea vines where snakes have been rumoured to hide, and caress a nodule with my lips and tongue, to suck a bud into openness. I have crunched my share of hibiscus buds, and they are pungent as leeks but fragrant, too, like Indian desserts, indescribably flowery. There are always new buds, freshly opened by morning and these I leave for my Lord.

I am what I am, a gaunt baritone with paranoid tendencies, a widow uncomfortable in his body. Not from my lips will you hear gender-shading: no widower I. In this phase of my life, I insist on absolutes.

2. This phase of my life I owe to an engaging teen-ager by the name of Boom-Boom Karakas. I have seen pictures of his room in happier days, his drums and a trophy-case. He is the son I never had: athletic, outgoing, a bit madcap. I have even met the lad, a direct descendant of Genghis Khan on his father's side, though the mother is a bit of a mutt.

I have shaken the hand that U-turned a Camaro across three lanes of the Eisenhower Expressway, down four miles of the northbound lanes warping an errant tapestry through a woof of horns, then plunging like a spawning salmon up the headwaters of a pinched suburban stream. Caroline, heading to O'Hare to pick me up, flipped him like a grizzly flicking a salmon from a shallow gravel-bar, gutting the Camaro from bumper to tailfin. He popped from the dorsal seam like a lichee from its skin. Our car sustained barely a scratch, just a folded fender and a starburst of shattered glass. It was a bloody spawn.

It went better for the boy that he was legally sober and not on drugs. He'd merely been watching old 'Sweetness' himself, Walter Payton, hitting the holes, accelerating, picking up his blocks. He snapped his fingers, kicked his heels and sang, 'I can do that!' They called it 'the Sweetness defence,' the surge of misplaced glory a high-school fullback must feel, finding the seam at night without lights, cutting back against the grain of onrushing cars and trucks, dashing the wrong way down the Eisenhower. No jury would convict, not after the Super Bowl. He'd done it safely, as the phrase went, many times: down the Eisenhower, up the Stevenson, across the Ryan.

Fiction, I'd always taught my students, is a sealed realm of pure and beautiful justice. A justice-dealing machine. The great novel exposes hypocrisy, tests every pretence; that is its only comfort. There are agents of savage justice in this world, most of them outlaws, many of them evil. I'd spent a lifetime teaching students to respect and even admire existential cowboys like Boom-Boom Karakas, the Belmondo of Brookfield Estates. My training in literature, which I took as training for pertinent realms of life and death, told me there was a string in there somewhere. Find it, and follow it through, no matter where it leads. To a ruined estate in Uttar Pradesh, crouched among the monkeys, seems entirely logical.

At that hour of the night, Caroline would have been far beyond the legal limit. I always figured our next sabbatical would be to a dry or expensive country, an academic's Al-Anon. Not that anyone could guess. She was always presentable. And since she was merging into the Eisenhower that night in the proper lane at the proper speed, and she was grey-haired and dressed in a wool skirt and a Scottish sweater we'd bought at Heathrow a few months earlier, they never took a blood sample. I spent three hours in the United Terminal, then took a taxi home, where the police were waiting.

She looked like the wife of a small-college president. I knew her suits and dresses by name: 'Wear your Oberlin sweater,' I'd say, 'your Denison suit.' Knox, Carlton, Bowling Green – the names roll before me now like cherished phrases of a dead, devotional language. I'd lectured in just about every college in the Midwest, been met in every poky airport, gotten liquored up in their gracious guest houses, and always put on an adequate show. We knew their institutional odours, saw them all as choices once offered but never taken, affairs not entered into, enmities spared.

She seemed dressed for a perpetual country auction, under a crisp autumn glaze. Something about her bottled ruddiness suggested high New England, a bright but blustery day with falling leaves. 'I'll bet you're a Smith girl!' one of my colleagues bubbled on first meeting her, 'I'll bet you knew Sylvia Plath!' She stayed trim, but not svelte, more sporting than sexy. She was credited with fitness, but actually she just never ate.

People assumed we lived on a country estate and commuted to campus from Wisconsin, perhaps. They came to me with bizarre requests about breeding their dogs and stabling horses. We actually lived in a late-fifties suburban development north of Evanston. We were reclusive because of Caroline's social unpredictability. She would start crying at dinner, or she would drop the crystal. Or fling it against walls, giggling.

In all fairness to myself, I could have passed for a small-college president. I used to wear corduroy jackets and cashmere turtlenecks. My hair turned silver fairly early, as did Caroline's, so we were always thought of as young-at-heart, good-sport senior citizens. On the night of Boom-Boom's intervention in my life, and termination of Caroline's, we were only forty-eight.

'And I almost made it,' he lamented. 'Your wife panicked, professor, and that's the truth. Now I'm looking at a two-year suspension of my licence – where's the justice in that? It's not going to bring her back.' He'd repressed his remorse so deeply, and continued to behave so normally – which is to say objectionably – that the therapists were worried about his recovery. They suggested reserving some of my settlement money for his treatment, should traumas ever surface.

The lad is clearly a force in the universe, a principle of pure destruction. I've paid my dues, I thought, let others pick up the bill. 'Your Honour,' I said, 'I have talked to this boy. He has not publicly expressed the grief I know he feels in his heart. I know these things; I am a literature teacher, a trained observer of life. The Arrangers of the Universe are behind this boy. I support his petition to retain his licence. It is unlikely he will play the Walter Payton game again.'

Let there be no inhibition in the free exercise of his will, I said. Let the rain forests fall, the seas run black. The Court was impressed by my compassion. An act of Christian charity, according to his lawyer. His mother threw herself on my neck. His father wrenched my hand and shoulder. The boy said, 'You're okay, professor.' I left the courtroom worth slightly over five million dollars.

3. 'Three children,' Caroline used to say, 'one of each.' She knew how to carry off outrageousness, sounding just a pinch British, despite having come from Cincinnati.

Carl's in ophthalmology at Iowa Hospitals; Renata's a young Boer in the Stanford Law School. It's Bayard, child of my Faulkner period, San Francisco's 'Cecil Beaton of Heavy Metal', who had been our only problem. Now it's his problem. He enjoys being up there with hanggliders and race-car drivers, in a very special uninsurable risk group. 'And you always thought I was a sissy!' he laughs.

By day, he's a landscape photographer, doing gardens of the rich and idle. At night he haunts the bars. He's the most debauched twenty-one-year-old I have ever met. He's said no thanks to his future. He gets messages on his telephone service: catch the overnight to Tokyo. KISS needs a glossy.

My question now is, what did we do to deserve Carl and Renata – stodgy even for these constipated times? Carl's friends – other residents in ophthalmology – could start a rotary club of health care professionals. The world is an eyeball and music's for the waiting room. He's twenty-six and getting bald. His girlfriend has three children.

For this I bought twenty years of season's tickets to the Chicago Symphony? For this I refused a television set till they were out of high school?

Renata is also doing well. She's in her final year of women's law. A partnership is guaranteed. I used to melt when she called me 'daddy'. Now she holds me responsible for Caroline's unfulfilment; hence her drinking; hence her accident. It is not comfortable to be called a murderer by the only person, until my bride, who had filled my whole heart.

Bayard you know about. I wish he could be here now. He revels in the debasement of love's design, he knows the shape of love's deformities.

I was becoming a curmudgeon. I was forty-eight, rich, single, and disaffected. My university offered, in their phrase, 'compassionate leave'. I sold the house and made a quarter-million on the inflationary ride. I put everything in mutual funds and started pulling out the equivalent of an endowed, Ivy-League chair. I moved into a north shore apartment with twelve-foot ceilings. I spotted Saul Bellow at our local pharmacy.

Before Caroline's death, the most exotic thing I had ever done was teach in Teheran for a year. I compiled a book while the Shah collapsed. My Iran book was called *Contingency and Character in the Contemporary American Novel*. It attempted to 'locate' (as I used to say) the modern hero in the multiple contingencies of language, history and culture, instead of paraphrasable psychology. The reviewers said it might have been a useful book, twenty years ago, before deconstruction. It's out of print.

And then the Fulbrights called again. Not out of compassion, but with a favour to ask. They were desperate. An obscure college in India had just become Fulbright-eligible, the result of an agreement negotiated by a lunatic who'd never visited the town or the campus. They'd throw in a second year, wherever I wanted, if I agreed to pick up the pieces. 'We owe you one for Iran,' is how they put it. I could be Dr America and Dr Modern Letters in a provincial backwater ('more a backsand, I'm afraid') that had never taught American Lit or anything later than Thomas Hardy.

4. Shri Viswanath Patel University was willed into existence in 1948, five pastel residences and a lecture hall overlooking a cracked griddle of swirling salts, the sunken floor of a dry lake. 'The Death Valley of India,' the Dean-cum-Chairman proudly explained, except when the monsoons made it Great Salt Lake. I was their first foreigner, except for a wayward Uzbek who'd taught *ghazals* by Omar Khayyam the year before.

For those familiar with India, the state is Bihar, a catchment of human misery draining, eventually, into Calcutta. My Fulbright salary, converted to rupees, not to mention the monthly cheques accumulating back in Chicago, probably exceeded the GNP of the entire district.

Viswanath Patel had been a Gandhian. He'd been a 'Sir' but dropped it during the Independence struggle. His vision dictated a college for tribals and untouchables. Some indeed are tribals: handsome, black-skinned men addicted to much adornment. Over the decades, however, ideals have gradually receded. Students come from the middle classes of neighbouring towns, or landowning families of surrounding villages. Despite reservation clauses guaranteeing their admission, tribals have set up trinket-stalls around the college, selling bows and arrows, drums and carvings made of bone. 'Backward castes' do the cleaning and heavy work. The land they beat a living on, by netting fish or raising sorghum, has been declared arid, saline, and terminally leached.

Yet, still, things grew. I arrived just after the monsoons, when the lakebed was already drying and my students were busy ploughing, planting and adding manure. I was given an 'apartment' in the guest house, a furnished room with a fan (though electricity was rarely available), and a bathroom on the Indian model with a hole in the floor between metal stirrups for squatting or taking a standing aim. There was no running water and no kitchen, but I did have a bell, attached to a grey-haired and elegant-looking gentleman who'd once worked in a Calcutta club. He seemed to be on duty twenty-four hours a day. His name was Dhiren.

He had a daughter named Meena.

I had asked for, and been graciously assigned, a graduate seminar in American literature. Every word in that sentence should have quotation marks around it. Once a week, a man vaguely familiar as myself (less and less so as the winter wore on and I dropped my Western clothes, grew a beard and lost forty pounds on Dhiren's fruits and yoghurt), called 'I', stood in a dark, stuffy intimate amphitheatre, candlelit and bug-infested, in front of twenty-five women ranging in age from fifteen to fifty-two, responding to astonishing questions and remarkable opinions on Time and the Universe, the English language and American Trivia. In my innocence, I had assigned the usual texts, from Benjamin Franklin and the Federalist Papers, through *Moby-Dick* and *The Scarlet Letter*. The books had been shipped, but resold in Patna by the bookseller's agent.

The absence of books confirmed something I had always suspected. For the inspired lecturer, the text is often distracting. That winter by candlelight (electrical supply then being in permanent disruption), I reconstructed American thought, American history, the rise and flowering of American literature. I stuck to the syllabus, and they asked questions and wrote papers on the assigned, but invisible, books.

5. Only the blind could ignore such beauty. It was spring by a Chicago calendar, though the seasons made little impression apart from dry and wet. Forster, being Forster, had noticed the deep-chested, wasp-waisted naked male bodies, the graceful limbs of labouring men bursting with muscle. I, being whatever I had become, noticed the women, faces cast more perfectly, skin more radiant, bodies straighter, yet more womanly, than any I had ever seen.

'How are you finding your students?' the chairman, Professor Narayan, inquired. I was feeling expansive. 'Intriguing,' I said.

'They are not, of course, sophisticated at all,' he apologized.

'I find some of them perfection itself,' I said.

'Oh, sir, you do us too much honour!'

'Some are exquisite.'

This was entering forbidden territory. In the Gandhian world, 'lascivious behaviour' can be revealed in a glance, an off-hand word, an innocent gesture. I was thinking of a girl named Meena who had delivered a paper on *The Scarlet Letter*, or should I say, had delivered a paper about a spirited young woman with a child, abandoned by her timid lover, who confronts him in a forest with her unbroken will and her thunderous determination to preach, to write, and to act. I had mentioned Hester in my lecture; I had even commented on Hawthorne's striking defence of art and independence in a Puritan society.

But in Meena's retelling, the forest was hot and snake-infested, the nefarious minister was a drunken and abusive landlord's son, and the young mother a virtuous girl of the serving-class who had been given to him at thirteen to settle her father's gambling debts.

Unsound pedagogy, you say.

She read her paper by candlelight. I had been sitting beside her at the front desk (a dissecting-table in the college's original design), and I lost myself, first in her tears and outrage, and then quite frantically as I studied the shadows under her sari, imagining her nudity from the midriff folds visible to me, a nudity so tangible that I yearned to reach out and dab the sweat, mash the mosquitoes buzzing her head and drinking from her arms, and to begin the delicious unwrapping of all six yards of that Christmas-coloured cotton.

I had been celibate for nearly two years. I had thought of my Fulbright year in an Indian desert as a kind of sexual Al-Anon, a safe removal from much temptation. I had seen my intellectual life as sterile, my paternity irrelevant, my bloated finances a joke.

This is computer-enhancement fuelled by passion: in the candlelight of a hot March Tuesday afternoon I plotted the intimate topography of a small, dark planet named Meena whose age and last name I had never learned. She had been anonymous and now she had erupted in my consciousness and wouldn't let go.

'Yes,' I said, 'beautifully done. Hawthorne would approve.'

We all had a picture now of *The Scarlet Letter* as a revision of Sita's testing in the forest, of a beautiful woman walking through flames to prove her faithfulness, holding out her hand to a doubting, fair-skinned Ram who had put her through the torture of his suspicions. Hanuman, the co-operative monkey-lord who had guided Ram through snake-dense forests and delivered him safely to the island fastness of Sri Lanka, stepped back into the forest's gloom, his duty discharged.

The oldest tableau in Hindu piety.

But what is this? As Ram approaches, slightly humbled by Sita's purity, slightly abashed by his lascivious assumptions, she withdraws her hand. She clutches the child to her breast. His child, perhaps; Ravanna's child – her abductor's – perhaps. 'Tell me,' Ram demands, but she laughs. He will not beg her forgiveness; he demands that she abandon the suspect child to the monkeys and accompany him back to his throne, where he is fated to rule long and benevolently with her at his side.

She laughs in his face. There can be no justice with me at your side, she mocks. I am not yours to command. I did not resist our enemies for fourteen years in order to follow your orders. I did not walk through flames only to serve you now.

He's enraged. What can he do but rule? What can she do but be his wife? It is their *dharma* and their *karma,* to rule and to serve.

'What can I do?' she cries in rebuttal. 'Preach! Write! Act!'

In Meena's tale, Sita and Mukta, her daughter, stay in the forest. Hanuman retrieves them. Ram wastes away in various disguises, wandering through his kingdom, claiming to be the true king. He is mocked, jailed, becomes a drunk and public nuisance. The throne is occupied by lesser and lesser kings, until it is lost to outsiders.

That was the Meena I had in mind, when I spoke of exquisite women to Professor Narayan. 'There is no Meena in our programme,' he insisted.

'Brilliant and beautiful,' I said.

He was smiling when he corrected himself. 'The only Meena I know is Dhiren's daughter. But she is a serving-girl! Most unfortunate, what happened. A mishap. Divorced, a bad husband, with a child.'

'Yes, I'm sure that's who I mean!'

He reached out to touch my arm, smiling benevolently. 'No, no, quite impossible, you see. As I have explained, she is not favoured in her appearance. She is very dark –'

'This Meena is very dark.'

'– and a servant's girl.'

'So?'

And that was the moment I fell from respectability. To have found comeliness in a dark-complexioned servant's daughter is to harbour lascivious attitudes, to express attraction where only one kind of attraction is possible.

'I see,' said Professor Narayan. 'This fellow Dhiren is very shifty. He asked permission for his daughter to attend your class. I thought, what is the harm? She may even improve her mind and get her thoughts off her problems. She had lived with her father in Calcutta for many years and developed urban ways. Dhiren became a scoundrel and fell in debt. His wife died, and he fell among bad types. The girl was not unattractive in a village sort of way, and so he sold her to bad fellows. Her husband allowed his friends to use her, for money. Then, in remorse for what he had done, Dhiren came to us and begged for honest work. I felt sorry for the chap, so I created a position. Now you tell me his daughter is brilliant and beautiful. I'm very sorry, sir, very sorry I did not warn you before. You are blameless, sir – I take full responsibility. I must release Dhiren immediately.'

'Fire him and you'll lose your Fulbright money,' I said. Lust and pity guided my words. The girl was Cinderella, Sita, Hester Prynne.

'Sir,' Professor Narayan stepped back now, rocking on his heels. 'Everyone here is knowing her story. If you do not cut yourself loose, the good name of your country will be tarnished.'

I heard myself saying it even before the thought occurred. 'I'm going to marry her, Professor Narayan.'

6. We were of course obliged to leave the college. There were, in fact, two children – a boy of seven by the name of Amal and a girl of five ... named Mukta. I have learned that the tent of the universe is pegged by coincidence, and that accumulated coincidence constitutes a pattern. I have learned that after fifty, a man encounters no more surprises, everything is vaguely predictable. By the age of fifty, the millions of random thoughts, the thousands of people we've met, the hundreds of thousands of separate articles, books, words, all begin to coalesce. Our character becomes multiple contingency. Meena also had three brothers and four sisters, most of them in Calcutta living precariously. They, along with their children and widowed in-laws, fifty people in all, began arriving a week after our announced intentions.

Dhiren – now known as 'Baba', my father-in-law, though

considerably younger than I, feared that his role of servant might cause me embarrassment. I should note that the college, in its excitement over landing an eminent American scholar (as I was then known) had confused the means with the ends and introduced me as Senator J. William Fulbright. Dignified attempts at reclaiming my identity had only met with hurt and alarm. To avoid further indignities to my high office, Baba proposed a reasonable solution.

He wished to return to his ancestral village in Uttar Pradesh and take up landlording. Many abandoned estates, including the one his own father had cooked for, could be bought for a few million rupees. There would be buildings within its walls for all his children and grandchildren. There would be fields attached and outlying villages of indentured labourers to pay him tribute. I was touched by his seigneurial ambitions. There would be an apartment suitable for the Senator and his bride.

We were married in a Christian service in Ranchi, though neither of us subscribed to that faith. Her last name, I learned at the service, was Kumar, common as Smith. We left for our honeymoon in Rajasthan, to walk the parapets of Rajah Singh's palace, to gaze at the *zenana* walls and lose ourselves in lust, while Baba and the family left for Uttar Pradesh with a line of credit for twenty lakhs – two million rupees.

Perhaps you think me trusting or even simple-minded. I draw your attention to the ballast I've shed in the cauldron of love. If Newton's laws hold true for the moral universe, consider an equal and opposite reaction to the surrender of my name and citizenship, my wealth and whiteness, my tenure and refinement, my three children and a spotless defence of culture and irony wherever they seemed imperilled. Consider the Giddiness of Being that follows when the memory-banks are spilled like water in the sands of Rajasthan.

I was being reborn, you see.

Seven feet tall and proportionally endowed, I waited at sunset on the Rajah's walk for a signal from *the maid on the parapet, awaiting her lover,* my bride. Secrets of the ancients coursed in my loins. My virgin courtesan had never been inside a hotel, had never eaten restaurant food, had never worn jewellery, a silk sari, or even a bra. Had never been taken in a gentle embrace by a man not bent on hurting her.

I have had affairs, yes, with students and with colleagues and with the wives of colleagues, and in all those tangled, expectant moments there inhabits the shadow of an ultimate purpose: what it means to be a man, to escape the old self, and to create something new. Don't look for profundity here, for I am out to extinguish all the markers I took to be normal and within the parameters of the Male American Self.

Those moments were not repeated with my bride.

She met me in the room, in her *Scarlet Letter* sari as I had requested, kohl-eyed, tinkling in her honeymoon gold and jewels. I turned off the air-conditioner. I turned off the fan. She put her hand on the back of my neck, and it was ice cold and trembling. I followed the hand, the thin arm ribbed with bangles, up the smoothness to the elbow, under the sari-end that hid the rest of her arm, and shoulder. My fingers followed the outline of the *choli*, where it scooped in the back and hooked in front and I eased the eyelets apart. Still no bra, no wonder I had not miscalculated a millimetre of that exquisite topography. The sari hid everything from my gaze. My hands slipped down her sides, bare and warm, to where the folds of her sari were nipped by a drawstring. She tugged and it came loose. I lifted the sari and she stood before me in a petticoat and opened top. She tugged again and now my white pyjama bottoms tried to fall unimpeded to the floor but, understandably, snagged.

I sing you no tales of love's disillusionment. Love is not a domestic animal and I have been spared the petty politics of its taming.

We returned to our new estate of marriage on these grounds that Baba bought: a crumbling mansion, servants' quarters, apartment blocks for minor relatives, orchards, animal-pens, and a high wall studded with glass. In one of those servants' pens, Baba had been born. He wept at the memory.

Money-lenders of the last century, fat merchant-princes of Calcutta who dabbled in landowning and the casual chatteling of seasonal labour had built this mansion, deeded these fields, indentured these surrounding villages. A consortium of owners, great-grandchildren of the merchants, now Calcutta wastrels little better than servants themselves except for exalted notions of their lineage, sold their interest to Baba for little more than back-taxes and a transfer fee. Baba hired a tax-official to do his negotiating, which amounted to threats of prison terms and fines bearing compound-interest from the British days, if the deeds were not turned over in compensation.

7. Special effort seemed called for. In these two years we have reclaimed three rooms of the mansion with paint and wood and plaster, we've unburied an Aphrodite sculpture that rioting Muslims had decapitated in 1947, we've repaired the outer walls and begun pruning the mysterious orchard – snake-choked, hazed with bats and resting monkeys – which should bear sweet lime and mango in a year or two if Boom-Boom's ladies co-operate. In olden times, five villages depended on this estate for inputs and simple justice before extractive greed brought everyone to their knees. Senator Fulbright has used his influence to bring electricity, a classroom, and a dispensary. He's even done some teaching of the servants' children. Gradually, in this life, I am finding my level.

With the possible exception of Baba and Lord Boom-Boom, I am the happiest man I know.

The money for playing both man and god should last another year or two. Meena writes me that her teachers are pleased with her progress, and with Amal's and Mukta's. They are American schoolchildren, as she had wished. They live in my north shore apartment with the twelve-foot ceilings. She is the only freshman at Northwestern with an MA (Sir V. N. Patel Univ.) in English literature. She writes that Chicago is very cold this winter.

Perhaps it is all a dream, but if it is, I am dreaming in colour, with a full palette of taste and texture. Boom-Boom and I have learned a game, on his evening visits. We sit on the warm stone balcony, rolling my evening orange back and forth, each of us feigning a bite, holding it close for inspection, pretending to keep it, licking it, then rolling it back. He finds this orange game vastly amusing, and he has permitted some of his ladies and children to join us, each of them rolling fruits or pebbles, licking them, and rolling them back to me.

Then comes the time when innocence ends.

This evening, biting off buds for tomorrow's worship as I always do, tongue parting the crevices between the leaves as Boom-Boom has shown me, lips grasping, teeth in readiness, moray-man in the reef of his bougainvillaea, I encounter the surge of new resistance, of low, astonished lizard-life, the green head no larger than a bud trembling in my mouth, its twitching tail jerking from my lips. My tongue is nipped – it could have been worse – and Lord Boom-Boom swipes once at my face and dashes the poor lizard to the floor.

And then he pushes me aside, for there, lured at last from the ladder of my vines, the giant head appears, awakened from its millennial sleep. My Lord squats on the parapet wall, the snake, its yellowed hood flaring wide, its tongue flicking, launches itself only to fail, to spray the stone with venom at Boom-Boom's dancing feet. The women begin their screaming, their flinging of fruits and pebbles. Hanuman, my guide and protector, dodges and leaps, landing astride the ancient god, pulling it from the forest of leaves and raking its flesh with his claws, battering its head against the parapet. When it is safe, the first of his women, and then I, join the general battle. We leave the snake bloody and twitching, under a pulpy sludge of burst-apart oranges. Boom-Boom studies my face. I read his brown, bag-rimmed eyes, his wrinkled face and cheeks. *This far and no further, O wanderer,* his eyes tell me.

He rises, whistles once, and his troop of women gather. Another whistle and they plunge over the stone railing still moist with venom, and gather again in my garden, to plunder my fields under the watchful eyes of their god.

Man and His World

1. IN THE SEASON of dust with the sun benign, a man of forty and a boy of twelve appeared at the Tourist Reception Centre, asking for rooms. Failing that, a house, with cook and servant.

The Centre was a modest concrete bunker with thirty rooms and a dining hall, and it was full. This was winter, the time for migrating Siberian songbirds and their Japanese pursuers. For the man and boy the situation was potentially desperate. Udirpur was a walled, medieval town baked on an igneous platter a thousand feet above the desert. To the east, no settlements for two hundred kilometres. To the west lay twenty kilometres of burnt, rusted tanks and stripped, bloodstained jeeps, a UN outpost manned by a bizarre assortment of ill-equipped troops, then barbed wire, mines, and fifteen kilometres of more trophy tanks and bloodstained jeeps. In the winter, buses dropped off passengers twice a week, picked up freight, and returned to the capital.

The man – who gave his name as William Logan – really should have booked a room through the central authority. That way, he would have saved the trip, and who knows, maybe his life.

2. They had been on the road six days from New Delhi. Sleeping on buses, standing on trains, paying truckers. By day, the thin air required a sweater, though the hot sun could burn with its mere intention. From March, when summer returned, the town would disappear from tourist maps and the national consciousness. The national highway would become the world's longest clothesline and camel dung kiln.

Wealth was counted in camels. Camels outnumbered bicycles in the district. Camels pulled the wooden-wheeled carts and plodded around the water-screws, drawing up monsoon rains from the summer before. They yielded their carcasses more graciously than any animal in the world. The first sight of camels grazing in the bush had been a wonder to William Logan. Something half evolved to mammalhood, comic and terrifying in its brute immensity. It had confirmed him, for the moment, in the rightness of what he was doing.

In the desert near the Rat Temple, the government maintained a camel-breeding station. The sight of a hobbled cow being mounted by the garlanded bull, their bellows and the swelling of their reptilian necks, suggested to the Japanese naturalists on their guided tours an echo of the world's creation, a foretaste of its agony and death.

3. Before the invasion of the Aryans, Greeks, Persians and British, the desert people had their own cosmology. The Mother of the World had given birth to identical pairs of camels, tigers, gazelles, elephants and rats. She did not distinguish among her children. She did not have a particular aspect or appearance; whatever their size or ferocity, the children all resembled her, perfectly. The people of Udirpur are still known as rat-worshippers.

When she was nearly too old for child-bearing and the world was already full, she found herself pregnant again. And for the first time, she suffered pain, foreboding, fatigue. She bled, lay down frequently and grew thin. And from her womb came rumbles, lava, fire and flood. When she gave birth, only one cub emerged. His strangled, identical brother fell from the womb and was hastily buried under the great stone anvil in the middle of the desert.

It is said that one brother was evil, but which one? They had struggled in the womb but the secret was kept. The tribes of animals divided. Those giving allegiance to the survivor became his servants. Others retired to the oceans and to the air and to the underworld, growing fins or scales or feathers, or shrinking themselves to become insects. They all kept faith with the one who had died.

It is said that the survivor, be he good or evil, is born with sin and with guilt and is condemned to loneliness. Nowhere on the earth will he find his brother or anything else like him. And with this birth, the Mother of the World died and the creative cycle came to an end.

4. Ten years earlier, from over the mountains a thousand kilometres to the north, a woman had arrived in Udirpur: the palest, whitest woman the people had ever seen. She'd been discovered outside the Rat Temple by a lorry driver who'd been praying to the God for a successful trip. He

had offered sweets and lain still while the God's children swirled over his hands and feet, licking his still-sweet fingers and lips.

Clearly the girl was a hippie – the only English word he knew – one of a tribe he'd heard about but never seen. She carried a newborn baby and nursed him like a village woman by the temple gates. She wore a torn, faded sari, something the lorry driver's own wife or widowed mother would be ashamed to wear. But she wore it well and seemed comfortable in it.

He spoke to her in his language, offering a ride to Udirpur, where at least there were facilities for foreign women and for babies. To his surprise, she answered in a language he knew. She gathered her sleeping baby and the cotton sack that held her possessions and followed him to his truck, without question. This was the way she had travelled and lived for the past three years. At some point in time lost to her now, she had been a girl in a cold small town on the edge of a forest, near a river frequented by whales. She had left that town on a bus to work in the city in the year of a World's Fair. And after that summer she'd not stopped her travelling, until it brought her here.

The lorry-driver knew where to take her. In Udirpur, the city of rats, the Rajah had travelled the world. He spoke every language and he welcomed any remnant of the world that managed to seek him out.

5. He lived in a tawny sandstone palace two kilometres from the centre of town, at the place where the igneous mesa began to split. A summer river fed a forest and residual privilege permitted the luxury of a gardener and family, the appropriation of water, and the maintenance of a very small game sanctuary.

In the British days, the various nizams and maharajahs had been afforded full military salutes. The British, with their customary punctiliousness over protocol and hierarchy, assigned each native potentate a scrupulously measured number of guns. Thus, powerful rajahs like those of Jaipur and Baroda enjoyed full twenty-one-gun salutes, and the no less regal but less prepossessing rajahs of Cooch Behar and Gwalior and Dewas Senior and even Dewas Junior (whose one-time employee, a reticent young English novelist, introduced Gibbon to the royal reading room) were granted fifteen, or twelve, or eight guns. The Rajah of Udirpur, grandfather of the current resident of the Tawny Palace, had been assigned a mere two guns on the imperial scale. He was therefore called the Pipsqueak Rajah, or Sir Squealer Singh, for the twin effect of his popgun salute and for the only worthy attraction in his district, the notorious Temple of Rats. It is not written how Sir Squealer, a genial and worldly man by all accounts, felt about his name or his general reception.

The grandson, Freddie Singh, occupied two rooms in the sealed-off palace. In those rooms he maintained the relics he'd inherited: swords, carpets, carvings, muskets, tiger claws, daggers, and the fine silk cords designed for the silent, efficient dispatch of one's enemies. Freddie Singh's private armoury was as complete as any rajah's but no visitor ever saw it. He kept in touch with his subjects, or those few hundred who still acknowledged his rule, and kept out of the way of the State, District and Conservation authorities who actually ran the town.

He had been out of the country once as a young man, then just graduated in business administration from the Faculty of Management in Ahmedabad. The First National City Bank (India, Pvt. Ltd.) had hired him as a stock analyst, and after two years of the fast life in Bombay, he'd been sent to an office in Rome, then Paris and finally New York, to learn stocks and bonds and how to trade in futures.

Those had been the beautiful years of Freddie Singh, those years on the Strand, in the Bourse, on Wall Street, an exiled princeling, smelling of licorice.

6. She and the baby – a rugged little chap, half-Pathan by the look of him – opened up a room on the second floor, assisted by the old Royal Groom and Keeper of Polo Ponies (now reduced to cook and gardener and feeder of the royal animals), his widowed daughter and her very small daughter who became a companion for young Pierre-Rama.

She seemed to bring some order, perhaps some beauty, into Freddie Singh's life. He no longer sat in his armoury, sipping tea by candlelight. For the majority of people in his ancestral city, the Rajah (though still a youngish man) was either a relic or an embarrassment. When he at last took the unwed foreign mother as a wife, they were prepared to call her Rani if it pleased him. Other names as well, in front of her but never him. The camel, bountiful in all things, provides an anthology of choice insults. The Rani was made to feel as worthy as the slime off a dead camel's tooth. Weeks, then finally years went by, without her ever leaving the compound.

7. Pierre-Rama was nearly ten when the man and his son appeared in town that cool day in late December. Since the Tourist Centre was filled with birdwatchers, someone asked if the visitor would object to accommodation in the Rajah's palace? No, he would not. Would the visitor mind sharing the second floor with the beautiful White Goddess? No, decidedly, he would not. Would he be patient with the Rajah, who, if he could not marry his guests, would often confer upon them land deeds or Moghul miniatures or dusty carpets that it had been his grandfather's privilege to bestow, but which now belonged to the State? Yes, he would be patient with the old gentleman.

They put the man and his son (a frail lad given to sneezing in the dust and to whining for the newly outlawed American soft drinks) in Youssef's camel-drawn cart and drove them to the gully-hugging yellow palace. They made their own way through the garden to the main gate, and pulled on a rusty chain to alert the *chowkidar*.

It was the Rajah, clad in pyjamas and a shawl and smoking an English cigarette, who opened the door. He was younger than the guest, a vigorous man no more than thirty-five, with a head and mane of glossy curls, a rounded face and rubbed, rounded body that glowed with a kind of polish the visitor had never seen. 'My wife is upstairs. She is just coming down.' He called up from the stairwell, 'Visitors, Solange! Come quickly!' Seeing confusion in his guest when the young woman appeared at the head of the stairs bowing shyly and murmuring 'Bonjour', the Rajah winked and said, 'My wife, the Rani. She is from Cue-beck, in Canada. And from where, sir, do you hail?'

'Winnipeg,' said William Logan. 'In Canada.'

8. That is how, this night in February two months later, under a sky pierced with stars, with meteorites flaring and bright silent things making their way across the heavens (not planes, satellites possibly, if indeed so many had been launched), under a sky that would embarrass a planetarium, a sky that thrills the way the ocean or a mountain range can thrill, a sky that suggests mythologies more potent than any yet devised, the two are talking, have been talking, for hours. She nurses the baby, Jacques-

Ravinder, the Rajah's son, four months old, honey-coloured, plump and good-natured.

How perfect a garment is the sari for nursing babies, thinks the man, William Logan. They sleep under a lavender or green or yellow gauze, free of flies and the glare of the sun, the mother sits with her baby anywhere, nurses him in a crowd with only the little toes peeking from the crook of her elbow to give the act away.

Such is the posture that night. Logan talks. The Rani listens. The Rajah is almost asleep in his wicker chair, contributing nothing but his benign royal presence. The older boys run through the palace undisturbed, chasing rats, confining them when possible to the unused rooms.

9. The stars over the winter desert are mythologically potent tonight. The sky is an ocean, thinks William Logan; I could watch it forever. The Milky Way is a luminous smear, meteorites rip and tear, blue-white stars glitter like messages. There is no sound in the universe but the sucking of milk.

Logan is speaking. 'Now this is a night for sea turtles,' he says very slowly, because English is the Rani's last language, the one she learned here, with a local accent, from the gardener and his widowed daughter. Sea turtles she does not understand, but lets Logan go on. Freddie is always there to translate.

'When sea turtles are hatched, they have maybe twenty minutes to memorize the exact location of their birth. Their exact twenty feet of sand, in the world. And these are among the stupidest animals on earth – can you imagine?'

'That is amazing,' she says.

'But I've seen them down on the beach at Grand Cayman. Caribbean sea turtles. The old she-turtle waddles ashore and digs a deep trough about fifty feet up from the water. And she drops in her eggs and pats down the sand and goes back to sea.'

'That is beautiful,' says the Rani.

'But they don't make it, see. No, no, the natives hide behind the trees, waiting for the old turtle to lay her eggs. They are too tired now to move....'

'Yes, I am knowing that tiredness....'

'And so the natives attack them, turn them all over on their backs.

And after a few hours they build fires on the beach and heat iron spikes red hot and then push them under the shell –'

'Oh, Mr Logan, please. This is terrible. No more, please.'

'Do not be upset, Solange,' says the Rajah, snapping awake. 'I too have seen this.' Because they are stupid, nature protected them with built-in star-charts. Their specialization is a form of stupidity, just as a stupid man will keep repeating his mistakes.

A long silence ensues. 'I have seen skies like this only up north,' says the Rani. 'The nights on the Black Sea and on the Caspian and in the desert of Kandahar and in the mountains of Kashmir were all like this. I could not live without stars like this. It is a head full of jewels, the people say. And in the monsoons when the stars are covered, the people say the camel has closed her eyes and people get sick.'

Mr Logan had not yet spent a monsoon. He wondered how Freddie knew about sea turtles, coming from a desert in India. He remembered the hundreds of hatchlings racing across the beach like fiddler crabs, the hundreds of birds, the natives with baskets. The elemental odds against survival had never seemed clearer then.

'Ten minutes to implant those stars, then a mad dash across the sand, and then he hits the ocean with all its monsters. All it knows is how to get back to this lone beach to spawn. The brain clamps shut and it lives on instinct for the next three hundred years.'

'That is very beautiful,' she agrees.

'We are the only animals who can get so lost, Mr Logan,' says Freddie Singh.

Under the sari, the baby is shifted to the other breast. For several minutes they watch the meteorites and the steadily moving things that the Rani thinks of as extraterrestrial.

'When our geese are flying south,' says Logan, 'it is said they can hear the Gulf waves crashing on the shores of Texas and they can hear the Atlantic surf in Ireland. From Winnipeg, or Montréal.'

The Rani says nothing but she feels that she has travelled as unerringly as any turtle or any goose and that even tonight she could hear every voice in every language that has ever been spoken to her. This man Logan, a countryman, is over-impressed with the brains of lower animals.

'You are a restless man, Mr Logan,' says the Rani.

10. The three-block frontage of William Logan's birth was Stiles to Raglan, between Portage and Wolseley, in the city of Winnipeg. Though life had stretched him, he often returned to that original scene, in his memory, to the house built by his father on land on the Assiniboine, purchased by his grandfather. In his way he had swum the world ever since. He had lost his bearings.

He had been in Montréal in 1967, living in Westmount and working in textiles. He'd just been divorced. He was thirty that year with a two-year-old boy and he remembered Westmount Park, the library, the sandboxes and the slides. He was, then and now, a tall, lean, bald, elegant man – in textiles, after all – walking slowly, fingers clutched by his little boy, eyes alert to the idle young mothers, so rich, so confident and attractive. They shared an idleness those afternoons – he was frequently in and out of Montréal and found himself with half-days to kill – there was a power in being the only man in the park, with a sturdy little child.

In the ten years with his mother after the divorce, the child had grown less sturdy. He was better now. Logan remembers a day when a new adventure began, when he was sitting at a reasonable distance (but on the same bench) from a blond, maturing woman in a lavender sweater. It was late April, perhaps snow still was pushed in ridges but the earth was dry and dusty. A little girl, pursued by an *au pair*, ran to the lady and took a good long look at William Logan.

'Mama, that man is *bald*,' said the little girl.

'Damn,' said the mother.

Logan, who'd never minded his baldness or the reputation it carried, found it a handy prop in establishing his essential harmlessness with younger women, said, 'That's okay, out of the mouths of babes, etc.'

The mother straightened the little girl's jacket and motioned for the *au pair* to take her back to the swings. 'Oh, it's not that. It's that now I have to sleep with you to restore your almighty male ego.'

'Pardon me?' He'd been out of the country.

She gave her address – a brick house on Lansdowne, just up from the park.

The Rajah stood and poured a final cup of tea.

The baby was sleeping and he took him back to the palace and bade his guest good night.

11. 'I'll never get back,' he says.

'To Montréal?'

'To Winnipeg. Not that I want to. I can't anyway. I'm a fugitive.'

The Rani is not disturbed. He has established his essential harmlessness.

'Tell me about the lady on Lansdowne,' she says.

He sips slowly. God forgive me, thinks William Logan: she reads minds and her breast excited me though she's my hostess, a Maharani, and nursing an infant.

The lady on Lansdowne was Hungarian. Thirty-five and very beautiful and bold and angry. She was an actress and her husband had left his wife for her. He had much older children and that obnoxious little girl.

'Her name was Laura,' says the Rani. 'Now, Mr Logan, tell me about the *au pair* girl.'

Before he can answer, he remembers it all. My God, he thinks. He'd lived long enough, accumulated enough points of reference, for his experiences to start collapsing, growing dense with coincidence.

'You looked familiar the first time I saw you. Solange – of course.'

'That day in the park. You called me the *au pair* girl but I noticed you alone in the park and I watched Mrs K watching you and she asked me, did I think you had a wife, and I could see you were both very experienced in the world … I was not, not at all. I wondered how you two would get together.' She took a long breath, and wrapped the sari-end over her head.

'You speak a lot more when your husband is gone.'

'My husband is never gone.'

She listened awhile to jackals on the plain, the leathery sway of palms in the desert, the distant clatter of wooden wheels, a cart and camel over cobblestones.

'May I call you Solange?'

She pondered the question longer than he thought necessary. 'I cannot stop you.'

'Then what are the chances of our getting together? Surely it means something, no? It can't just be' (he thought of the stars) 'coincidence.'

'Perhaps you are too restless, Mr Logan.'

'It's just that I don't wait for things any more.'

On his last flight from Egypt to Montréal, Logan had sat next to a pleasant, moon-faced young man bound for Athens, and maybe

Montréal. He'd asked Logan shrewd job-hunting questions and Logan had been flattered by his interest. Then he'd asked him what time it was. They were south of Athens. Logan told him and the man jerked into a new posture. He stood and opened one of the Red Cross emergency medical bags that was in the storage area immediately overhead. At the same time, six other young men stood and opened other emergency boxes. *Oh, no,* Logan had thought: the boxes were full of grenades.

There is nothing in the modern world quite like eight days of siege to focus a man's attention on final matters. They had landed a few hundred yards from the hillside home of the Delphic oracle. *Low has fallen the prophet's house,* quoted one passenger. Women and children were released; Logan made his peace. As good a place as any to die; as good a reason as any. His life was a hostage-taking anyway, he was a passenger only, detained by fanatics. He vowed, if he survived, to live his life from that moment on as if the person next to him were a terrorist, as if every package contained grenades, as if every flight would end on a hillside surrounded by troops.

12. Just a few weeks before, but a millennium ago, he had landed in Montréal, flown to Toronto, taken the airport limousine to the door of the expensive school he paid for and asked for Billy Logan, a boy who was a stranger to him and whom he'd come to dislike just a little. He'd taken Billy with him back to the airport and they'd flown to London, bought tropical clothes and Logan had sent telegrams to his boss and ex-wife. *Resign effective immediately ... I have Billy don't look you'll never find us.* He bought tickets to a dozen destinations, under various names. Not merely restless, he'd become impulsive.

Some nights, sleep is an act of will requiring as sharp a focus as thought itself. Under such heavens there can be no sleep. Listening to the Rani is like listening to an Indian woman, only better. It's strange but familiar, and behind it is something he can understand. It's erotic, terribly erotic. He cannot control his love, not for her, not for his host, not for his child; he wants to displace the Rajah; he feels at last he has found his home.

In the second week of residence at the Tawny Palace, Logan had boldly proposed to the attractive lady who did his rooms, the gardener's widowed daughter. Perhaps she had not understood; it was instead, her daughter, an exquisite child of – what, thirteen? – who had appeared. And then to say to the girl, 'No, I meant your mother' when she had presented herself so wondrously to him would have offended his morals in some new way. To turn from beauty is a sin, thought the new William Logan; to refuse the daughter would embarrass us all, and be insulting, he feared.

But he had not intended this, any of this, and there could only be one honourable way to act. To enjoy the love of the girl and to try to love the mother. What incredible complications this would lead to, William Logan could not say: only that he was ready to face them. Somehow, marriage was expected, perhaps to the widow. The adjacent space, he had learned, may always be evil, or it may open into the next world, the next level, a higher existence. The girl comes to him after bathing while the mother prepares his lunch. The Rani and Rajah, he feels, have no suspicion. It is a very private, second-floor affair. The daughter must know – though she has never asked – that in the evenings after the main meal has been cooked and the sweeper has cleaned the rooms and she has washed the dishes, that her mother returns, laden with fruits and a small clay pot of sweets, makes tea, then lies beside him.

Is this corruption? At one time he would have known but now he cannot say. He feels at times that he has entered a compact, nothing down, no interest, small monthly payments, but that an unpayable price will be extracted. It is like a nightmare in which he is ice-skating out on the Assiniboine, and he can feel the dark waters oozing from the slashes of his blades; there is still time to skate ashore but a wind is pushing him out to the black open water and he can't turn back.

13. Freddie Singh sits in his armoury, wondering if this is the night. He has come to like the visitor. The boys have become inseparable; there is hope for the boy. But Freddie Singh is still the Rajah of the Tawny Palace; he knows what happens on his grounds as his grandfather once knew what happened in his larger *durbar*. He knows that an uprooted man is the principle of corruption and will spread it wherever he goes. When you announced yourself from Canada, the Rani said *Get rid of him immediately* but I could not. You needed rest, just as the Rani had needed rest. But she has healed, and you have not, my friend.

The people here know of dualities, of coincidence. Every day they see the sand turn to embers. Every night to ice. Ten months of the year, never a drop of water. Two months, walls of mud.

The Rani arrived in India with a friend, another girl from Lévis, in Cue-beck. But the other girl met a handsome Frenchman at the airport and the Rani struggled onward, to the desert. Her friend followed the handsome Frenchman to Bangkok, Hong Kong, Djakarta, Nepal. She loved him, she cooked for him, she became his slave and she helped poison people for him, maybe dozens of young travellers, like herself, like the Rani. She will die in jail. She was not evil, not born evil, but she had become lost.

We have known others, thinks Freddie Singh. A fourteen-year-old girl gives birth in a paddy field in Bangladesh nine months after a week of raping, after her mother's rape and murder, her village's rape and butchery. She slashes the wrists and throat of the hated infant, hacks up the body like a fish's, then throws herself successfully on the knife. But someone comes by, picks up the smaller body and takes it to a hospital and the corpse is resurrected. And the baby is adopted by a family in Lévis who name her Marie-Josée and now she's the best student and the best figure-skater in her school.

The people here have seen enough of life to know that coincidence itself is no motive for action. Coincidence on your level, Mr Logan, is a turtle's coincidence, nothing but instinct.

The gardener arrives with a fresh pot of tea. 'You called, sir?' he asks.

'The animals are fed?'

'*Ji*, sahib.'

'Your daughter is sleeping?'

'*Hanh, ji.*'

'You may see Mr Logan now,' says the Rajah.

Coincidence is coincidental, thinks Freddie Singh.

14. 'We have a visitor.'

Logan, sipping the last of his cold tea, turns in his wicker chair. 'Nothing more, Ram, I –'

In the gardener's hands is stretched taut a valuable artefact from one of the desert tribes. In the old days they had joined caravans across the desert, offering their services as entertainers and animal-handlers. And those caravans never reached their destinations. The people were called *thuggis* and they worshipped the principle of creation no less than other tribes, though their ultimate loyalty was to the brother who had died.

Death moves swiftly across the heavens, obliterating the stars at a point just short of meaning, and across Logan's brain like some long-sought solution made suddenly apparent, only to retreat again. He looks up, about to speak, and across to the Rani who now is standing, and turning away. Then he looks down at himself, sees his head perched crazily on his chest and the widening dribble of tea on his luminous white *kurta*, and the stain spreads to fill his universe.

Dear Abhi

I WATCHED HIM this morning juicing a grapefruit, guava, blood orange, mango, plums and grapes and pouring the elixir into a giant glass pitcher. Beads of condensation rolled down the sides, like an ad for California freshness. Chhoto Kaku, my late father's youngest brother, is vegetarian; the warring juices are the equivalent of eggs and bacon, buttered toast and coffee. He will take tea and toast, but never coffee, which is known to inflame the passions. Life, or the vagaries of the Calcutta marriage market, did not bless him with a wife. Arousal, he believed, would be wasted on him and he has taken traditional measures against it.

Ten years ago this was all farmland, but for the big house and the shingled cottage behind it. No lights spill from the cottage, yet Chhoto Kaku makes his way across the rocks and cacti to her door. *Don't go,* I breathe, but the door opens. Devorah was alone last night. Usually she comes out around eight o'clock with a mug of coffee and a cigarette, sometimes joined by one of her stay-overs. On our first visit she produced a tray of wild boar sausage that a friend had slaughtered, spiced, cooked and cased, after shooting.

Her hair changes colour. I've seen it green and purple. Today, there are no Mercedes or motorcycles in the yard, she was alone last night. She wears blue jeans and blue work shirts and she smells richly resinous, reminding me of mangoes. Her normal hair is loose and greying.

She told me the day after we'd moved in, 'Your uncle is a hoot.' She calls me Abby, my uncle Bushy. His name is Kishore Bhushan Ganguly. We call her Devvie, which in our language approximates the word for goddess. 'He looked at my paintings and he said, "You have the eyes of god." Isn't that the sweetest thing?' I count myself a man of science, so I must rely on microscopes and telescopes and X-rays to glimpse the world beyond. 'He said I see the full range of existence. He said, "I tremble before you." Isn't that beautiful?'

When I reported her assessment, Uncle said, 'I think she is an advanced soul.' I asked how he knew. 'She offered me a plate of cold meats. I told her meats inflame the passions.' Youngest Uncle is a Brahmin of the old school. 'So, she's giving up meats, is that it?' I asked. He said, 'I believe so. She said, "Maybe that is my problem."'

Six months he's been with me, my cherished Youngest Uncle, the bachelor who put me and two cousins through college, married off my sisters and cousins with handsome dowries and set up their husbands, the scoundrels, in business. He delayed, and finally abandoned all hopes of marriage for himself.

When he was an engineer rising through the civil service, then in industry, there'd been hope of marriage to a neighbour's daughter – beautiful, smart, good family from the right caste and even subcaste. Her father had proposed it and even Oldest Uncle, who approved or vetoed all marriages in the family, declared himself, for once, unopposed. Preparations were started, horoscopes exchanged, a wedding house rented. Her name was Nirmala.

I came home from school one day in my short pants, looking for a servant to make me a glass of fresh lime soda and finding, unimaginable, no one in the kitchen. The servants were all clustered in Oldest Auntie's room joining in the loud lamenting of other pishis and older girl-cousins. I squeezed my own limes then stood on a chair from the kitchen across a hallway open to the skies. I had a good view into Youngest Uncle's room. He was in tears. He had been betrayed. In those years he was a handsome man in his middle thirties, about my age now, with long, lustrous hair and a thin, clipped moustache. Older Uncle had voided the engagement.

Something unsavoury in Nirmala's background had been detected. I heard the word 'mishap'. Perhaps our family had given her the once-over and found her a little dull, flat-chested or older than advertised, or with a lesser dowry. It could have meant a misalignment in the stars, a rumour of non-virginity or suspicion of feeble-mindedness somewhere in her family. Or Nirmala might have caught a glimpse of her intended husband and found him too old, too lacking in sex appeal. Every family can relate a similar tale. A promising proposal not taken to its completion is an early sign of the world's duplicity. My parents who married for love and never heard the end of it, did not call it duplicity. They called it not striking while the iron is hot, an image in English I always had difficulty picturing.

In time 'Nirmala' stood as a kind of symbol of treacherous beauty. In this case, the rumours were borne out. She had a boy on the side, from an unsuitable community. They made a love-match, disgracing the name of her good family and rendering her younger sisters unmarriageable to suitable boys. They had two boys before she was eighteen. The sisters scattered to Canada and Australia and had to marry white men. A few years later, Nirmala divorced, and once, I'm told (I had already left for California), she showed up at Youngest Uncle's door, offering her body, begging for money. Proof, as my mother would say, that whatever god decides is for the best. God wished that Youngest Uncle would become middle-aged in the service of lesser-employed brothers and their extended families and that he not spend his sizeable income on a strange woman when it could be squandered on his family instead.

You will see from this I am talking of the not-so-long ago Calcutta, and surmise that I am living, or more properly, was living until a few months ago – with my wife, Sonali, our sons, Vikram and Pramrod – in the Silicon Valley and that my uncle is with us. You would be half right. My wife kicked me out six months ago. Not so long in calendar days, but in psychological time, aeons.

My Christmas bonus eighteen months ago was $250,000. In Indian terms, two and half lakhs of dollars; multiply by forty, a low bank rate, and you come up with ten million rupees: one crore. My father, a middle-class clerk, never made more than two thousand rupees a month and that was only towards the end of his life when the rupee had started to melt. What does it do to a Ballygunge boy, a St Xavier's boy, to be confronted in half a lifetime with such inflation of expectation, such expansion of the stage upon which we strut and fret. Sonali planned to use the bonus to start a pre-school. She was born in California and rarely visits Calcutta, which depresses her. Her parents, retired doctors who were born on the same street as I, live in San Diego.

There are three dozen Indian families in our immediate circle of friends, all of them with children, all of whom share a suspicion that their children's American educational experiences will not replicate the hunger for knowledge and rejection of mediocrity that we knew in less hospitable Indian schools. They would therefore pay anything to replicate some of that nostalgic anxiety, but not the deprivation. She could start a school. Sonali is a fine Montessori teacher. Many of the wives of our friends are teachers. Many of my friends would volunteer to tutor or teach a class.

We would have a computer-literate school to do Sunnyvale proud. She spoke to me nightly of dangerous and deprived East Palo Alto where needs are great and the rents are cheap.

If I stay in this country we would have to do it, or something like it. It is a way of recycling good fortune and being part of this model community I've been elected to because of the responsible way I conduct my life. You name it – family values, religious observation, savings, education, voting, tax-paying, PTA, soccer-coaching, nature-hiking, school boards, mowing my lawn, keeping a garden, contributing to charities – I've done it. And in the office: designing, programming, helping the export market and developing patents – I've done that, too. America is a demonstrably better place for my presence. My undistinguished house, bought on a downside at a mere $675,000 for cash, quadrupled in value in the past five years – or more precisely, four of the past five years. It is inconceivable that anything I did would not be a credit to my national origin, my present country and my religious creed. When something is missing it's not exactly easy to place it. I have given this some thought – I think it is called 'evidence of things unseen'. Despite external signs of satisfaction, good health, a challenging job, the love and support of family and friends, no depressions or mood swings, no bad habits, I would not call myself happy. I am well adjusted. We are all extremely well adjusted. I believe my situation is not uncommon among successful immigrants of my age and background.

I went alone to Calcutta for two weeks, just after the bonus. Sonali didn't go. She took the boys and two of their school friends skiing in Tahoe. She has won medals for her skiing. I am grateful for all those comforts and luxuries but had been feeling unworthy of late. It was Youngest Uncle who had paid for the rigorous Calcutta schools and then for St Xavier's and that preparation got me the scholarships to IIT and later to Berkeley, but I lacked a graceful way of thanking him. The bonus check was in my wallet. I would be in Calcutta with a crore of rupees in my pocket. I, Abhishek Ganguly of Ballygunge.

Chhoto Kaku is now sixty-seven, ten years retired from his post of chemical engineer. The provident funds he'd contributed to for forty years are secure. One need not feel financial concern for Youngest Uncle, at least in a rupee zone. He had no legal dependents. Everyone into the remotest hinterland of consanguinity has been married. He was living with his two widowed sisters-in-law and their two daughters plus husbands and children in our old Calcutta house. The rent has not been substantially raised since Partition when we arrived from what was then East Bengal and soon was to become East Pakistan, then Bangladesh. Chhoto Kaku was then a boy of eleven. I believe the rent is about fifteen dollars a month, which is reflected in the broken amenities. A man on a bicycle collects the rent on the first of every month. They say he is the landlord's nephew, but the nephew is a frail gentleman of seventy years.

It is strange how one adjusts to the street noise and insects, the power cuts, the Indian-style bathroom, the dust and noise and the single tube of neon light in the living room which casts all nighttime conversations into a harsh pallor and reduces the interior world to an ashen palette of greys and blues. Only for a minute or two do I register Sunnyvale, the mountains, the flowers and garden, the cool breeze, the painting and rugs and comfortable furniture. And my God, the appliances: our own tandoori oven and a convection oven, the instant hot-tea spout, ice water in the refrigerator door, the tiles imported from Portugal for the floor and countertops. Sonali is an inspired renovator. You would think it was us, the Gangulys of Sunnyvale who were the long-established and landowning aristocracy and not my uncle who has lived in his single room in that dingy house for longer than I've been on earth.

Youngest Uncle is a small man, moustached, the lustrous long hair nearly gone, fair as we Bengalis go, blessed with good health and a deep voice much admired for singing and for prayer services. He could have acted or sung professionally. There was talk of sending him to Cambridge in those heady post-Independence years when England was offering scholarships to identify the likely leaders of its newly liberated possessions. Many of his classmates went, stayed on, and married English girls. He remained in India, citing the needs of his nieces and nephews and aged parents.

The tragedy of his life, if the word is applicable, was having been the last-born in the family. He could not marry before his older siblings and they needed his unfettered income to secure their matches. And if he had married for his own pleasure the motive would have appeared lascivious. This, he would never do. My father, that striker of, or with, hot irons, had been the only family member to counsel personal happiness over ancestral duty. He called his sisters and other brothers bloodsuckers. When my parents married just after Independence under the spell of Gandhian idealism, they almost regretted the accident that had made their brave and impulsive marriage also appear suitable as to caste and sub-caste. My father would have married a sudra, he said; my mother, a Christian, Parsi, Sikh, or maybe even a Muslim, under proper conditions.

I am always extravagant with gifts for Youngest Uncle. He has all the high-tech goodies my company makes: an e-mail connection and a lightning-fast modem though he never uses it, a cell phone, a scanner, a laser printer, copier, colour television, various tape recorders and stereos. The room cannot accommodate him, electronically speaking, with its single burdened outlet. But the gifts are still in their boxes, carefully dusted, waiting to be given to various grandnephews still in elementary school. He keeps only the Walkman, on which he plays classic devotional ragas. He's making his spiritual retreat to Varanasi electronically.

I touch his feet in the traditional *pronam*. He touches my shoulder, partially to deflect my gesture, partially to acknowledge it. It is a touch I miss in the States, never giving it and never expecting to receive it. It is a sign that I am home and understood.

'So, Chhoto Kaku, what's new?' I asked, the invitation for Youngest Uncle to speak about the relatives, the dozens-swollen-to-hundreds of Gangulys who now live in every part of India, and increasingly, the world.

'In Calcutta, nothing is ever new,' he said. 'In interest of saving money, Rina and her husband, Gautam, are here.' Rina is the youngest daughter of his next oldest sister. Thanks to Youngest Uncle's dowry, Rina had got married during the year and brought Gautam to live in her house, an unusual occurrence, although nothing is as it was in India, even in polite, conservative, what used to be called *bhadralok*, Bengali society.

'Where do they stay, Uncle?'

'In this room.'

There are no other spare rooms. It is a small house.

'They are waiting for me to die. They expect me to move in with Sukhla Pishi.'

That would be his oldest sister-in-law, the one we call From Room Auntie for her position at the window that overlooks the street. She is over eighty. Nothing happens on Rash Behari Avenue that she doesn't know. The rumour, deriving from those first post-Partition years, is she had driven Anil Kaku, her young husband, my oldest uncle, mad. He'd died of something suspicious which was officially a burst appendix. Something burst, that is true. Disappointment, rage, failure of his schemes, who can say? It is Calcutta. He was a civil engineer and had been offered a position outside of Ballygunge in a different part of the city, but rather than leave the house and neighbourhood, Sukhla Pishi had taken to her bed in order to die. (I should add that modern science sheds much light on intractable behaviour. Sukhla Pishi is obviously agoraphobic; a pill would save us all much heartache.) Anil Kaku turned down the job and she climbed out of bed and took her seat on the windowsill. All of that happened before I was born. There had been no children – they were then in their middle twenties – so she became the first of Youngest Uncle's lifelong obligations.

'This is your house, Uncle,' I said. 'Don't be giving up your rights.' As if he hadn't already surrendered everything.

'Rights were given long ago. Her mother holds the lease.'

I should say a few words about my cousin-sister Rina. She is most unfortunate to look at, or to be around. I was astonished that she'd found any boy to marry, thinking anyone so foolish would be, like her, a flawed appendage to a decent family. We'd been most pleasantly wrong. He was handsome, which goes a long way in our society, a dashing, athletic flight steward with one of the new private airlines that fly between Calcutta and the interior of eastern India. We understood he was in management training. Part of the pre-marriage negotiation was the best room in the house, that would allow him to pocket his housing allowance from the airline while subletting the company flat, and his own car, computer, television, stereo, printer and tape recorder. He'd scouted the room before marriage since the demands were not only generic, but included brand names and serial numbers.

'I cannot say more, they are listening,' said my uncle.

It was then that I noticed the new furnishings in the room, a calendar on the wall from Gautam's employer. This wasn't Youngest Uncle's room any more, though he'd lived in it for over fifty years. He'd sobbed over Nirmala on that bed. The move to the sunny, dusty, noisy front room, rolling a thin mattress on Sukhla Pishi's floor, had already been made. Next would be Gautam's selling on the black market of all the carefully boxed, unopened electronics I'd smuggled in.

'Let us go for tea,' I suggested, putting my hand on his arm, noting its tremble and sponginess. I kept an overseas membership in the Tollygunge Club for moments like this, prying favourite relatives away from family scrutiny, letting them drink Scotch or a beer free of disapproval, but he wouldn't budge.

'They won't permit it,' he said. 'I've been told not to leave the house.'

'They? Who's they?'

'The boy, the girl. Her.'

'Rina? You know Rina, Uncle, she's –' I wanted to say 'flawed'. On past visits I'd contemplated taking her out to the Tolly for a stiff gin just to see if there was a different Rina, waiting to be released. '– harmless.'

'Her mother,' he whispered. 'And the boy.'

I heard noises outside the door. 'Babu?' came my aunt's query. 'What is going on in my daughter's room?'

'We are talking, Pishi,' I said. 'We'll be right out.'

'Rina doesn't want you in there. She will be taking her bath.'

The shower arrangement was in uncle's room. His books, the only ones in the house, lined the walls but Rina's saris and Gautam's suits filled the cupboard. It was the darkest, coolest, quietest, largest and only fully serviced room in the house. Not for the first time did it occur to me that poverty corrupts everyone in India, just as wealth does the same in America. Nor did family life – so often evoked as the glue of Indian society, evidence of superiority over Western selfishness and rampant individualism – escape its collateral accounting as the source of all horrors. I suggested we drop in at the Tolly for a whisky or two.

'I cannot leave the house,' he said. 'I am being watched. I will be reported.'

'Watched for what?'

'Gautam says that I have cheated on my taxes. The CBI is watching me twenty-four hours a day from their cars and from across the street. I must turn over everything to him to clear my name.'

'Kaku! You are the most honest man I have ever met.'

'No man leads a blameless life.'

'Gautam's a scoundrel. When he's finished draining your accounts, he'll throw you in the gutter.'

'They are watching you too, Abhi, for all the gifts you have given. Gautam says you have defrauded the country. We are worse than agents of the Foreign Hand. He has put you on record, too.'

All those serial numbers, of course – and I thought he was merely a thief. Every time I have given serious thought to returning to India for retirement or even earlier, perhaps to give my children more direction and save them from the insipidness of an American life, I am brought face to face with villainies, hypocrisies, that leave me speechless. Elevator operators collecting fares. Clerks demanding bribes, not to forgive charges, but to accept payments and stamp 'paid' on a receipt. Rina and Gautam follow a pattern. I don't want to die in America, but India makes it so hard, even for its successful runaways.

And so the idea came to me that this house in which I'd spent the best years of my childhood, the house that the extended Ganguly clan of East Bengal had been renting for over fifty years, had to be available for the right price if I could track down the owner in the three days remaining on my visit. It was one of the last remaining single-family, one-storey bungalows on a wide, maidan-split boulevard lined with expensive apartment blocks. I, Abhishek Ganguly, would become owner of a house on Rash Behari Avenue, Ballygunge, paid for from the cheque in my pocket and my first order of business would be to expel those slimy schemers, Gautam and Rina and her mother, and any other relative who stood in the way. Front Room Pishi could stay.

Perhaps I oversold the charms of California. I certainly oversold the enthusiasm my dear wife might feel for housing an uncle she'd never met. Rina and Gautam would not leave voluntarily. Auntie would cause a fight. There'd be cursing, wailing, threats, denunciations. Nothing a few well-distributed gifts could not settle. Come back with me for six months for good food and sunshine, I said, no CBI surveillance, and you can return to a clean house and your own room, dear Youngest Uncle.

Bicycle Nephew was more than happy to trade a monthly eight hundred rupees for ten million, cash. And with India being a land of miracles and immediate transformation as well as timeless inertia, I returned to California feeling like a god in the company of my liberated Chhoto Kaku, owner, *zamindar* if you will, like my ancestors in pre-Partition East Bengal, of property, preserver of virtue and expeller of evil.

It is America, contrary to received opinion, which resists cataclysmic self-reinvention. In my two-week absence, my dear wife had engaged an architect to transform a boarded-over, five-shop strip mall in East Palo Alto into plans for the New Athens Academy, the Agora of Learning.

Where weeds now push through the broken slabs of concrete, there will be fountains and elaborate gardens. Each class will plant flowers and vegetables in February and harvest in May. Classes will circulate through the plots. I can picture toga-clad teachers. New Athens will incorporate the best of East and West, Tagore's Shantiniketan and Montessori's Rome, Confucius and Dewey, sports and science, classics and computers, all fuelled by Silicon Valley resources. She'd started enrolling children for two years hence.

And then I had to inform her – that outpost of Vesuvius – that my one-crore bonus check now rested in the account of one Atulya Ghosh, the very cool, twenty-year-old grandson of Bicycle Ghosh, nephew of old Landlord Ghosh, the presumably late owner.

One of the Ghoshes, it might have been Atulya's grandfather, had been the rumoured lover of a pishi of mine who'd been forced to leave the house in disgrace. She killed herself, in fact. Young Ray-Bans Ghosh was a Toronto-based greaser, decked out in filmi-filmi Bollywood sunglasses and a stylish scarf, forked over a throbbing motorcycle – all I could ask for as an on-site enforcer. He took my money and promised there'd be no problems: he had friends. Rina, Gautam, and Rina's mother deserved to share the pokey company flat bordering a paddy field on the outskirts of Cossipore.

Sonali wailed, she broke down in tears, sobbing, 'New Athens, New Athens!' she cried. 'My Agora, my Agora! All my dreams, all my training!' What had I been thinking? And the answer was, amazingly, she was right. I hadn't thought about her or the school, at all.

'You don't care about me. You're always complaining about our boy's education, you think I'm lazy, you only care about your goddamn family in goddamn Calcutta –'

'I should return home,' said Chhoto Kaku.

'Oh, no,' she cried. '*I* should return home! And I'm going to!'

She stood at the base of the stairway – I could rhapsodize over the marble, the recessed lighting under the handrail, the paintings and photographs lining the stairwell, but that is from a lifetime ago. And her beauty. I am easily inflamed, I admit it, and I will never see a more beautiful woman than Sonali, even as she threw plates at my head. 'Boys! Pramrod, Vikram! Pack your bags immediately. We're leaving for San Diego!'

Chhoto Kaku began to cry. I held him. Sonali went upstairs to organize the late-night getaway. The boys struggled to pack their video games and computers. The ever-enticing, ever-dangerous phenomenon of the HAP, the Hindu American Princess, had been described to me by friends who'd urged me not to marry here, but to go back to India. Do not take on risky adventures with the second-generation daughters of American entitlement. Did I listen? Did she love me for my money, had she ever loved me? Was this all a dream? I sat on the bottom step, hiding my tears, cradling my eyes and forehead against my bent arm, while Chhoto Kaku ran his fingers through my hair and sang to me, very low and soft, a prayer I recognized from a lifetime ago.

Well, enough of that. Justice is swift and mercy unavailing. The property split left Sonali and the boys in the big house and my uncle and me in this tiny rental. Last Christmas there was no bonus. My boss, Nitin Mehta, called me aside and said, 'Bad times are coming, Abhi. We have to stay ahead of the wave. I want you to cut twenty percent of your tech group.' So I slashed, I burned. Into the fire went everyone with an H-1B visa; back to Bombay with Lata Deshpande who was getting married in a month. Off to a taxi in Oakland went Yuri, who'd come overnight from Kazakhstan to Silicon Valley, thinking it a miracle. This Christmas there will be no job, even for me. Impulse breeds disaster, I've been taught.

In a month or two we'll be free to move back to Calcutta. Ray-Bans Ghosh informs me the 'infestation' has been routed. But Youngest Uncle has found a girlfriend in America. Kaku and the Goddess; my walls glow with her paintings. The turpentine smell of mango haunts the night.

In the summer of my fourteenth year, Youngest Uncle was given a vacation cottage in Chota Nagpur, a forest area on the border of Bihar and West Bengal. Ten members of the family went in May when the heat and humidity in Calcutta both reached triple digits. The cottage was shaded by a grove of mango trees too tall to climb. Snakes and birds and rats and clouds of insects gorged on the broken fruit. The same odour of rotting mango envelops the Goddess and the sharp tang of her welcome.

She is a well-known painter in the Bay area and represented in New York. The first time we visited, Youngest Uncle said, 'You smell of mango,' and she'd reached out and touched him. 'Oh, sweeties,' she said, 'it's just linseed oil.' She never seems to cook. On garbage collection days there is nothing outside her door yet she can produce cold platters of the strangest foods. She has an inordinate number of overnight guests who doubtless return to their city existence, trailing mango fumes. My uncle brings her sweet lassi, crushed ice in sweetened yoghurt, lightly laced with mango juice. I hope that in place of a heart she does not harbour a giant stone.

That summer in Choto Nagpur, I had a girlfriend. There was another cabin not so distant where another Calcutta family had brought their daughter for the high-summer school holidays. We had seen each other independent of parental authority, meaning we had passed one another on the main street of the nearest village, and our eyes had met – in my twenty-four years' memory I want to say 'locked' – but neither of us paused or acknowledged the other's presence. The fact that she didn't exactly ignore me meant I now had a girlfriend, a face to focus on and something to boast about when school resumed and the monsoons marooned us. I had the next thing to a wife, a Nirmala of my own. Knowing her name and her parents' address in Calcutta and trusting that she was out there waiting for me when the time would come, I was able to put the anxieties of marriage aside for the next five years.

When I was eighteen I asked Youngest Uncle to launch a marriage inquiry. I provided her father's name and address – I'd even walked by their house on the way to school in hopes of seeing her again and perhaps locking eyes in confirmation. Youngest Uncle was happy to do so. He reported her parents to be charming and cultured people with a pious outlook, whose ancestral origins in Bangladesh lay in an adjoining village to our own. Truly an adornment to our family. It seemed that the girl in question, however, whose name by now I've quite forgotten, was settled in a place called Maryland-America and had two lovely children. And so, outwardly crushed but partially relieved, I took the scholarship to IIT and then to Berkeley, met Sonali at a campus mixer thrown by outgoing Indo-Americans for nervous Indians, had my two lovely children, made millions and lost it and the rest is history, or maybe not.

All of my life, good times and bad, rich or poor, married and alone, I have read the Gita and tried to be guided by its immortal wisdom. It teaches that our life – this life – is but a speck on a vast spectrum, but our ears are less reliable than a dog's, a dolphin's or a bat's, our eyes less than a bird's in comprehending it. I have understood it in terms of science, the heavy elements necessary to life, the calcium, phosphorus, iron and zinc that settle on us from exploded stars. We are entwined in the vast cycle of creation and destruction; the spark of life is inextinguishable. Today human, but who knows about tomorrow? We are the fruit and rot that infects it, the mango and the worm.

Ray-Bans Ghosh now wants to put his crore of rupees to work in Toronto. Dear Abhi Babu, he writes, tear down this useless old house, put up luxury condos and you'll be minting money. Front Room Pishi, who misses nothing outside the window, reports that she has seen evil Gautam in various disguises sneaking about the property. Dear Abhi, she pleads, come back, that man will kill me if he can and your cousin Rina and her mother will bury me in the yard like a Christian or worse, and please send my love to Chhoto Kaku and your lovely wife and children, whom I've still not met.

Perhaps my Nirmala waits for me in Calcutta, perhaps in Tokyo or Maryland or the ancestral village in Bangladesh. Youngest Uncle will stay here just a while longer, if he may, keeping my house clean and ready for whatever God plans. He has bought himself some brushes and watercolours, and takes his instruction from the Goddess who guides his hand and trains him to see, he says, at last. His old middle room has been vacant these past several months. It will suit me.

This life, which I understood once in terms of science – the heavy elements, the calcium, phosphorus, iron and zinc, settled on us from exploded stars – is but one of an infinity of lives. The city, the world, has come and gone an infinite number of times. One day I expect my Nirmala, whatever her name, to come to my door wherever that door will be, our eyes will lock, and I will invite her in.

The Sociology of Love

A MONSTROUSLY TALL GIRL from Stanford with bright yellow hair comes to the door and asks if I am willing to answer questions for her sociology class. She knows my name, 'Dr Vivek Waldekar?' and even folds her hands in a creditable namaste. She has researched me, she knows my job-title and that I am an American citizen. She's wearing shorts and a midriff-baring T-shirt with a boastful logo. It reads, 'All This and Brains, Too'. She reminds me of an American movie star whose name I don't recall, or the California Girl from an old song, as I had imagined her. I invite her in. I've never felt so much the South Asian man: fine-boned, almost dainty, and timid. My wife, Krithika, stares silently for several long moments, then puts tea water on.

Her name is Anya. She was born in Russia, she says. She has Russian features, as I understand them, a slight tilt to her cheeks but with light blue eyes and corn-yellow hair. When I walk behind her, I notice the top of an elaborate tattoo reaching up from underneath. She is a walking billboard of availability. She says she wants my advice, or my answers, as a successful South Asian immigrant, on problems of adjustment and assimilation. She says that questions of accommodation to the U.S., especially to California, speak to her. And specifically South Asians, her honours project, since we lack the demographic residential densities of other Asians, or of Hispanics. We are sociological anomalies.

It is important to establish control early. It is true, I say, we do not swarm like bees in a hive. 'Why do you criticize us for living like Americans?' I ask, and she apologizes for the tone of her question. I press on. 'What is it we lack? Why do you people think there is something wrong with the way we live?'

She says, 'I never suggested anything was wrong –' She drops her eyes and reads from her notes.

'– That there's something defective in our lives?'

'Please, I'm so sorry.'

I have no handkerchief to offer.

Perhaps we have memories of overcrowded India, when everyone knew your business. I know where her question is headed: middle-class Indian immigrants do not build little Chinatowns or barrios because we are too arrogant, too materialist, and our caste and regional and religious and linguistic rivalries pull us in too many directions. She hangs her head even before asking the next question.

No, I say, there are no other South Asian families on my street. My next-door neighbours are European, by which I mean non-specifically white. I correct myself. 'European' is an old word from my father's India, where even Americans could be European. Across the street are Chinese, behind us a Korean.

That's why I'm involved in sociology, she says, it's so exciting. Sociology alone can answer the big questions, like where are we headed and what is to become of us? I offer a counter-argument; perhaps computer science, or molecular biology, or astronomy, I say, might answer even larger questions. 'In the here and now,' she insists, 'there is only sociology.' She is too large to argue with. She apologizes for having taken my name from the internal directory of the software company I work for. She'd been an intern last summer in our San Francisco office.

I say I am flattered to be asked big questions, since most days I am steeped in micro-minutiae. Literally: nano-technology. I can feel Krithika's eyes burning through me.

The following are my answers to her early questions: We have been in San Jose nearly eight years. I am an American citizen, which is the reason I feel safe answering questions that could be interpreted by more recent immigrants as intrusive. We have been married twenty years, with two children. Our daughter Pramila was born in Stanford University Hospital. Our son Jay was born in JJ Hospital seventeen years ago. When he was born I was already in California, finishing my degree and then finding a job and a house. My parents have passed away; I have an older brother, and several cousins in India, as well as Canada and the U.S. My graduate work took four years, during which time I did not see Krithika or my son. Jay and Krithika are still Indian citizens, although my wife holds the Green Card and works as special assistant in Stanford Medical School Library. She will keep her Indian citizenship in the event of inheritance issues in India.

Do I feel my life is satisfactory, are the goals I set long ago being met?

Anya is very persistent, and I have never been questioned by such a blue-eyed person. It is a form of hypnosis, I fear. I am satisfied with my life, most definitely. I can say with pride and perhaps a touch of vanity that we have preserved the best of India in our family. I have seen what this country can do, and I have fought it with every fibre of my being. I have not always been successful. The years are brief, and the forces of dissolution are strong.

Jay in particular is thriving. He has won two junior tennis championships and maintains decent grades in a very demanding high school filled with the sons and daughters of computer engineers and Stanford professors. As a boy in Dadar, part of Bombay – sorry, Mumbai – I was much like him, except that my father could not offer access to top-flight tennis coaching. I lost a match to Sanjay Prabhakar, who went on to Davis Cup. 'How will I be worthy?' I had asked my father before going in. 'You will never be worthy of Sanjay Prabhakar,' he said. It is your fate. You are good, but he is better and he will always be better. It is not a question of worth. I sold my racquet that day and have never played another set of tennis, though even now I know I could rise to the top of my club ranks. I might even be able to beat my son, but I worry what that might do to him. I was forced to concentrate on academic accomplishment. In addition, public courts and available equipment left much to be desired.

Do I have many American friends? Of course. My closest friend is Al Wong, a Stanford classmate, now working in Cupertino. We socialize with Al and Mitzie at least twice a month. She means white Americans. Like yourself? I ask, and she answers 'not quite'. She means two-three-generation white Americans. Such people exist on our street, of course, and in our office, and I am on friendly terms with all of them. I tell her I have never felt myself the victim of any racial incident, and she says, I didn't mean that. I mean instances of friendship, enduring bonds, non-professional alliances ... you know, friendship. You mean hobbies? I ask. The Americans seem to have many hobbies I cannot fully appreciate. They follow the sports teams, they go fishing and sailing and skiing.

In perfect frankness, I do not always enjoy the company of white Americans. They mean well, but we do not communicate on the same level. I do not see their movies or listen to their music, and I have never voted. Jay skis, and surfs. Jay is very athletic, as I have mentioned; we go to Stanford tennis matches. I cannot say that I have been in many American houses, nor they in mine, although Jay's friends seem almost exclusively white. Jay is totally of this world. When I mention Stanford or Harvard, he says Santa Cruz, pops. He's not interested in a tennis scholarship. He says he won the state championship because the dude from Torrance kept double-faulting. Pramila's friends are very quiet and studious, mostly Chinese and Indian. She is fourteen and concentrates only on her studies and ice-skating. I am not always comfortable in her presence. I do not always understand her, or feel that she respects us.

We will not encourage Pramila to date. In fact, we will not permit it until she is finished with college. Then we will select a suitable boy. It will be a drawn-out process, I fear, but we are progressive people in regard to caste and regional origins. A boy from a good family with a solid education is all we ask. If Pramila were not a genius, I would think her retarded. When she's not on the ice, she lurches and stumbles. Jay does not have a particular girlfriend. He says don't even think of arranging a marriage for me. Five thousand years of caste-submission will end here, on the shores of the Pacific Ocean.

'So, you and your son watch Mike Mahulkar?'

'Mike?' I must have blinked. 'It is Mukesh,' I say. 'My son models his tennis game on Mukesh Mahulkar. Some day Mukesh will be a very great tennis player.'

Neither my son nor I would ever be able to score a point off Mukesh Mahulkar.

My father has been dead nearly twenty years. I think he died from the strain of arranging my marriage. Krithika's parents never reconciled to my father's modest income. In my strongest memory of him, he was coming from his bath. It was the morning of my marriage. His hair was dark and wet. We will never be worthy, he said. A year later, I was sharing a house with Al Wong and two Indian guys. Jay was born that same year, but I was not able to go back for the birth, or for my father's funeral services. Fortunately, I have an older brother. My father was head clerk in Maharashtra State Public Works Department. In his position, he received and passed on, or rejected, plans for large-scale building and reclamation projects. Anywhere in Asia, certainly anywhere in India in the past twenty years, such a position would generate mountains of black money. Men just like my father posed behind the façade of humble civil servant, living within modest salaries, dressed in kurta and pyjama of rough khadi, with

Bata sandals on their dusty feet. They would spend half an hour for lunch, sipping tea under a scruffy peepal. But in the cool hours of morning or evening, there would be meetings with shady figures and the exchange of pillow-thick bundles of stapled hundred-rupee notes. They would be pondering immense investments in apartment blocks and outlying farmhouses and purchasing baskets of gold to adorn their wives and daughters.

But Baba was one of the little folk of the great city, an honest man mired in universal graft. He went to office in white kurta. At lunch, he sat on a wall and ate street-food from pushcart vendors and read his Marathi paper. He came home to a bath and prayer, dinner and bed. Projects he rejected got built anyway, with his superiors' approval. He was seen as an obstruction to progress, a dried-up cow wandering a city fly-over. So we never got the car-and-driver, the club memberships and air conditioning. He retired on even less than his gazetted salary, before the Arab money and Bombay boom.

I suddenly remember Qasim, the Muslim man whose lunch cart provided tea and cigarettes and fried foods to the MSPWD office-wallahs. My father and Qasim enjoyed a thirty-year friendship without ever learning the names of one another's children, or visiting each other's houses, or even neighbourhoods. Dadar and Mahim are different worlds. We never learned Qasim's last name. But whenever I dropped in on my father on lunch or tea breaks, I would hear him and Qasim engaged in furious discussions over politics, Pakistan, and fatherhood. Qasim had four wives and a dozen children, many of them the same age, all of them dressed in white, carrying trays of water and tea. Qasim and Baba were friends. To me, they are the very model of friendship. You might find it alien. You might not call it friendship at all. If, as rarely happened, Qasim did not appear on a given day, my father would ask a Muslim in the office to inquire after his health. Once or twice in a year, when my father took leave to attend a wedding, a strange boy would appear at our door, asking after Waldekar-sahib. I'm certain my father expressed more of a heartfelt nature to Qasim than he ever did to his wife, or to me. In that, I am my father's son.

'My father, too,' says the blue-eyed girl in the T-shirt. All This and Brains, Too. Suddenly, I understand its meaning, and I must have uttered a muted 'ahhh!' and blushed. Breasts, not height and blondness. I feel a deep shame for her. Krithika reads the same words, but shows no comprehension. I have a bumper sticker: My Son Is Palos High School Student of the Month. When I put it on, my wife said I was inviting the evil eye. For that reason, we have not permitted newspaper access to Pramila. We are simple people. Our children consume everything. To pay for tennis and ice-skating lessons takes up all our cash. I could have bought a Stradivarius violin with what I've spent. When she was ten years old, after a summer spent in Stanford's Intensive Mathematics Workshop with the cream of the nation's high school seniors, Pramila wrote a paper on the Topology of Imaginary Binaries. I do not mention it, ever.

'My father says that if he'd stayed in Russia and never left his government job, he would be sitting on a mountain of bribes. Over here, he started a Russian deli on Geary Boulevard.'

'You have made a very successful transition to this country,' I say. All this. 'I personally have great respect for the entrepreneurial model.'

She takes the compliment with a shy smile. 'Appearances can lie, Dr Waldekar,' she says.

Krithika brings out water and a plate of savouries.

I am of the Stanford generation that built the Internet out of their garages. I knew those boys. They invited me to join, but I was a young husband and father, although my family was still in India waiting to come over, and I had a good, beginning-level job with PacBell. I would be ashamed to beg start-up money from banks or strangers. My friends said, well, we raised five million today, we're on our way! And I'd think you're twenty-five years old and five million dollars in debt? You're on your way to jail! I have not been in debt a single day of my life, including the house mortgage. It all goes back to my father in frayed khadi, and three-rupee lunches under the dusty peepals.

'I notice an interesting response to my question,' she says. 'When I asked if you've fulfilled your goals, you mentioned only that your son is very successful. What about you, Dr Waldekar?'

Krithika breaks in, finally, 'We also have a daughter.'

'I was coming to that,' I say.

'She is enrolled in a graduate level mathematics course,' says Krithika.

'That's amazing!'

'She is the youngest person ever enrolled for credit in the history of Stanford. She is also a champion figure skater. My husband forgot to mention her, so I thought you might perhaps note that, if you have space.'

'I believe I mentioned she is very studious,' I say.

Anya breaks off a bit of halwa.

I rise to turn off the central AC. The girl is underdressed for air conditioning, and I am disturbed by what I see happening with her breasts, under the boastful logo. They are standing out in points. Krithika returns to the kitchen.

'I am content, of course.' What else is there on this earth, I want to ask, than safeguarding the success of one's children? What of her father, the Russian deli owner? Is he happy? What is happiness for an immigrant but the accumulation of visible successes? He cannot be happy, seeing what has happened to his daughter. Does the Russian have friends? Does he barge into American houses? Do Americans swarm around his? Who are his heroes? Barry Bonds, Terrell Owens, Tiger Woods, Jerry Rice? We share time on the same planet; that is all. We will see how much the Americans love their sports heroes if any of them tries to buy a house on their street. Mukesh Mahulkar is big and strong and handsome and he is good in his studies and I'm sure his parents are proud of him and don't fear the evil eye. He'll play professional tennis and make a fortune and he won't spend it all on cars and mansions. He will invest wisely and he will be welcomed on any street in this country.

'My father works too hard. He's already had two heart attacks. He smokes like a fish. He dumps sour cream on everything. Everything in his mouth is salty, fatty meat, and more meat, and cream, and cheese and vodka. Forgive the outburst.'

'We are vegetarian. We do not drink strong spirits.'

'So's Mike. Veggie, I mean. He's teaching me.'

'You mean Mukesh, the tennis player?'

'His name is Mike. He's my boyfriend, Dr Waldekar.'

The ache I feel at the mention of a boyfriend is like the phantom pain from a lost limb. If I could even imagine a proper companion for this Russian girl, he would be as white and smooth as a Greek sculpture, built on the scale of Michelangelo's David. The thought that it is a Mumbai boy who runs his hands over her body, under those flimsy clothes, makes my fingers run cold.

'I might as well come out with it, Dr Waldekar,' she says. 'We've broken up. His parents hate my guts.'

Good for them, I think. Maybe you should dress like a proper young lady. I knew a Mahulkar boy in Dadar. I knew others in IIT, but no Mahulkars of my generation in the Bay Area. So many have come. Given my early advantage, the opportunities I turned down, I am a comparative failure.

'This is my honours project, but ... it's personal, too. I love India and Indians, I love the discipline of Indians. No group of immigrants has achieved so much, in so little time, with such ease and harmony. I love their pride and dignity. I even love it that they hate me. I can respect it.' She is smiling, but I don't know if I should smile with her and nod in agreement, or raise an objection. She might be a good sociologist, but there is much she is missing in the realm of psychology. So she goes on, and I don't interrupt.

'But what I don't love is that Mike won't stand up to them, for me. You know what his father said? He said American girls are good for practice, until we find you a proper bride. When Mike told me that, we laughed about it. I'm friendly with his sister and I said to her, your game's a little rusty. Think you need some practice? and we laughed and laughed. Mike said he'd show me Mumbai, and I said I'd take him to Moscow. He's twenty-two years old, but the minute his father said to stop seeing me, he stopped. One day we're playing tennis, or at the beach or he's cooking Indian vegetarian and I'm learning, and then, nothing. Nothing.' She lets herself go, drops her head into the basin of her hands, and sobs. It is a posture I, too, am familiar with. Krithika rushes in from the kitchen, stops, frowns, then goes back inside. I will be questioned later: what did I do, say, what didn't I do, didn't say? She will suspect some misbehaviour.

So, I think, Mahulkar has found a bride for his son. This is very good news. Who could it be? Why hadn't I heard that the famous Mukesh Mahulkar was getting married? It means there is hope for every Indian father with a son like mine.

'Please, take water,' I say. I would be tempted to hold her, or pat her back, but my arms might not reach. It would be awkward, and perhaps misinterpreted. Now that she has pitched forward, I see deep into her bosom; she has a butterfly tattoo on one breast, well below the separation-line. A girl this big, and crying, in my living room, wearing such a T-shirt, has brought chaos from the street into our life.

'I'm so sorry,' she says. 'That was inexcusable. You must think I came under false pretences. Mike's getting married in Mumbai in three weeks. It's very hard, to be told, without warning, without explanation, that you're just... unworthy.'

She has a beautiful smile. It's as though she had not been crying at all, or knew no sadness, or had a Russian childhood and a father with a mouthful of meat and vodka. I will ask around and discover the bride's name.

I stand. 'I must ask you quietly to leave. I must pick up my daughter from practice. My son will be home soon.' I do not want her defiling my house, spreading her contagion into our sterile environment. She has no interest in successful immigrants, or in me. 'I have no special Bombay advice to offer.' When I open the door, my fingers brush the white flesh of her back, just above the tattoo. I don't think she even feels it. She says only, 'you have been very kind and hospitable. Please forgive me.'

I could not go home for my father's funeral. I did not see my son until he was four years old and had already bonded with my wife's family. I think he still treats me like an intruder. So does my wife. It has pained me all these years that I permitted my studies and other activities to take precedence over family obligations. I have been trying to atone for my indiscretions all these years.

In three of the four years I shared a house with Al Wong and the Mehta boy who went back and a Parsi boy who married an American girl and stayed, I remained steadfast to my research. I got a job at PacBell, where they immediately placed me in charge of a small research cell with people like myself, debt-free, security-minded team players. Suddenly, I had money. I bought a car and a small bungalow in Palo Alto, suitable for wife and child. No one in the group knew I was already married, and a father. We were all just in our twenties, starting out in the best place, in the best of times.

In my small group there was an American girl, a Berkeley graduate. Her name was Paula, called Polly. Pretty Polly, the boys liked to joke, which embarrassed her. On Fridays, our group would join with others for some sort of party. I would allow myself a beer or two, since carbonation lessened the taint of alcohol. Those sorts of restaurants made vegetarianism very difficult; I was admired for my discipline. Polly was naturally less restrained than I, especially after sharing a few pitchers of beer, a true California girl from someplace down south. Watching closely, I could gauge the moment when a quiet, studious girl, very reliable and hard-working, would ask for a cigarette, then go to the bathroom, come back to the table, and sit next to someone new. She sat next to me. One night she said, 'You're a very handsome man, Dr Waldekar.' No one had ever told me that, and to look fondly at one's reflection in a mirror is to invite the evil eye. 'Take me home,' she said. 'I don't know where you live,' I answered. She punched me on the arm. 'Ha, ha,' she said, 'funny, too.'

It's that transformation, not the flattery that got to me. All week in the office, she was a flattened presence. She totally ignored me, and I, her. I imagined she was one of the good girls, living with her parents.

The passion that arises from workplace familiarity is hotter than hell. It is hell, because one must hide certain feelings, erase recurrent images, must put clothes back on a girl you've been with through the night. Above all, it must be secret. On Friday nights, she must not sit next to me. 'May I call you Vivek, Dr Waldekar?' she would ask. After the first time, I told myself it was the beer, but I knew it wasn't. The sexual acts that had resulted in the birth of my son back in India, a boy whose pictures I now had to hide, had seemed, in comparison to Polly, a continuation of tennis practice, slamming a ball against a wall and endlessly returning it. She took drugs, expensive drugs, and I was helpless to stop her, or complain. 'Go to her, if that will make you happy,' says Krithika. 'I know your secrets.'

'What foolishness.'

'You were staring at her. You shamed me. You behaved disgustingly.'

'If you were interested in the facts you would know I threw her out.'

'Remember,' she mumbles, 'I get half.'

I reach out for her, but she pulls away. This is the woman, the situation, I left Polly for. Eventually, I left PacBell because of her, which has worked out well for me. Polly left California because of me. Al Wong is the only person I confessed it to; I think he's mentioned it to Mitzie because of the ways she sometimes scrutinizes me. What do you think of her, Vivek? she'll ask me, as though I have a special interest in attractive women, instead of Al. Maybe she's mentioned it to Krithika. The promiscuous exchange of intimacies, which passes for friendship in America, is a dangerous thing. It is the sad nature of the terms of a marriage contract that the strongest evidence of commitment is also the admission of flagrant unfaithfulness.

One night fourteen years ago, I went up to SFO to meet Krithika and

THE SOCIOLOGY OF LOVE

Jay who were arriving in my life after a thirty-hour flight from Bombay. I got there early and pressed myself close to the gate, but Sikhs from the Central Valley, rough fellows with large families and huge signboards, pushed me aside and called me names. It was a time of deep tensions between Hindus and Sikhs. If I had stood my ground, they threatened to stamp me into the floor. The Indian passengers poured through, fanning out in every direction, pushing carts stacked high with crates and boxes. Waiting families ducked under the barriers to join them, and I waited and waited, but no wife, no child. The terminal is always crowded, but the number of Indians diminished, to be replaced by Mexicans and Koreans. Perhaps she was having visa problems, I thought, or the bags had been lost.

After two hours, just as I'd decided to go back to my empty house, I heard my name on the public announcement. Please pick up the courtesy phone, Vivek Waldekar. Your wife wants you to know that since you were not here to meet them, she and her child have gone to a safe address provided by a fellow passenger, and she will contact you in the morning.

Two days later, I got that call. Perhaps you forgot you have a wife and son, she said. Perhaps you no longer remember me. She has remained on friendlier terms with that generous family who took her home on her first night in America than she ever has with me.

At four a.m. when the streets are dark and only the dogs are awake, the rattling of food carts begins. Barefoot men and boys dressed in white khadi push their carts heavy with oil, propane, and dozens of spiced tufts of chickpea batter ready for frying, all prepared during the night by wives and daughters. Each cart is lit by a naphtha lamp; each man fans out to his corner of the city near big office buildings, under his own laburnum, ashoka or peepal tree. Qasim died one morning as he pushed his cart through the streets of Mahim. His son Walid appeared the next day, with his father's picture and a page of Urdu pasted to the cart's plastic shield. Even Hindus knew what it meant. My father took his retirement a month later – his superiors were truly sorry to see him go, since he was the obstruction that enriched everyone around him. He arranged my marriage, I received my Stanford scholarship and went to America, leaving a pregnant wife behind. After three years of bad health, Baba died. And I didn't attend the services because I was involved with an American girl named Polly who thought burning one's father's body in public was too gross to contemplate.

Partial Renovations

JULIA ARRIVED to baby-sit at precisely eight o'clock. The lady was waiting on the front porch, a small concrete slab with a wrought-iron grille. Her name was Shirley Rogers and she was a plain, nervous lady who had just frizzed her hair and bleached it a very bright yellow. The baby, who'd been put to sleep, was called Christopher. The nursery was in the rear on the second floor.

Julia was fifteen and considered a fine baby-sitter, mainly because she was thought of as too stupid to pry. It was a street in downtown Toronto of restless unmarried mothers. Most of them were in their thirties and trying to look younger, like Shirley Rogers. Around thirty-five was when they stopped trying to get remarried and started taking strange kinds of evening courses, coming back around midnight with scraped knuckles, and smelling of things they'd cooked, smoked, or rolled in. The world was divided between women who'd kicked out their husbands and women (like Julia's mom) whose husbands had walked out. Julia often dreaded what the next fifteen years would bring her. She was looking for short cuts. She'd save herself a lot of time and worry if she went through it all in the next four or five years. Twenty seemed comfortably far away. By then she'd be through it all and have a Visa card. At twenty she'd still be fairly young, but at least she wouldn't be stupid and no one could push her around. The only thing she would never do was have a baby. When you had a baby you automatically lost about ten years of living from your life.

Shirley Rogers took her into the kitchen and showed her a counter laid out with apples and oranges and a plate of granola bars. This was the usual thing. Even at Hallowe'en kids on this street got packets of unsalted nuts and granola bars. Then she showed her a pantry loaded with Fritos corn chips, pretzels and licorice whips. 'I didn't know which kind of girl you were,' she said, to which Julia assumed the proper humility. She thought well of her skin and figure but when the time came, she'd rather have corn chips than an apple. There were Cokes in the fridge and Mrs Rogers said she didn't mind if Julia took a beer if that was usual with her.

Christopher was a sound sleeper and on no condition should he be disturbed.

The house smelled slightly of talcum powder and baby oil. Mrs Rogers' assertiveness class lasted till 10:30, then she'd go out for coffee. She'd be back by midnight. She had a taped answering machine attached to the downstairs telephone. Julia was not to answer the phone unless it rang three times. That would mean it was Mrs Rogers herself ringing through. Julia told her not to worry about coming back. It was a summer weekend and she could sleep in.

None of the women on the street who had hired Julia would have called her curious or even intelligent. In fact, she was famously stupid on the street, since it was a very well-educated block. But curiosity was her only pronounced passion. She was curious about the physical arrangements of men and women. Not the sexual thing, which was something she knew about, but how they accommodated each other for months and even years in some cases. Over on Marlborough Place she'd read a scroll hanging in a bathroom. It said that marriages were either benign or malignant. You could live with them till they got uncomfortable or unsightly, or else you had to cut them out immediately and hope you got it all. Most of the women she baby-sat for had interesting ways of dealing with men. No matter how hard they hid the evidence, Julia usually found it. Some of them had so many men they had to post timetables in their closets. Her own father had wandered off a long time ago and her sister had just separated after seventeen months of marriage, so Julia knew she'd probably get married to the first guy who turned her on and really wanted to, and then they'd fight and they'd get a divorce.

Her mother said that what killed marriage was having to live together. The more you saw of a person, the more you were sure to hate him. This was also the case between Julia and her mother. That had been the case between her sister Stephanie and Rodney. Stephanie said that if you were the kind who had to have a man around, you should at least housebreak him to show up only when you called him and to leave when you told him to go. Even Stephanie said she was off men for a while, which meant she was cutting back, not counting Rodney, who was still around.

Julia liked to open drawers and feel men's clothes. She found them surprisingly soft for the kind of work they had to do. It bothered her that she liked the sound of men in a house. There hadn't been any in her mother's life since her father had left. She trusted their sounds in the bathroom. Her father had always let her stir up the lather in his shaving mug. She liked the dull plunk of the wooden brush handle on the thick glass mug. She would probably marry the first guy who still shaved that way. The earliest memory she had of her father was of him standing over the toilet bowl every morning. She would make the biggest circle with her arms that she could and her father would pee right through it.

Mrs Rogers got a lot of phone calls, which the tape took down and held. She didn't seem the type for so many calls. She must have been at least thirty-eight, and the way she curled her hair and bleached it and dressed in CHUM T-shirts made her look even older. She was flat as a board on top, but getting soft and squishy down below. The thought of Mrs Rogers without any clothes on and doing it with Mr Rogers or whoever was disturbing to Julia. Almost anything that had to do with bodies and babies struck Julia as gross. Bodies made her think of the word 'disrobe' which had to be the ugliest word she'd ever heard. The first time a doctor had asked her to disrobe for him she'd known that she was old enough to start causing trouble.

She knew about taped answering machines. Her father had one, and whenever she visited him he made a special point of turning it off. He told her it was for business messages (he was a salesman), but Julia managed once to hear a full day's tape and it was very different. One lady called five times from places all over the city saying, 'I'm on Queen Street, you bastard, and I saw you take that Chinese chick out to lunch.' On the last tape she had threatened suicide if her father didn't call, and since her father was taking her to a movie that evening, Julia had erased the whole tape. She often wondered what the woman had done. She hadn't sounded right for her father.

Shirley's messages from men were very short. 'Hi, just me. Catch you later.' Then the same voice a few messages later, with noises in the background like boxers in a gym. 'I'm waiting, Shirl. You've got half an hour, then I split.' Julia loved listening to voices like that, to harmless anger she could cut off and replay till it sounded funny. She imagined the guy in a cage behind thick glass, snarling and pounding the glass, while a gang of school kids and their Chinese teacher sat in front of him, eating their box lunches and throwing popcorn like at the zoo.

Another voice, a lady this time, had called a dozen times. First sort of chirpy with a recipe she'd seen. Then with an idea she'd had about a vacation trip, just the two of them, no men. Then in tears, 'I'm not doing well with my life, Shirl,' she said. 'Sometimes it doesn't seem worth it any more. How come you never call me, Shirl? What did I do to you?' Julia didn't like complainers and so she erased it.

By 10:15 she'd had her fun downstairs. The baby was probably wet, or would be soon. She took a bottle out of the fridge and let it stand in hot water, then went upstairs.

Since they were on the same street, Julia's and Shirl's houses were basically the same. She knew how all the rooms were arranged, where the bathroom would be and where the nursery would be in the back. Of course, Shirl had knocked out walls and hung up bright graphics from Marci Lipman's, but that didn't change the space, which still had only fourteen feet of width. This was a street of old row houses that had once been slums, but which architects had discovered and scraped clean and sandblasted and totally reconstructed. Not Julia's house, of course, which was falling apart. Her house leaked from the roof and around the windows and the kitchen floors were always wet and now were slimy and rotting. Shirl had rearranged her staircase to go up the side instead of the middle, and she'd pushed the kitchen back to the end of the ground floor and made it so small that two people could only hug each other if they got caught in there accidentally.

Julia had to pull herself up the metal staircase. It was narrow and steep and had no landing. And when she got to the top she had to lift a trap door, like a hatch on a submarine, a carpeted manhole cover. She was in a bedroom in a sea of grey carpet and mirrored walls, but she felt she'd been climbing a long way, up the sides of a slick, straight hole. There was a king-sized bed with a grey satin cover and a dresser with a mirror that picked up Julia's image and threw it back a hundred times on the walls. She felt like Alice in that old Grace Slick song.

Around the mirror frame, starting at the lower left, Shirl had wedged a panel of dog photos, taken in colour on a Polaroid. In the background were a group of men and women in bathing suits, sitting around a swimming pool. The dogs were a big Dalmatian and a golden cocker spaniel. At the top of the mirror were gross-out scenes of the Dalmatian mounting the smaller dog and getting stuck. The Dalmatian first was high on his hind legs and Julia could almost hear his whining, and the cocker looked ready to snap. But by the lower right their passion had cooled to the point of not looking at each other. They just stood joined like sausages embarrassed and staring in opposite directions. In the final shot a very muscular man and one of the girls had taken off their swimming suits and were squatting on all fours in the grass with their naked bums touching, just like the dogs.

She wondered why anyone would need to keep pictures like that out in the open. Usually Julia had to pry and pry and turn things carefully upside down before she found the magazines and the letters and the pictures – worse ones than these – that were always there.

She'd delivered papers to most of these houses two or three years before. Different people, of course. She was the only native kid on the block. The street was hers by stealth and experience, though she possessed none of it. She was like an Indian, her reservation fourteen feet of rundown frontage. She was there when the moving vans came and she'd be there when For Sale signs went up a few months later. She'd be there till her mother kicked her out. Her house was unpainted and unrenovated. They didn't have a deck on the back but they did have a real front porch with a roof and a swing, one of the last ones on the street, and her mother even sat on it.

As in a dream, Julia headed to Shirl's bed, to a large ceramic boar's head kept on the leather-padded ledge above the headboard, and she knew even before she lifted it that half of the head would come off and that she'd find a small Baggie of grass sealed up tight, grass enough for a good two weeks of before-and-after smoking up. Above the bed Shirl had framed what looked like a 'Personals' ad from the *Star*, only it was blown up maybe a hundred times so that you noticed the raggedy paper and the ink-skips first, and you had to stand back to read it all. It didn't make good sense, even then.

WOOD BURNING TORONTO DF
SEEKS KINDLING
PURPOSE COMBUSTION
Apply NYR Box 1439

It was hard to make out any exits except for the bathroom, which led out directly without any door. It was all pink tile and mirror and gold faucets, with a standing shower stall that slanted down steeply enough to form a kind of half-tub. There was a bubble overhead, light enough for trees and ferns to be growing from the shower stall and from hooks in the ceiling and from shelves in the corner. The medicine cabinet was huge, wider than the double sink, and there were lotions and perfumes and gadgets inside that Julia had never seen before. There were buffers for nails and for calluses and there were hot combs and hair dryers and all sorts of fancy appliances that spelled out age and boredom to Julia, the hand-held autoerotic devices that were usually more carefully hidden. It made her curious about what Shirley might think of actually hiding, if all these foams and diaphragms and pink plastic machines were so up-front. All in all, it was one of the best bathrooms on the street and after carefully replacing things and wiping off the mirrors, she took a copy of *City Woman* with her into the toilet stall for a long christening.

She almost screamed when she returned to the bedroom. On the bed, loosely propped against the headboard and looking as if they'd been there all night instead of only five minutes, were two giant-sized stuffed dolls, Raggedy Ann and Andy. They had not been there before she'd used the bathroom. The walls reflected a hundred images of a frightened girl, totally alone. Whoever had put the dolls there had *just* done it while she was reading *City Woman* in the bathroom. The dolls had the faces and freckles of Raggedy Ann and Andy but the bodies were very different, since they'd been sewn together and Ann's clothes were torn off and Andy's pants were halfway down. Julia was almost afraid to come near for fear that Andy would reach up and grab her. They were like the marionettes in horror movies, secretly alive and in control of the human-looking dolls around them.

She was aware of the phone ringing, somewhere, then shutting off. She wanted to get out of that room and she started pushing against the mirrored panels. One whole wall was a wardrobe that opened into an enormous closet. Normally Julia loved to search through pockets, finding crumpled dollars in off-season overcoats. She made her way around the huge central island of the bed with its grinning redheaded couple staring up at her, using her fingernails to tap on the glass walls so that she didn't leave a smudge, avoiding the little carpeted bulkhead that was the hidden stairway back down to the living room. The only wall she hadn't explored had to lead to the hallway and the nursery, and probably a couple more guest rooms, so she kept tapping and testing the mirrors with her elbow until one finally yielded.

It was black and musty back there, out of the range of central air conditioning. When her eyes got used to it, she made out rolls of carpet in the hall and stacks of bundled newspapers and somewhere at the far end a final door painted white with animal cutouts on it. She found a light switch. The hallway was much like her own house's, with two bedrooms and a bathroom branching off, and a steep narrow staircase at the far end leading up to the third floor. She started walking.

In her house she had a third-floor room, the kind with a bed pushed next to the small attic window. There was only a narrow area under the peak of the sloping roof where she could stand up straight. When people remodelled their houses, that was something they corrected right away. They usually knocked out the back wall and made it a wall of sliding glass, leading out to a sun deck. And they would knock out the little attic window and the wood around it and replace it with one huge solid triangular panel, and they would stick a couple of potted trees behind it. That was one sure sign of remodelling you could see from the street. A lot of people on the street lived more on their third floors or second floors than on the first. In the summer they lived on their decks and in the winter they lived under the third floor slope behind their potted trees and they could look out of their triangular windows and see the CN Tower and some of the yellow neon at Yonge and Bloor. Of course, Julia's little window was on the wrong side of the street for that. She could only look north to the triangular windows across the street. And she didn't have a deck to look out of on the back. Most of the houses that she baby-sat had skylights of frosted plastic that were very good for all their plants. Julia had old floor lamps with frayed cords in her room and she'd wedged her cot next to the little window for breeze and for looking into other people's houses. She'd done that all her life. Looking into other houses was like a hobby with her.

The hall creaked as she walked it. From what she could tell, the two bedrooms (or what were bedrooms in her house) were empty. She opened one of the doors and knew suddenly from the smells she was wrong. She knew the smell of old people's sleeping and smoking and drinking, how they could live in any kind of filth and how they contributed to it. Sour clothes, old smoke, cat smell. There weren't any shades on the windows and street lights from outside and the hall light from inside weren't really strong enough to tell her much. Only that there was a brass bed with a grey lump on it, but no sheets. The shape of the lump told her it was a man sleeping with his arm slung over his eyes the way a drunk sleeps day or night in a coin-wash or in a park. And when she took a step inside, a sharp wooden creak from the window alerted her to another presence in a chair, and to the tiny red nub of a cigarette moving from the arm of the chair and disappearing behind its high upholstered back. An old woman coughed.

The second bedroom was much darker, and it smelled of sickness. A man in an undershirt and striped pyjama bottoms sat at an old plastic dining table. He had long, dark hair but a sunken face and body. Julia knew the look of a heavy drinker. She used to think (applying it to an uncle of hers) that drinking kept old men's hair from falling out or turning grey. That was before she learned that her uncle was only twenty-eight, and had a right to his full, dark head of hair. He only looked like sixty everywhere else. This man, now standing and holding the front of his pyjamas like a wad in his fist, could have been one of her uncles. 'Hi,' she whispered, then closed the door on him. The old bathroom's door was open but the smells from it reminded her of her father's unflushed toilet at the cottage, odours backing up from all the pipes. She passed the steep carpeted stairwell leading to the third floor, and opened the nursery door.

The night light was strong enough. There was a crib, a wicker bassinet, another white dresser with stuffed dolls propped on top. She could see the baby's leg peeking out from under the quilt, but, thank God, there were none of the smells she was so good at detecting. The kid really was a dream. She reached through the crib slats to tuck the baby back under the quilt, then she stopped, just before touching his heel.

Someone was behind her, watching. She expected a strong hand to come clamping down on her mouth and for her head to be jerked back so suddenly she'd lose full consciousness, the way Rodney, Stephanie's husband, had done it to her the first time. She waited, knowing that in this house any kind of fighting back would be useless and dangerous, and she knew she wouldn't be the fool she'd been those other times. She turned instead, slowly, holding the crib with one hand, just to brace herself in case he slammed into her real hard. At least she wouldn't have to put up with a wrenched back. Last time the guy had wrenched her back so hard it was almost *that* that had made her go to a doctor. But she hadn't.

It was Shirl. Julia was prepared for a man, some carpet-person rolled up on the floor in an unlit room, someone who just lay in there week after week in case some girl came walking down the hall. Someone who was awake only at night. At first, Shirl's features didn't seem familiar.

'God, you scared me!'

'I called through. I told you I'd call through when the class was over. You didn't pick up the phone, so I raced home.'

'I couldn't find it,' said Julia. She tried to laugh, it sounded absurd, but she knew that Shirley knew she'd been prowling upstairs. The phones were hidden only up there.

'I told you never mind about Christopher. You're looking after the house. The baby is fine.'

There was a man in the hall, very tall, with hair curled like Shirl's, in a white silk shirt with the top three buttons open. He laid a wide hand with many chunky rings on Shirl's shoulder.

'Let me take care of it,' he said. He peeled dollars from a metal clip, the rasping sound of new bills on new bills – he was the kind who handled only crisp bills, who wouldn't take old bills even in change from Becker's or from kids with a paper route. Money made a special noise in hands like his.

Her hands slithered down the crib slats, resting briefly on the waterproof mattress. She wanted suddenly to feel something smooth and reassuring, like baby's skin. She patted the heel.

'Five crisp ones do it?' he asked, forking them over.

This time Julia didn't flinch. Not when the baby's heel wasn't cool to her touch, nor warm, nor anything. It wasn't living. It was cloth. She moved her fingers quickly. No one saw.

'He didn't cry, did he?'

'No,' said Julia. 'You've got a great baby.'

'Boys are so easy,' said Shirley to the man, who seemed to agree. 'Didn't even have to change him, I'll bet.'

'I'd *just* come in,' said Julia. 'I didn't even get a chance to straighten his blanket.'

She took the five green ones and let Shirl quickly close the nursery door and guide them down the hall. The other doors were all closed. 'I *must* do something up here,' she was saying to the man, 'I wanted to spare you an upsetting sight.' He said something Julia didn't catch, but from the jerk of the head she knew it was about her. 'Don't be silly,' Shirl giggled, 'she's only fifteen.' Julia had gone past the rear stairwell and the first closed bedroom door when Shirl called out, 'Where do you think you're going?' Julia turned; she was headed for the front bedroom and carpeted bulkhead.

Shirl opened a door that Julia hadn't noticed, or else had assumed was a closet. 'Just how do you think you got up here?' she asked. She snapped on a light. It was the servants' staircase leading down through the broom closet and the pantry and back down to the kitchen.

'I don't think I'll be needing you again,' she said from the top of the stairs. Julia could hear the hallway creaking as the two of them headed to the master bedroom. Shirl called down one final instruction to make sure the front door was locked on her way out.

She didn't consider crossing the street and going home. She had some money and the night was hot and she hadn't eaten and Yonge Street was just a block away. There were nights like this one when all the things she thought she knew seemed worthless and she felt unwelcome even in places that she thought were hers. She felt so light and empty that she could blow away and no one would know that she'd ever been born.

It was only midnight and boys were calling for her from their cars. After a doughnut and a Coke, she took a ride with some boys who said there was a party they'd heard about somewhere on the Danforth.

Afterword

IN STORY COLLECTIONS, context is all. Many of these stories have appeared in earlier books (notably, *If I Were Me* and *Man and His World*), but here they stand alone, bouncing off each other in a revised sequence, a different display.

Fate, family and marriage have conspired to make me into a hydroponic writer: rootless, unhoused, fed by swirling waters and harsh, artificial light. In Canadian terms, a classic un-Munro. A Manitoba mother and a Quebec father, an American and Canadian life split more or less equally, can do that to an inquisitive and absorptive child. I never lived longer than six months anywhere, until my four-year Pittsburgh adolescence and fourteen years of Montreal teaching. As a consequence, when I was a young writer, I thought that making sense of my American and Canadian experience would absorb my interest for the rest of my life.

But a five-minute wedding ceremony in a lawyer's office in Iowa City forty-two years ago delivered that inquisitive child an even larger world than the North American continent. I married India, a beautiful and complicated world, and that Canadian/American, French/English, Northern/Southern boy slowly disappeared. (I wonder what he would have been like, had the larger world never intervened.) The stories in *World Body* reflect a few of those non-North American experiences. I now live in California, but my California, strangely, presents itself through Indian eyes.

– *Clark Blaise*,
San Francisco

BHARATI MUKHERJEE

Clark Blaise has taught in Montreal, Toronto, Saskatchewan and British Columbia, as well as at Skidmore College, Columbia University, Iowa, NYU, Sarah Lawrence and Emory. For several years he directed the International Writing Program at the University of Iowa. Among the most widely travelled of authors, he has taught or lectured in Japan, India, Singapore, Australia, Finland, Estonia, the Czech Republic, Holland, Germany, Haiti, and Mexico. He lived for years in San Francisco, teaching at the University of California, Berkeley. In 2002, he was elected president of the Society for the Study of the Short Story. In 2003, he was given an award for 'exceptional achievement' by the American Academy of Arts and Letters.

Clark Blaise and his wife, Bharati Mukherjee, live in San Francisco and Southampton, Long Island.